# The Ghost of You Lingers

Cat Washington

ISBN: 979-8-9932056-1-8 (paperback)

Cover design by Van Garcia

Edited by Carolina VonKampen

**Content Warning**

This story deals with difficult family relationships, depression, and suicide. Please take care of yourself while reading.

If you want to talk to someone, the 988 Suicide & Crisis Lifeline is available (in the United States).

Live chat services are also available at 988lifeline.org.

# Chapter 1

I grabbed my battered suitcase from the stack of luggage that came off the ferry. It was covered in duct tape and, like me, had seen better days. As I extended the handle and walked toward the interior of the island to find my new cottage, a man took it from my hands.

"What the—"

"This you?" He held up a placard with the name "Veronica Cartwright" on it, then pointed at my bag.

When I bought it from a thrift shop, I'd put stickers in the shape of letters in different fonts on the front. It made my name look like a ransom note. No one alive would've paid a ransom for me, so it seemed funny at the time. Alone on an island nine hundred miles from home, it was less funny now. The letters spelled my chosen name, Gibson Cartwright.

"Close enough." I hadn't answered to Veronica for almost twenty years, but it was technically still my legal name. Whatever.

"This way." He walked into the crowd of tourists, dragging

my bag behind him, wheels scraping against uneven concrete. The porter must have been at least seventy-five, with a stoop and neat white hair. If he had been a young dude, I would have ripped my bag out of his hands and told him to fuck off. Instead, I followed him through the plaza. I could be an asshole but I wasn't about to scream at a senior citizen.

Kids I recognized from the ferry ride to the island ran with reckless abandon toward an ice cream stand. A group of women I'd overheard gossiping about their plans to celebrate being divorced power-walked with equal glee to the first bar in sight. Some of them were cute, but without leather or tattoos, they weren't exactly my type.

I pushed a strand of wet-noodle hair out of my eyes and silently cursed humidity in general. Then Michigan humidity in particular.

Downtown Mackinac Island was full of fudge shops, novelty gift stores, and more fudge shops. Flower boxes and bicycle racks lined the streets. Because cars weren't allowed, people strolled down the middle of the street holding hands. A quaint little town you couldn't easily leave—it gave me the creeps.

The porter turned onto a small road leading into the residential part of the island. I almost stepped in several piles of manure casually dropped by the gigantic horses that clop-clopped around the car-free island. Some were attached to carriages holding swooning couples, others ridden by giddy tourists. My black shirt was already soaked through with sweat.

I followed the older man down an even smaller road lined with densely crowded cedar trees and tall lilac bushes. The trees on my block back home in New York were friendly, but these loomed like nosy giants. The sound of happy vacationers faded, replaced by birdsong and the whispering wind. I shivered at the change, and a chill came over me despite the damp summer heat.

We turned down a private lane marked with a small wooden sign that said Abaddon Cottage. It cut through a dark mass of trees that opened to reveal my newly deceased great-aunt's house. We'd never met, so I didn't understand why her dying wish was to give me her house. I didn't want the house. Cash would've been great, but just like everyone else in my family, she didn't give a shit about what I wanted.

But Mackinac was full of rich fucks with rich-fuck real estate, so I was ready to cash in on the unexpected inheritance.

"Here, miss," the porter said. "Good luck."

"Uh, thanks."

"Give ya two days," the man muttered as he turned toward the road.

"What?"

The porter turned back around. He raised bushy white eyebrows and nodded at the house. "Couldn't pay me to live in there. Good luck, girl."

~

Abaddon Cottage was enormous. I thought a "cottage" was supposed to be small and charming. Cute, even. This was large. Formidable, even.

The front yard was a tangled mess of vines that choked out any charm the grounds may have had. I unclipped the key ring from the carabiner on my belt loop and approached the house. It was a dilapidated, three-story wood-and-brick-faced miniature mansion with a wraparound porch. On it sat a pair of Adirondack chairs that badly needed a coat of paint. The entire place needed a coat of paint. Or a time machine.

For half a second, I thought I saw someone with long hair standing in the third-floor bedroom. But when I blinked and looked again, it was just the outline of an old lamp.

"Okay, Aunt Agatha," I said, unlocking the door. She had been my mother's aunt, not mine. A simple blood relationship that was anything but simple, seeing as both were dead and neither had wanted anything to do with me while they were alive. "Let's get this over with."

My boss Babs didn't give a shit if I worked from the office or Timbuktu as long as I turned in assignments on time. But the longer I remained, the more likely it was that another shitstain guitar player would steal my spot in the band whose career I'd helped launch. They thought of me as nothing but a sideman. But with their regular guitarist in jail, the lead singer had promised me the gig, full time. And she was hot, but all we'd ever done was fool around, so I wanted a shot at making her my full-time gig, too.

Pushing away thoughts of Brooke, I entered the house. I tried the boot scraper mounted next to the door, then pulled off my manure-encrusted shoes.

The tile entryway led to a giant curved staircase. Off to one side was a grandfather clock, its pendulum swinging lethargically. A huge chandelier hung in front of the staircase. Beyond the entryway, cream-colored wallpaper with a swirly texture covered the walls, accompanied by a warm wooden trim. Dust bunnies gathered in the crevices. Agatha's furnishings had been left as part of the estate transfer, and the caretaker had covered them in white sheets, leaving the impression of a ghostly gathering.

I pulled off one of the sheets, then regretted it when I uncovered a hideous pink couch.

I left my bag next to the staircase and ran a finger over the baluster. My fingertip came away dark with grime, so I wiped it on my pants. I whistled, then shivered at how the house swallowed the sound.

On the other side of the staircase was an alcove with a floor-to-ceiling bookcase. It even had one of those rolling ladders. I ran my hands over the spines, expecting dust, but my hand came away clean.

The kitchen and bathroom made up the rest of the first floor. A basic wooden kitchen table was nestled against the wall next to the door leading to the backyard. The table was clean and empty. In the bathroom, I flipped the light switch, but nothing happened. The shower was basic, tiled in grimy white squares. I tried not to think of the stabbing scene from *Psycho*, but it appeared in my head anyway.

Before heading upstairs, I flipped a switch labeled "chand." The lights in the chandelier came to life, twinkling and sending warm shards of light around the hallway. Except one bulb on the bottom, which stubbornly remained dark like a tooth punched out of a smiling face.

Upstairs were two bedrooms, one with mint-green wallpaper and one with a more tasteful rose pattern. Both were old-fashioned, but in a cozy way. I didn't hate it nearly as much as I should. In spite of myself, I saw potential. Someone could stay here. Someone who wanted to escape the real world. Someone who wanted to live in a creaky Victorian-era house on an island they couldn't easily leave. Someone who wasn't me.

The third floor consisted entirely of the master suite. It had a detached wardrobe and a bathroom with an old claw-foot tub and decently clean tile. None of it was my style, but I could live with it until I found a buyer.

A chime from the downstairs grandfather clock jump-started my heart. I told it to calm the fuck down.

Looking back at the empty room, this time I saw sadness. The four-poster bed stood stalwart against the march of time, covered by a quilt made by hand long ago. I purposely distanced myself from my family, including whoever made that quilt. Although on purpose, my disconnection from them now made me feel isolated and small.

A loud scream ripped through the silence of the room.

It was high-pitched, almost a whistle. My shoulders rose, and my entire body tensed with fear.

"What the—"

After a moment of frozen indecision, I skipped down the stairs two at a time. Halfway to the landing, I stopped, realizing what the sound was.

A tea kettle?

I mentally replayed my walkthrough of the kitchen, trying to remember a tea kettle. I couldn't remember seeing one, but it didn't matter, because there was no one else in the house. I unlocked the door. I was the only person with keys.

The sound abated. I strained my ears and, sure enough, heard the sound of water being poured into a mug. Someone else was in the house.

I counted to ten, breathing deeply, then shouted, "Whoever you are, you're trespassing on private property!"

Racing down the stairs, I skidded around the base of the staircase and thundered into the kitchen like a bat headed into hell. I stopped at the entrance with a hand against the old refrigerator, breathing heavily.

The kitchen was empty.

But something caught my eye and held it, anchoring me in place.

The empty table wasn't empty anymore. A mug, white porcelain with angel wings, sat off to one side. Next to it was an open book with a ribbon for a bookmark. A chair had been pulled out as if someone had been sitting there, curling their hands around the mug to feel its warmth. Wisps of steam rose from hot, dark liquid within.

As I fixated on the objects on the table, I heard the creaking of door hinges that badly needed grease. The door between the kitchen and backyard swung open, then shut again. There weren't any curtains on the window, so I could clearly see the empty deck.

I slowly backed away.

Then I picked up my shoes and ran out of the house, slamming the door, not bothering to lock it.

*Shit.*

The house was haunted.

# Chapter 2

The divorced ferry women were seated at the Purple Stallion when I arrived. Based on their rosy cheeks and empty glasses, they were several drinks ahead of me. I sat at the bar and watched purple-clad servers carrying trays of margaritas to sunburned tourists in polo shirts.

I ordered a beer from the bartender, a kid in his twenties who mixed throwback styles by sporting both a mullet and a fanny pack. While he poured, I convinced myself the door and ghost mug were simply my imagination at work. A breeze opened the door. I hadn't looked closely enough to *actually* see steam coming from the mug. Someone forgot to put a cup away while they were dealing with Agatha's possessions. No one had been in the house making tea. I was tired.

And, yeah, the house was spooky, so my mind was playing tricks. Stress, not *Casper*.

I frowned. My shaky mental health wasn't the only explanation. Someone might have broken into the house. Mackinac marketed itself as a haven away from crime-ridden big cities, but it was also a tourist trap. The cottage had been empty while Agatha was in hospice. Someone might have noticed and made a move, not knowing the new owner was about to arrive.

Glancing around, I scanned the restaurant for locals who might know about recent home invasions. A man who looked like a pile of rags come to life sat on the other side of the bar. His facial hair couldn't be called a beard but was more than stubble. He looked like he lived in that bar seat and knew the island. But he also looked like he might start ranting about mermaids if given the chance, so I looked away.

I ordered a veggie burger. When I set aside my menu, a woman with bright orange hair sat next to me.

"You look just like Agatha, you know." She stared at me with a smile that was kind, if a little too friendly for my liking. "How's the house treating you?"

"Do I know you?"

She smiled again, crinkling the heavy makeup around her eyes. "News travels fast."

I nodded, unsure what to do or say. The bartender delivered my food, so I nibbled on a french fry.

"I'm Miranda." She extended a hand, and I took it. She was wearing large rings on three of her fingers. They matched her chunky necklace, which sat atop a bright green dress. Her entire outfit was loud and her smile was genuine, but it also held something back. Miranda seemed like a woman who was delighted by the secrets she kept.

"Gibson."

Her penciled eyebrows raised. She didn't remark on my unusual name. Someone younger might've asked for my pronouns, to which I would've answered, "whatever, she is fine, I don't give a fuck," but the woman just smiled.

"Have you heard of any houses broken into recently around here?"

"Goodness, no." She handed me a card. "You'll find me off Verbena Way. Your dear auntie and I got up to all sorts of trouble." She batted extremely thick fake eyelashes.

Since I didn't know my great-aunt Agatha existed until recently, I had no idea what to make of that. My mother had been estranged from her family due to religious differences, and when I became old enough to, I estranged myself from her. Religion was only one of the many differences between us.

I glanced at the card. Miranda's title was listed as "Spiritual Medium. Tarot Readings by Request." Inwardly, I groaned. There was no way I'd visit a medium—haunted house or no.

She concentrated, then said, "Let me guess. . . Capricorn?"

I opened my mouth to deflect, but she was right.

A man appeared at her elbow. "Miranda! Ms. Cartwright doesn't care about that crap." He was an imposing presence, built like a fridge and smiling like he owned the place. "Seymour Anderson, Mackinac High-End Homes. You and me should chat about that land."

Miranda clicked her tongue. "How do you know Gibson is interested in selling?"

"Of course she is!" Seymour guffawed, throwing his head back and putting his hands on his hips. He was wearing a pristine athleisure tracksuit in a shade of light blue. Odd choice for such a macho guy. "This young lady knows what a goldmine that dump could be. If it gets in the right hands, that is."

My jaw automatically clenched at being called a "young lady." I had always hated being called a lady, because it was usually meant as an insult. Well into my thirties, the "young" part was definitely insincere. But I wanted insight into the island's real estate, and here it was, in the form of a douchebag in sky-blue sweats.

He handed me a card. "Call me. You will *not* regret it."

"Like Mrs. Montclair didn't regret letting her home go?" Miranda's voice was as sweet as honey, but the look in her eyes was sharp.

"That was different—"

A voice yelled, "Leave 'er alone!" Pile-of-rags man heaved off his stool and left a stack of bills on the bar. "Disgraces, both of you. The cottage is hers."

He met my gaze and nodded, then shuffled out of the restaurant, almost knocking into a family buying souvenir T-shirts in the attached gift shop. Miranda and Seymour trailed after him, leaving me sitting at the bar with a cold burger and the feeling that dealing with this house would be more of a hassle than I anticipated. I wanted the money enough to deal with colorful local characters but that didn't mean I was eager to be friendly about it.

~

It was windy on my walk back to Abaddon Cottage. I had a jacket in my suitcase, but I had rushed out of the house convinced it was haunted, so I hadn't exactly gotten a chance to unpack. I crossed my arms and rubbed them to keep warm. The hot dog and ice cream stands at Windermere Point were closed, but the rest of downtown came alive as night fell. Music and happy people drifted out of the restaurants and hotels. I wandered among the crowds, feeling totally alone.

A group of kids rushed by on bicycles, almost knocking me over. Their leader, a curly-haired kid of about ten or so, called a quick "sorry!" over his shoulder. I scowled at the kids, but they were gone before I could yell at them.

Using the GPS on my phone to figure out which direction to go, I headed back to the cottage.

Within a few minutes, I left the old-fashioned lamps and cheery flowers of Main Street behind and entered the dark world of the rest of the island. A paved path circled the entire island, so unless I ventured into the forested park in the middle, there was little chance of getting lost. All the streetlights weren't lit, though, leaving patches of the path completely dark. The enormity of the lake on my left and the heavy damp feeling of the woods pressing in on my right made me uneasy. It's not that my life in the city was perfect, but walking home at night, I never felt alone. It was rarely hard to find somebody worse off than you or a substance to distract you from the shitty nature of everyday life. Out here, there was nothing to fill the silence, just dark woods and the lapping of cold water at the rocks.

I used my phone flashlight to light my way down the little private lane to the house. After I pushed open the door, the sight of the ghostly furniture made me jump, even though I knew it was there.

The house was quiet in an altogether different way.

Abaddon Cottage was like a deserted train station at 2 a.m. It was the kind of quiet where a light flickers somewhere in your periphery and you know the train isn't going to come but something else might. Quiet that makes the hairs on your arms stand at attention. Where anything at all could happen. The cottage was a living being that slumbered, waiting to wake up.

The chandelier reflected my phone flashlight back at me in weird shards of artificial light. I walked past my bag on the floor at the foot of the stairs and into the kitchen. My heart sped up as I checked the kitchen table.

No mug. No book. Just me, imagining things.

I breathed in and out slowly, staring at the empty table. Of course it was empty. There hadn't been anything there in the first place. I was losing my mind—in Michigan.

Returning to the hall, I grabbed my phone charger out of my luggage, which had fallen when I rushed out of the house. The main zipper was starting to come apart, and a few socks escaped onto the floor. I hadn't considered unpacking before hightailing it to a bar. I was thirty-seven years old and still spreading my shit all over the place. My mother would've had a fit.

I shook my head, dispelling those thoughts. My mother was long dead. She couldn't nag me about being messy from beyond the grave, though god only knows she would certainly try.

Sighing, I found an outlet in the hallway but when I plugged in my phone, sparks flew and the wall emitted a terrible smell. I snatched the charger from the wall and waved my hand in front of my nose.

Giving up on power, I sat on the stairs and scrolled through social media with my remaining battery. I had texted Brooke a few times as I made my way out to the island, but she left me on read without responding. My thumbs hovered over the messaging app, but I forced myself not to send another text until she responded to any of the previous ones. She knew I made it here without dying. That's all I could expect from her because she wasn't my girlfriend. Was she? I never seemed to know where we stood.

I switched over to Instagram, where Brooke had posted a picture of her and the rest of her band, Call Me Kate Kane. My face cracked in a smile at the sight of them on stage, sweat pouring off their bodies. Brooke's mouth was open in a shout. She was wearing a neon over-the-shoulder sweater with skintight pants that gave her the illusion of having an ass when her behind was as flat as any vinyl record in her collection. And Doc Martens. No matter how many times I told her Docs didn't mean what she thought they meant anymore, she kept wearing them. I had a bad habit of going after girls in their twenties instead of women my own age. Women my own age thought I was too old to pursue my dream of being a full-time musician. My ex certainly had.

Stephani, a young guitar player from a band that had recently broken up, posted a comment saying, "can't wait to jam with y'all next week." She followed it with a kissy face emoji, and without thinking, I threw my phone across the hall. It clattered against the door and ricocheted into the library where it came to a stop on the ugly green carpet.

"Fuck it," I said out loud. "You're not going to replace me, Stephani With One E. I'm a better player than you'll ever be. Brooke likes me, not you. Plus, you're too young, and your bangs are stupid."

I flipped on the light switch, bringing scattered light to the foyer. Then I picked up my wayward socks and threw them in my suitcase haphazardly, fixing the zipper and extending the handle.

Real adult behavior, Gibson, well done.

"What else?"

There was a weird shadow on the floor from the missing light in the bottom row of the chandelier. I focused on it, directing all my rage onto the little square patch of darkness.

"I can fix that," I said. "Then I'll sell this dump and get the fuck out of here. . . And I'm still talking to myself."

The hallway closet was home to several spiders that scurried away when I opened the door. Tugging on the lightbulb chain, I half-expected to be electrocuted. But, miraculously, the light turned on without killing me. I moved aside dusty boxes and eventually found one with chandelier-specific bulbs. There wasn't a date on the box, but the typography was dated and it was covered in dust. I took it into the foyer anyway, along with an old metal stepladder.

The stepladder wasn't tall enough to reach even the bottom row of the chandelier, so I dragged the wingback chair from the reading alcove over and stacked the ladder on top of it.

"Fix your shit, Gibson," I said, then climbed the improvised ladder.

I reached for the darkened lightbulb, trying to bring some sense of order into the chaos of my life, and immediately lost my balance.

My heart shot from my rib cage to my throat. I realized, with a clarity I'd felt once before, that I was going to die. The stone tile would crush my skull, and that would be that. Completely alone, in a house on an island where no one knew me, I would die.

A cold blast of air whooshed in from the sitting room.

The nearest couch, the uncovered pink suede one, flew across the room. Its wooden legs scraped loudly across the floor. The pink sofa slammed into the wingback chair I'd dragged under the chandelier, and I slammed into the pink sofa. The impact knocked the air from my lungs, and my head hit the armrest, hard.

A searing pain—then darkness.

# Chapter 3

The back of my head throbbed. Something watery was dribbling down my neck to my shoulder, pooling in the collar of my shirt.

Instead of being smashed to bits on the floor, I'd landed on the arm of an ugly pink couch. I was lying on my side, arms and legs strewn across the uncomfortable Victorian sofa like a fainting maiden. The throbbing in my head was joined by a quick stab of pain behind my right ear.

Wait— Was I dead? My head wouldn't hurt if I was dead, would it?

I winced and opened my eyes.

Above me, a woman's face hovered, lit by moonlight drifting in from the windows and the mottled light thrown by the chandelier that had tried to kill me. Her face wasn't quite solid. She was the most beautiful person I had ever seen.

"So, I *am* dead," I said to the angel hovering over me. "That's a fucking bummer, I guess."

She frowned, then gave me a skeptical look, like she thought

I was being very stupid. "No, you're not."

I tried to sit up, but the whole room started spinning, so I closed my eyes and set my head carefully back on the arm of the sofa. When I opened them again, the woman was still staring at me. I could see through her face to the ceiling. "Okay, but you're an angel, so. . ."

"I'm not an angel," she said in a prim English accent. Her voice was clear as a bell, but it was like someone had turned down the opacity setting on her body. Her eyes were a brilliant pale blue with perfectly curly lashes. Her blond hair flowed to her shoulders and hovered there like it knew this was the perfect length to frame her face and it had no intention of growing any further.

I breathed in deeply, fending off a panic attack. That was the last thing I needed. I counted to five and focused on my breaths, willing my heart to stop pounding. I could feel my pulse throbbing in my scalp behind my ear in the spot where I hit the couch.

"I'm really not dead?" I said this as much to myself as to the strange woman hovering over me.

"No." She huffed, turning her full lips into a pout. "Though you *would* be if I hadn't been watching."

I managed to sit up, and she flowed backward to give me space.

Her body wasn't anchored to the floor, which was similar to how I felt at the moment. But in her case, her legs just. . . weren't there. She was wearing a white neck-tie blouse with bell sleeves. I wasn't so out of it that I didn't notice how nicely she filled out the blouse. She also wore high-waisted navy trousers, but after her shapely thigh, her legs faded. The ghostly woman's concern turned into an exasperated expression—like she was the one who was put out by this situation instead of me.

"Okay, I get it." I pressed my hand to the tender spot on my head, realizing as I did how much I was still bleeding. It dripped down my hand onto my forearm in a bright line. Although I knew it was my blood and not some intruder's, the whole thing felt like it was happening to someone else instead of me.

I giggled, feeling lightheaded and silly. "I'm being Scrooged. I probably deserve it."

"Scrooge?" She shook her head. "No, dear, *Marley* was the ghost in that novel. Do they not teach Dickens to young Americans?"

"I know *A Christmas Carol*! I'm not an idiot."

"I never said you were. I said you're not dead."

"But—"

"You're not dead, Gibson. I am." She reached out as if to pat my arm, but stopped the gesture a few inches from me. "Let's get you some tea."

The woman stood. Her legs went all the way to the floor now, and her pant legs swished as she walked straight through the sofa. She called over her shoulder, "Do you like Earl Grey?"

A stream of blood pooled in my elbow, tickling the skin there. My head throbbed, and I was still halfway convinced I was dead.

Earl Grey. The tea I'd seen steaming in that stupid angel wings mug.

I turned and stood, still holding my throbbing head. The motion made me dizzy, but I threw out my other hand to balance the unsteady rocking of the room.

"It was you! You were the one making tea."

"Yes, dear." She disappeared into the hallway, literally fading for a moment before reappearing in the doorway of the kitchen. "That's what I've been trying to tell you. Do keep up."

"My house is haunted. I have my own Jacob Marley," I said, latching on to that name. *Dead to begin with.*

"No, my name is Annabelle. You should get checked for brain damage tomorrow."

I stood in the hallway, looking down at an ugly couch, now with a dark patch of my blood staining the arm.

Abaddon Cottage was haunted. And its ghost was a beautiful woman who shoved a couch under my ass to save me from splattering my brains all over the hardwood floor. She was humming a tune as she poured water in the kettle. The strangest feeling came over me, but it wasn't fear or the visceral displeasure I felt on the journey to this strange house. I couldn't give it a name.

As if in a dream, I followed my ghost into the kitchen.

# Chapter 4

I left a little trail of blood on the floor as I walked down the hall. My head felt like it was stuffed full of straw with bits leaking out.

At least I wouldn't get lost if I decided to make myself a midnight snack.

The ghost, Annabelle, handed me a cup of tea in a chipped yellow mug. She smiled sweetly as she handed it over, her fingers not quite solid on the handle. I took it, staring at the brown liquid in the cup. Was all this actually happening? Or had I died under the chandelier and someone was pulling a prank on me in the afterlife? Blood was still dripping onto my shoulder through my fingers.

"Let's get that wound sorted, shall we?" Annabelle rushed past me to the hall closet.

As she did, her shoulder went right through my arm. I shivered as she went through me—it felt like all the nerves where my body met her spirit glitched for a moment, before returning to normal.

I sat at the kitchen table in the spot opposite to where Annabelle's mug had caught my eye earlier. She bustled back into the kitchen, carrying an old first aid kit and several towels. Still feeling disconnected from everything happening to me, I half expected my own personal horror movie to begin and a swarm of bees to come swirling out of the kit.

But Annabelle set the kit on the table and pulled out a series of normal things: two hand mirrors, antiseptic, gauze, tape, and scissors. "Here we go," she said, passing me a mirror and a pair of scissors. "Head wounds usually look worse than they are."

She smiled reassuringly, but her words made me realize I hadn't seen the back of her head since she appeared in the hallway. For all I knew, Annabelle had a matching head wound— one that had actually been deadly.

I said "Okay," but the sounds that came out were mangled. Blocked by words I'd never screamed, still stuck in my throat.

She gestured for me to raise the mirror in my hand. Then she stood behind me holding another mirror so I could see the back of my head through it. "Can you see?"

The hand mirror had a handle with a delicate pattern in mother-of-pearl. It definitely belonged to an eighty-year-old woman. Or this old-fashioned ghost. The ghost in my kitchen. *Shit*. The room started to spin.

"Hold on, I—"

There was a faint pressure on my head, like a cool breeze but focused in one spot. My scalp tingled. Cold pressure moved up and down the back of my head, sending little pings of electricity down my spine. It was like an ice cube being slowly and gently pressed against the back of my head. I breathed out slowly, feeling my panic subside.

When I felt steady again, I held up my mirror. I could see

my own face and, behind me, the reflection of the back of my head in the other mirror. If I didn't know Annabelle was there, I would say the other mirror was suspended in the air, with no one holding it up.

Annabelle chuckled. "I'm not much to look at in the mirror, I'm afraid."

I turned to face her.

Behind me, clearly visible, was Annabelle: a beautiful woman with a sad smile on her face, clasping a mirror in one hand and reaching out to me with the other.

She'd been stroking my head. Her touch had felt like I was being petted by Frosty the Snowman. But instead of being ridiculous, the moment held a sort of strange intimacy. The ghost had saved my life and was caring for me even though we'd just met. And she was dead. And I was an intruder in her house. Yet I missed the tingly, cold sensation of her ghostly touch as soon as she stopped.

What the hell kind of ghost story was I in? I should've been afraid of her but I wasn't. I was definitely losing my mind.

Annabelle put her hand back at her side. As she moved her arms, her lace sleeves swished, even though they weren't made of a solid material. Her hands were delicate and looked like they would be soft—the opposite of my rough skin and thick, calloused fingertips.

"I can see you but can't touch you? Is that it?" I reached out a hand tentatively, palm out.

Annabelle met my eyes and reached back. Her hand passed right through mine. As it did, a cold tingling sensation traveled all the way up my arm.

"Marley," I whispered, staring at our hands. "Dead to begin with."

Annabelle withdrew her hand.

"I can't hurt you, Gibson," she said. "But I can't do much to help, either. Not directly, anyway." Her expression was soft, but her eyes held a timeworn sorrow. "And my name isn't Marley, it's Annabelle Williams."

I smiled. "Nice to meet you, Marley Annabelle Williams."

She returned my smile, then said, "Turn around, please. We need to assess your wound, though it appears to have stopped bleeding." Annabelle murmured to herself as she scrutinized my head.

I felt her and saw glimpses of her in my peripheral vision as she peered at me. My face flushed as a strange, beautiful woman—ghost—tried to take care of me without touching me.

"You might need to trim your hair right behind your ear," she said, clicking her tongue. "You have such beautiful hair."

"Literally no one has ever said so, but thanks." I felt around the bump starting to form on my head and took a bunch of hair in hand. "Here goes."

I cut it as close to the skin as I could. "How does that look?"

"No brains falling out, so that's a plus."

"Good. Not sure I have any extra gray matter to spare."

She chuckled. "You'll have a sizable bump on your noggin, though. You should have the doctor look at it tomorrow. Hopefully, it won't leave too much of a scar."

Annabelle's face was so close to mine. If she had been alive, her breath would've puffed on my ear, but instead, all I felt was a cold breeze. I shivered again, but I wasn't afraid. It was unnerving to be so close to someone who wasn't really there. But Annabelle smelled like the tea she'd just made, and her not-quite-there presence was almost comforting.

She opened the antiseptic bottle and dabbed a small amount

of liquid on a gauze pad. She handed it to me and said, "Now, apply this to the wound, and let's get some gauze on you."

Annabelle held a mirror behind my head so I could see what I was doing. Together, we awkwardly cleaned my head and applied a bandage with tape that would probably pull out the rest of my hair when I ripped it off. She gave bad directions as I worked on the back of my own head, telling me, "Left! Up, no, up! More to the left! Do listen to me, dear, I can see the back of your head and you can't."

When she was satisfied with my state, Annabelle packed up the first aid supplies and toyed with the zipper on the pouch. She stood close enough that I could have reached out and tried to touch her.

"Thanks, Marley," I said. "Hope the ghost of my Christmas past is as nice as you are."

"That's kind of you, but it's just me in this house. You'll have to make do with only one ghost." Her smile was brighter than all the lights of the stupid chandelier in the hallway put together. Like a lighthouse beacon with the power to break through the thickest fog.

I couldn't handle so much cheerful beauty, so I glanced down; her legs had disappeared again. "You, uh, lost your legs."

"Oh!" She flushed, her face becoming noticeably pinkish even though I could still see through it to the wall behind her. "Sorry. I forget, sometimes."

"How does that work? Can you control how much of your body is solid?"

She glanced down at the end of her wide-legged trousers, now completely visible. Her feet were encased in fuzzy white slippers.

"Generally speaking, yes," she said. "I can interact with the physical world just as you can. I can touch objects, as you've seen. But I do have some added. . . perks."

"Walking through walls and shit?"

"Walking through walls and such, yes."

I looked down at my hand, which had gone right through hers. "But you can't touch me?"

"No. When I try to touch living beings, it's like they're water running through my hands. But otherwise, my body is solid when I choose to be solid." Annabelle smiled, but it was perfunctory. Then she turned and took the first aid supplies back to the hall closet.

"Huh," I said, astutely.

I wrapped my hands around my now-cold mug of tea, feeling strangely calm. As if conversing with a ghost in a haunted house hundreds of miles away from normal life was no big deal. Annabelle should have been terrifying—a spirit from beyond the grave haunting a creepy-as-fuck house. But all the fear and all the frustration had drained out of me, leaving only exhaustion. I still had no idea what kind of ghost story this was, but it could wait until morning. Apparently, the dead woman in my house wasn't going anywhere.

"I'll make more tea," she said instead of asking if I wanted any.

"For reals, how much tea is there in this house?"

She gave me a mischievous look that was flat-out adorable. "Loads."

I really didn't want more tea. I drank three cups anyway while Annabelle chatted at me about topics I wouldn't for the life of me remember the next day.

# Chapter 5

It took me showing Annabelle four different sources on my phone for her to accept that it was no longer necessary to keep people with concussions awake. She didn't believe "wee-keepedia" or anything from the first page of Google results, but she finally accepted it when I showed her an article from the BBC. Her forehead creased when she read the other headlines on the page, and I took my phone back before she asked me to explain Brexit.

When I woke the next morning, I had a patch of hair missing, a terrible headache, and the old-lady smell of the house all around me. I got up and brushed my teeth, grumbling the whole time, then headed downstairs to see if my house was still haunted.

Annabelle greeted me at the bottom of the stairs holding a steaming cup of tea and a sunny smile. She was wearing the same clothes she had yesterday and looked exactly the same— still partially transparent and still totally gorgeous. "Good morning, dear!"

"Morning, Marley."

"Don't start that again," Annabelle said, dramatically rolling her eyes. But the wide smile stayed on her face, making her eyes crinkle cutely and making my insides do a little flip. If she smiled like this every time, I would definitely keep calling her that.

She followed me to the kitchen, then sat down at the table and watched while I hunted through the cabinets for coffee. My great-aunt apparently didn't share my need for a double espresso in the morning. I turned back to Annabelle, questions competing with my need for caffeine.

"Did Agatha know you were here?" I asked.

"Oh, yes, of course." She smiled sweetly, but it didn't quite reach her eyes. "It took a while for us to adjust to each other's . . . living arrangements. But once we did, we became good friends."

If that was true, then Agatha knew she was passing down a haunted house to me, a grand-niece she'd never met. Was this inheritance a prank? Was my great-aunt pranking me from beyond the grave? I had never met Agatha, so I had no idea if that was something she might do. But from colorful characters like Annabelle and the kooky medium Miranda that surrounded her while she was alive, I supposed I couldn't rule it out.

I gave up searching in the cabinets. "Is there any coffee in this house?"

The look of barely contained distaste on Annabelle's face answered my question.

"There must be a coffee shop on this island somewhere," I said. "I'll get some."

"If you must." Annabelle waved her hand in the air as if dismissing me. "Do get your head examined, dear, I'd hate to have you expire after going to all that trouble to fix you up. Not to mention the sofa." She glanced at the stained pink couch, still in the middle of the hallway where it caught my fall.

I shoved the couch back to its place and added "whatever gets blood out of suede" to my Notes app shopping list.

"Right. What's on your docket today?" I asked, then grimaced at how awkward I sounded. I reminded myself that Annabelle wasn't a hookup who stayed overnight instead of leaving. She was the one who belonged here, not me.

But the beautiful ghost didn't react to my terrible attempt at conversation. She glided across the hall to the alcove with all the books. "I was thinking of revisiting the Brontës this morning."

I followed her, eyeing the extensive cottage library. "These are your books?"

"Yes." She beamed at her collection. "Though I can't leave the house physically anymore, these transport me anywhere I'd like to go."

"You can't leave the cottage?" I hadn't stopped to consider whether the whole island was haunted or just my house.

"Not anymore, no." Her bland smile and breezy tone didn't hide the full stop at the end of that sentence. Annabelle wasn't going to elaborate.

Before I could follow that thought any further or press her on the subject, the grandfather clock in the sitting room interrupted, chiming nine times. My stomach growled, loudly reminding me that the only sustenance in this house was a tin of sardines and endless bags of tea. Annabelle waved cheerfully as I left the house, wishing me a good day in her adorable accent, and instead of feeling awkward, I couldn't help but smile.

~

I found coffee at a small shop I found charming despite my natural resistance to being charmed. Then I wandered through downtown for a while. The friendly crowds and sun overwhelmed my senses, which were calibrated for haughty pedestrians and city traffic, not chubby children and more bicycles than the fucking Tour de France.

The face of the real estate guy I met last night was plastered on flyers and signs all over town advertising his services. I hadn't given him a second thought after leaving the bar, too distracted by my near-death experience to remember the smarmy guy in blue sweatpants. One sign boasted that he could sell a house to a turtle, which made very little sense, but the sign proclaimed it with confidence anyway. His ads made him look like a pompous ass, and he had acted like one in the bar last night. But if the man could sell Agatha's house at a good price, fast, I needed to talk to him. I snapped a photo of one of his ads with my phone and added "call real estate guy" to my to-do list.

The day was hot, and my hair clung to my forehead like a moist mop had been plopped on my head. I pushed it back, annoyed, then hissed in pain when my hand brushed against the bandage on my head. I had stopped on the doorstep of one of the gazillion fudge shops on the island. Two teens sat on the bench in front of the door, looking at me like I was a middle-aged alien in a sweaty thrift store outfit.

Right. I was wandering around the island with a homegrown haircut and a head wound. Like a Final Girl in a horror film walking around *The Truman Show*.

I started walking, eager to leave before the youths started filming me to post on social media, and searched for a hairdresser with my phone. There were several salons inside swanky resorts, but I'd rather buy a pair of clippers and shave my head myself than step inside one of those. Luckily, there was also a barbershop a few streets over.

Before I reached the end of the street where I needed to turn, I passed a window with a row of real estate listings. I slowed down to peruse the houses for sale on the island, and my jaw dropped. The prices were astronomical. The houses were immaculate. The flowers in the yards were blooming. Presumably, the electrical situation inside these houses was up to code, instead of borderline dangerous.

There was no way I could sell a run-down, haunted house. Who would want to buy my dump instead of one of these normie, no-ghost houses?

I pulled up a picture of Abaddon Cottage on my phone and compared it to the listings. Where they had bright porches with built-in swings and homey furniture, Abaddon had rotting wood and protruding nails. They had open-concept kitchens with brand-new appliances, whereas Abaddon had an ancient gas stove and a refrigerator that was still labeled "ice box." All the homes for sale on the island, and even the recently sold ones, looked perfectly ready to host a new family. My house had already tried to kill me, and it came with a ghost.

~

I found Burn Your Bridges Barbershop in a smallish house in the residential neighborhood not far from Main Street. Unlike the mini-mansions in the real estate listings, or Abaddon Cottage for that matter, this house looked like a reasonably comfortable fit for a small family. There was a gaggle of bicycles out front. Many of the neighbors had immaculate lawns, but this one was small and messy, with a row of vegetable garden beds instead of flowers. It looked like people actually lived in this house, instead of having it maintained by a landscaping company.

On the front door, there was a hanging sign with a logo of the Mackinac Bridge on it. The bridge was being cut in half by a pair of giant scissors, and underneath it, the Great Lakes were on fire. I cracked a smile at the weird logo. Below the sign, on the glass windowpane, was a teeny tiny rainbow sticker.

I knocked on the door. "Hello?"

From inside, a voice called, "In here! Come on in!"

I entered the sitting room of the cozy house. The indistinct chatter of a group of teens drifted down the stairs. The front room had been converted into a barbershop, with a high chair and large mirror dominating the space. Hairdresser's tools in homemade jars sat on plastic shelves. They had cutesy slogans and children's drawings adorning the labels. A coatrack in the hallway held jackets of various kids' and adults' sizes. The house was the sort of messy that implied a busy life with children and, possibly, a pet. Not dirty or cluttered, just lived-in.

Looking at it, I felt like an anthropologist tiptoeing around the life of an unknown culture.

A woman entered from the back of the house, cleaning her hands on a dish towel.

"What can I do you for?" She was young but not too young, with a friendly sort of face and beautiful brown hair that fell halfway down her back. Somehow, it was shiny without being greasy and hadn't frizzed like mine in the humidity.

"I was hoping to do a walk-in. Nothing fancy."

The woman introduced herself as Rebecca Johnson, owner of the shop. She came closer, evaluating my messy mop of hair with a critical but not unkind eye. When she spotted the bandage above my ear, she said, "What happened there?"

I opened my mouth to respond but paused to formulate an answer that wouldn't make me sound insane. The truth was I almost died last night because I'm an idiot who doesn't want anything to do with this fucking island, but a ghost saved my life. Now she lived with me, or I lived with her? And I found her stupidly adorable.

Nope, that wouldn't work.

I cleared my throat. "Light in the hallway was out. I, uh, had a fall. It's not a big deal. Just need to deal with the hair situation."

Rebecca tsked lightly. "Why don't you get the doc to look it over?"

"I honestly have no idea what kind of network coverage my insurance has out here, and I really can't afford to find out the hard way."

"Valid. Hang on a sec." She yelled up the stairs, "Honey! Can you come down here and bring your stuff, please?"

"I'm fine. I don't need—"

"Don'tcha worry about it." Somehow, she had maneuvered me into the barber's chair. "Do you mind if I remove this?"

I nodded, and she gently removed the bandage over my ear. A few moments later, another woman skipped down the stairs carrying a black bag. Her dark hair seemed to float around her head in an uncontrollable cloud. Rebecca pointed to my head, awkwardly trimmed on one side and slightly swollen. "New-comer. She's had a fall, mind having a look?"

"You really don't have to," I protested.

But the cloud-haired woman was already turning my head gently. I closed my eyes and let her, feeling a hot lick of shame rising to my hairline.

"Doesn't look too deep, and you cleaned it fairly well," she said. "But let's go over it again, shall we?"

I swallowed. Apparently, no one on this island took no for an answer. "You're a doctor?"

"Yep." She reached into her bag to retrieve supplies that looked similar to the ones Annabelle had used, but much newer and cleaner. "Sorry, this might sting." She dabbed my head with antiseptic. "I'm Dr. Johnson. Rebecca's my wife. You're in Agatha's house then? Abaddon Cottage, she called it?"

She was holding my head, so I couldn't nod. "Yeah. She was my great-aunt, I guess. My name's Gibson."

"Well, Gibson, you could use a stitch. Won't take long, and it'll dissolve in a week or two so you needn't come back."

"I mean, I'm just here for—"

Dr. Johnson waved her hand and gave me a stern look. "No charge. Give me a moment, and I'll let you get back to your 'do."

I closed my eyes while Dr. Johnson worked on my head. There was a brief pinch as she set the stitch, then I heard her opening a new bandage. She gently placed it on my head, then stepped back.

The whole process took roughly five minutes, but I felt indebted to these women in a way that made me flush. I hadn't asked for their help, but they'd sensed how pathetic I was and helped me anyway. It reminded me of how small I'd felt as a child. How inadequate. My skin crawled with shame. I wanted to smash my hand into the mirror and throw the homemade jar into the wall.

I took a deep breath.

"Thanks, love," Rebecca said to the doctor.

"No problem." Dr. Johnson packed up her bag of supplies, then pressed a kiss to her wife's cheek. "Call me if the wound becomes red or more painful than it is now. It might itch a little.

But if it starts oozing, get your butt back in that seat, you hear?"

I nodded.

"So, what're you going to do?" Rebecca asked.

The obvious answer was that I would sell the house and get the hell out of here. I could take the money and run back to my normal life where no one helped me because I never asked anyone to.

I came all this way to evaluate the property, consult with a local real estate agent, and settle on a price. Abaddon Cottage and the land it sat on were mine to cash out—if I got enough for it, I could keep living in New York. I might still have to rent even if I made a million bucks on the deal, but I could find a better place. Maybe quit my day job in marketing. Go on the road playing with Brooke and the rest of Call Me Kate Kane.

Instead of saying any of that, I said, "The house needs a lot of work. Figured I'd see what the market is like, but I'm not sure it'll sell unless I gut it. And I'm not sure how long that'll take."

Rebecca gently placed her hand on my shoulder. "I meant your hair."

"Oh. Right."

She smiled. "But I'd be lying if I said the year-rounders weren't dying to know your plans for the cottage, too."

I ducked my head, trying to recover an ounce of dignity and failing miserably. "I don't know. Never been big on plans."

"Understandable. Need one for the hair, though."

In the mirror, I saw a person I barely recognized staring back at me. My brown eyes looked tired. My neck skin was starting to become turkey-like, and I was clenching my jaw without realizing it. In the mirror, I saw someone who'd been hurt once, then several times more. A mop-haired fool who'd been running from the hurt ever since. There were more lines on my face than I remembered, and they hadn't been put there by smiles.

"Cut it all off." I mimicked a buzz cut, complete with sound effects. "You can leave some in the front, but otherwise, full Rachel Maddow."

Rebecca hesitated, then gave me a nod and said, "Okay." She didn't ask if I was sure, or tell me I might regret the decision, just got down to business in a comfortable silence I was profoundly grateful for. She turned my head this way and that, moving my chin gently but firmly. I felt myself relax as pieces of hair fell away. Gradually, we returned to a conversation that didn't go near any exposed nerves. I told her about my to-do list and that I'd put off my day job by telling my boss my phone service was too bad to set up a Wi-Fi hotspot.

"Been to the fort yet?" she asked.

"Nah, I'm not really one for propaganda."

"That's fair." Rebecca smiled. There were pictures on the walls of the hairdresser, her wife, and a kid that aged and de-aged depending on which picture I glanced at. "The kids have fun doing accents and reenactments, though."

"Accents?"

"They play British soldiers."

I vaguely remembered the ferry captain saying something about the War of 1812 figuring into the history of the island. I hadn't much cared at the time, though. Rebecca worked silently for a few moments, and I drifted, feeling the odd sensation of a person flitting about behind me, actually able to touch my head.

"Wait—you said British soldiers?" I wanted to slap my forehead, but my arms were trapped inside a hairdresser's robe. "There were British soldiers here?"

"Yeah, they were here before we were." She paused. "I

mean, obviously, the Native Americans were here way before anyone else, though. Look down, please." She tipped my head down and shaved the back of it. I listened to the buzzing of the clippers while my thoughts swirled.

British soldiers—was that why Annabelle was British? Of course. Why didn't I realize how ridiculous it was to have an English ghost in an American house? Then how old was she?

I felt stupid for not connecting the dots earlier. But then again, it wasn't any of my business who Annabelle was or how she was connected to the house. Once I sold it, the next owner could interrogate Annabelle's connection to the colonialist history of this weird, gentrified island. I didn't need to know Annabelle's story, I just needed to tolerate her long enough to pawn her off on whoever I could convince to buy a haunted house.

But I wanted to know.

We stayed quiet for the rest of the cut. I tried not to think about how long it would take to fix the house up enough to sell it. I wondered what Brooke was doing. She'd probably be waiting tables, dreaming of being on stage. My day job writing copy and strategizing for an advertising firm was more "adult" than many of the musicians I hung with, but no less soul-sucking. At least no one cared if I put on my headphones and listened to Patti Smith's back catalog all day.

What kind of music did Annabelle like? She probably didn't know anything more recent than Beethoven.

To distract myself from the women living rent-free in my head, I glanced around at the cluttered house. I pointed to the business cards with the bridge logo on them, neatly stacked in a little homemade ceramic bowl. "What's with 'Burn Your Bridge'?"

"Well, the Mackinac Bridge, obviously," Rebecca said.

"Longest suspension bridge in the West and all that."

I hummed politely, not giving a crap about the long-ass bridge.

"And . . ." Rebecca hesitated, giving me a thoughtful look. It felt like she was appraising me, trying to decide if I was worth whatever she would say next. "Have you ever had a moment where you knew you needed to do something dramatic? But the prospect of change is so terrifying that in order to force yourself to do it, you have to burn your bridges? Because if you have the ability to go back, you will?"

I met Rebecca's eyes in the mirror. Her presence behind me was solid. She smelled like the light perfume of a hairdresser in her thirties comfortable in the skin she wore. I couldn't help but contrast her with Annabelle, an ephemeral woman in old-fashioned clothes who smelled like the tea she constantly made and couldn't drink.

"I guess I've burned a bridge or two," I said. "So, you had your big epiphany and burned your bridges to open a barbershop on Mackinac?"

Rebecca threw back her head and laughed. "Hell no. You think I wanted to stay here and be . . ." She pursed her lips and glanced upstairs, where her wife had returned. She didn't say "Mackinac's palatable lesbians."

"The thing is, you gotta make sure the life you're setting on fire is worth burning, and you gotta get it done. Over with. Nothing left, but ready to start anew. If you're on fire when you reach the other side of the bridge, then the place you're trying to get to isn't different from the place you left behind."

She put the finishing touches on the shaved hair around my bandage. The tickling vibrations sent tingles down my spine.

"Tell you what," she said, "if you stick around Mackinac for a while, buy me a drink and I'll tell you about my bridge and how I burned it."

I smiled, surprised to find that it was genuine, not a polite, forced smile. "Deal."

# Chapter 6

When I returned to the house, I was armed with four paper bags full of food, grumbling at the idea of staying here long enough to need a bicycle with a basket. My punk image was already bruised enough by becoming a homeowner on an island full of rich white people. I refused to set the bags down while detaching the keyring from my jeans.

Once inside, I set the bags on my hip and called out, "Hello?"

A strange sense of déjà vu came over me—but for a memory I didn't have. There was never a time in my life when I came home to someone eagerly waiting for me. My parents were always busy and rarely home. Then I didn't have a permanent address for a good decade and change. Before Jesse, living with Babs was the closest thing I had to stability in my twenties, and she kicked me out after I punched a hole in the wall. Fair enough.

Then Jesse and I got together and things were good, until they weren't. Even when Jesse still tolerated me, she was usually asleep when I got home from jamming with friends or watching someone else play. If I came home when she was awake, she greeted me with clenched teeth. Why expect anything different now?

"What a lovely haircut!" Annabelle appeared suddenly at my elbow, making me jump.

I lost my grip on the shopping bags, sending one of them careening sideways before I managed to catch it. A carton of eggs spilled, breaking open and smashing several eggs on the entryway floor. Bright yellow and orange innards splattered across the tile.

Damn. Well, if I couldn't eat them, maybe I'd use the shards to tell my future. Egg haruspicy . . . Yeah, I was losing my mind.

My heart rate slowed when I saw Annabelle's terribly cute, chagrined expression.

I said, "This is not going to work."

She cocked her head to the side, looking down regretfully at the eggs. "What isn't?"

"You. Appearing out of nowhere. Can you put a bell on or something? To let me know when you're going to appear?"

Annabelle pouted, pushing her rosy lower lip out. "I'm not a cat, Gibson."

An image of her pouting face with a collar around her neck popped into my head, and I banished the too-alluring thought.

"But I will try to be better about sudden appearances. I promise."

"Thank you."

"And in return . . ." Now Annabelle bit her lip and wouldn't meet my eyes. She was glancing at the open door, letting in humid summer air and a horde of bugs.

"What is it, Marley?"

"I'd appreciate your discretion about my . . . continued in-habitation of the house." Now Annabelle looked longingly at her library alcove, where she'd stacked a handful of novels on a side table next to her reading chair. I spied *Jane Eyre* and some-thing by Oscar Wilde but didn't recognize the rest.

"Sure," I said. "Who am I going to tell? Your secret is safe with me."

Until I sold the house. And even then, who would believe me anyway?

I gathered the rest of the groceries and set the bags down in the kitchen, then returned to the hall to clean up the eggs. A few unbroken ones remained, so at least I could have breakfast this week.

Before placing anything inside the ancient refrigerator, I wiped it down and made a note on my to-do list to hire a cleaner to do a deep clean. The pantry shelves were disgusting, so after putting away the food, I wiped them down and put the ancient jars in a pile by the door. I set an unopened bag of coffee and a box of tea on the counter next to the kettle. When I plugged my phone into the outlet next to the stove, sparks flew out of it. Unsurprised, I unplugged it and added, "get an electrician" to the list.

I sat down in Annabelle's spot at the table, suddenly feeling exhausted. Taking a deep breath in, I prepared myself to check my email but noticed the humid, almost fishy smell that plagued the house occasionally. It was like the smell of fish—if the smell of fish was made pleasant, somehow. Just then, Annabelle ap-peared in the chair opposite me, despite my request that she signal me beforehand.

"Would you like a snack?" she asked.

"Well . . ."

Without waiting for an answer, she headed into the some-what clean kitchen and started opening cabinets. "I'll make you something. It's been ages since I cooked for anyone. Agatha had the strangest tastes, and once she was moved to the care home, all the goods she had just went stale."

"Okay, but—"

A loud knocking on the front door made us both jump in surprise. I let out a breath and forced myself to relax. "Hold that thought."

When I opened the door, the woman from the restaurant last night was standing outside, smiling brightly. She clutched a large handbag and was wearing a scarf around her head despite the heat. "Good to see you again, dear."

"Okay," I said.

I didn't open the door wide enough for her to enter, but she pushed it open with her foot. Miranda entered the hallway and looked around with a placid smile. As if she was trying to put on a brave face about being in my house when she was the one who barged in.

"Oh good, all her things are still here."

"Excuse me?" I didn't close the door behind her, hoping she'd take the hint and leave. My established policy of not yelling at senior citizens might have to change.

"The estate people wouldn't let me in to take care of her things." Miranda's voice was shaky now. "Agatha had every-thing worked out ahead of time, but she could be so bullheaded about other people's feelings."

I had no idea what to say about that, but she seemed like she needed a moment, so I gestured her to a chair in the sit-ting room. She took a seat on one of the sitting room sofas. She glanced at the bloodstained one, but her expression didn't change.

"Uh . . . Tea?"

"Love some," she said, crinkling her eyes in a friendly way. It made her heavy mascara stand out among the many happy wrinkles around her eyes.

Feeling completely out of my depth, I made her a cup of tea and poured it into the only cup and saucer set I could find among a sea of mugs in the cabinet. Annabelle was sitting at the kitchen table, reading a novel and making tutting noises. I cleared my throat.

"Yes, dear?"

"You're . . . look, I don't want to sound rude, but—"

Annabelle set the book aside and folded her hands. She looked amused.

"I just . . . this lady showed up, and I can't explain you to—"

"It's quite all right, Gibson. I'll make myself scarce." She found a serving tray from one of the cupboards and put the tea I made on it. Then she vanished into thin air.

"Thank you?" I said to the empty kitchen.

I returned to the living room and set the tray on a low end table and handed Miranda the cup.

After a few moments of awkward silence, we fell into a conversation that became more enjoyable the longer it went on. I served Miranda three cups of tea while she peppered me with tales of séances gone sideways. I couldn't put a finger on her age. Since she knew Agatha, she had to be fairly old, but she somehow seemed both older and younger than she appeared. The conversation, of course, turned to the house and what I was going to do with it.

"First things first, I need an electrician. Or the house might burn down before I can sell it, anyway." I frowned. Checking things off my to-do list and getting closer to the payout that would let me leave this 1950s fever dream island was all well and good, but finding an electrician would mean *making phone calls.*

"I can help with that," Miranda said. "I know just the man! He doesn't have the most pleasant bedside manner, but he's a pro and he'll give you a fair price."

"I guess that would be nice, but you don't have to—"

"Of course I do, love." She clapped her hands together, then brought out an iPhone that was so many generations old it was practically obsolete. "In fact, I'll just call him now. He and I go . . . way back."

The way she said "way back" was so suggestive I blinked in surprise. Way to go, Miss Miranda.

She delicately pressed her fingers to the screen, angling them up to avoid scratching the phone with her fake nails. A man picked up after three rings, and she stood to pace the hall while they talked. I didn't hide the fact that I was listening.

"Now, Pete, you turn down that television and give me a listen or there'll be no leftover lutefisk for you come this Christmas." Miranda rolled her eyes and listened to a shouty tirade from the other end. When the speaker's voice faded, she gave him the address and said, "Very well. And you'll be on your best behavior while you're here. You already know how much work this place needs."

Miranda hung up and turned back to me. "All set. He'll be here tomorrow. Can't have us burning down this lovely old house, now, can we?"

I stuttered, feeling completely overwhelmed that she'd simply taken this task off my plate for me. "You don't need to help me. Why are you helping me?"

Miranda's dangly green earrings lightly brushed one shoulder as she cocked her head to the side. She pursed her lips. Her teacup now had a bright pink lipstick stain on it. "Because you need it, dear," she said gently.

I couldn't reply. It was too much. All the words stuck in my throat before I could get them out. I wanted to yell at her and make her leave. I wanted to hug her. The mixture of feelings was too large for my body.

"Thank you," I managed.

She smiled sweetly. We shared a moment of comfortable silence together in my great-aunt's home. Then the grandfather clock chimed, and she seemed to awaken from a dream.

"Oh, my, look at the time." Miranda helped me gather the teacups and bring them into the kitchen. She knew where everything went already and insisted on washing the dishes as I watched. Annabelle's cup and book were still on the table where she'd left them. I hoped Miranda wouldn't notice the extra cup and saucer.

Before she left, she turned and said, "Until next time, Gibson."

I nodded politely. Next time? How many times was I going to play hostess to my weird great-aunt's best friend?

She added, "It's just that I'd love to catch up with my old friend."

"What?"

She looked over my shoulder at the bookshelves, before glancing back and clearing her throat. "*My Old Friend.* It's a book I borrowed from your great-aunt. I'll bring it next time."

I shrugged. "Okay."

"Have a lovely evening," Miranda said, blowing a kiss over her shoulder as she left. "Both of you."

"Wait . . ." I turned.

Behind me, visible and waving, was Annabelle.

"Wait, you knew?" I shouted. "You *knew*!"

But she was halfway down the walk and either didn't hear or pretended not to.

~

While cooking dinner, Annabelle hummed a tune. She swayed her hips as she sang under her breath. Shoving down memories of my mother singing arias at my father over the breakfast table, I couldn't help but laugh when I recognized the song. Annabelle was singing a badly out-of-tune rendition of "Daydream Believer." I was sitting in an old house listening to The Monkees while a ghost cooked for me.

When was the last time someone made dinner specifically for me? Not since Jesse. God, that was so long ago. And even then, we fought over every little thing. I couldn't even salt the damn food well enough to please her.

"Here you are!" Annabelle said with a smile, setting a full plate of pasta in front of me.

"I don't know how you did that with the sketchy-ass appliances in here." I gave the stove the stink eye. No way I was going to use that thing. I'd probably leave the gas on somehow and die in my sleep. Maybe I'd haunt the house, too. God, what a depressing thought.

"Nothing to it," she said. She sat next to me and leaned over my plate, taking a deep breath in. "That stove may be almost sixty years old, but I'm over two hundred!" She chuckled to herself as if she'd personally put one over on the stove. She looked so pleased that I would never cook again if asking Annabelle to do it would put that look on her face.

"Try it, please."

I took a bite. The pasta was rich and creamy, cooked to the perfect firmness. "Mmm. It's so good."

"And? The texture? Tell me about the flavor."

"Creamy. And just the right amount of pepper."

She sat back, satisfied. "Oh, good." The look on her face was dreamy—as if she'd been the one savoring the meal. "Glad to know I haven't lost my touch. Although it's hard to go wrong when you add that much butter."

I nodded, unsure what to say that wouldn't make me sound like an idiot who had no idea how to describe pasta. I could write B2B marketing copy all day, but if I tried to imitate Anthony Bourdain and describe food to a pretty girl, my tongue tied itself in knots.

"'S really good, Marley. Thank you."

Annabelle smiled that brilliant smile at me again, and I had to look away from the intensity of it.

"You're most welcome, my dear."

We sat in amiable silence while I ate, trading smiles. Annabelle sat very close, leaning in every now and then to smell the food. I knew it wasn't about me—she was vicariously enjoying the meal through my consumption of it. But I had a hard time convincing my heart to slow down anyway. She watched me eat with an intensity that would've been scary if she'd been any other ghost. She set her elbows on the table and leaned forward, as close as she could get without sitting in my lap. The thought of that made me squirm—not in a bad way.

After a few moments of silence, I had to break it or I'd burst. "Chives!"

"What?"

"Chives. Would go good on this. With this. Not that it's not perfect as is, I mean." I paused to wrestle control over the sounds coming out of my mouth. "Do you know if there's any in the garden?"

"There might be," Annabelle murmured. There was a look on her face I couldn't interpret, and she'd gone a little fuzzy around the edges.

I got up from the table and put on rubber gloves to do the dishes. This earned me a suggestive side-eye from Annabelle that caused me to flush in return. I swallowed and turned to the sink, listening while she chatted about nothing in particular. The kitchen, once a source of anxiety, now felt like a bubble removed from the rest of reality. It felt like as long as I stayed in the moment, with me washing up after a meal Annabelle had cooked, the rawness of the outside world was held at bay.

It wouldn't last. I'd always found a way to mess up any safe space I was a part of.

I brought a bottle of wine out to the table and dusted off two chairs. Then I remembered that Annabelle's butt wouldn't mind a bit of dust, since it wasn't there. I stared out at the darkening sky. The garden was already mostly shades of blueish gray. The moon was but a sliver of silver light and stars were coming out to watch over us.

Curious, I went back in the house and found a flashlight. With its help, I poked around in the vegetable bed at the corner of the lot. There were so many bugs. The remnants of decaying plants I couldn't identify were rotting in the bed, having gone through at least one cycle of the seasons without human interference, maybe more. I found an onion, still alive and happy, tucked among decaying greens. Pulling out the bulb, I said, "Aha!" and returned to the table.

Annabelle was sitting on the chair I'd dusted. Up close, I could see her face clearly even in the dim light of the twilit evening. She seemed to glow faintly with an evanescence I couldn't stop marveling at. Again, I was struck by how beautiful she was.

I cleared my throat. "Look what I've got!" I held up the onion, which wasn't much more than a mangled mess of dirt and rotten vegetable matter. I plunked it down on the table between us and poured myself more wine.

"Is that an onion, or are you just happy to see me, darling?"

Darling.

The word dropped through my chest like a stone down a well, clanging against the sides of my ribs as it fell. It was nothing but a figure of speech. Annabelle spoke like a character from a Dickens novel—she was Marley, after all. It didn't mean anything.

And yet, when she smiled at me, the effervescent glow seemed to extend out from her to envelop me, too.

"Agatha was a gardener, then, I take it?"

"Well," Annabelle said, her smile still lingering, "she grew vegetables and a few herbs. But mostly she was interested in the ingredients she needed for her potions."

"Potions? Yeah, we are going to have to circle back to the potion thing."

Annabelle heaved a put-upon sigh. "I have no doubt. Though I'd much rather not think of them again. Stinkweed is ever so stinky."

I laughed again, and that feeling of something floating free in my chest grew stronger. "You don't strike me as the green thumb sort, either, Marley," I said. She was far too posh. "No offense."

It was meant as a tease, but instead of reciprocating, Annabelle stilled. She looked out at the dark shapes of the trees and shrubs, lurking, lit by the glow from the kitchen window. Their shadows played games with the mind, becoming monsters ready to strike. Or to dance.

"No. You'll have to tend to the gardens yourself, Gibson. I won't be able to help you." The way she said this was delicate. There was more she could have said, but she chose not to.

Then Annabelle reached out as if to pick up the onion, but her hand passed right through it. "I generally cook with dried herbs and spices," she said. "Fresh ingredients are hit and miss; it all depends on how long they've been out of the ground."

"I don't understand."

She repeated, "When I touch living beings, they're like water running through my hands. That includes your onion, so long as it's still alive."

"Oh," I said. "Marley, I—"

I wasn't sure what to say. It's not like I was a gardener myself. Before escaping to the city, I grew up in the desert, where watching things shrivel was just a part of life. But I had the power to try. Annabelle could only watch. Earlier, I had thought of her smile as a lighthouse beacon. But I hadn't considered how hard it would be to keep smiling while looking out on a world you couldn't touch.

"It's all right, dear." She gave me a small, pained smile, then looked out at the darkness. From somewhere nearby, a horse whinnied, then fell quiet.

The features on her face slowly set into a bland smile. She would have had two hundred years to practice using it to hide her real feelings. How often did she have to make herself disappear? How often had the occupants of this house been unwelcoming? Or afraid of her like I had been at first? Annabelle tried so hard to keep her face neutral, but something always gave her away. Whether it was a nervous fluttering of her hands or her twinkling eyes, Annabelle had a hard time hiding her feelings—a strange deficit for an old ghost.

I wished I had my guitar. I'd play her all the things I couldn't seem to say.

"Wait a second—" I got up and dashed back into the house. "Don't go anywhere!"

"I quite literally can't," she replied.

Grabbing my phone, I cursed the fact that I hadn't brought proper speakers with me. I opened my music app anyway and scrolled through my usual favorites as I returned to the deck. It took a while to get to something that wasn't screamy or intensely sad. None of my usual genres would fit the moment, but somehow, I figured that Annabelle might appreciate the blues. I selected a song and turned up the volume. Nina Simone's soulful voice entered the night air.

Annabelle brightened, sitting up straight and listening intently. Even the terrible sound coming out of my phone speakers couldn't ruin the magic of Nina's powerful voice.

"Did you always live here?" I asked. "In the house?"

Annabelle didn't look at me, staring at the back fence instead. "For many years, I moved more freely about the island. Before it was a house, this was a meadow. I walked among the trees and didn't need to worry about startling anyone with my appearance. Then things kept changing, and I found that as they did, I wasn't able to stay . . . solid. Not unless I was here."

"Do you remember . . . before?"

"When I was alive, you mean?"

I nodded. The humidity of the quiet night enveloped us in a silky embrace.

"I believe so, yes. But it's far away. I know some things with certainty, but other memories are . . ." Her face went through a complicated series of emotions, then settled on an expression of sad reserve. "It's as if there's a fog in between me and the life I used to have. Sometimes I can see things clearly, but most of the time, my memory is hazy. Even the brightest light won't pierce through to the other side and let me fully remember." Her eyes were sad, but she smiled nonetheless.

"I'm sorry."

"Don't be sorry, my dear." Annabelle reached out a hand and placed it carefully on top of mine. She held it just above my skin, not passing through and not touching. It made the nerves on the top of my fingers sing with an electric hum.

She shook herself. When she moved her hand away, I missed it immediately.

"My goodness, you've got me speaking in an overwrought metaphor. Imagine! A ghost talking about bright lights—how derivative."

I snorted. "It's not derivative, Marley. Just a metaphor."

"Yes, but it's a little on the nose, don't you think?"

We both chuckled.

I watched the shadows of the garden settle into flat darkness. My tailbone ached from sitting so long on the hard surface of a wooden patio chair. Splinters worked their way into my butt cheeks, but I didn't care. Annabelle's edges ebbed and flowed as we continued chatting, the sound of soul behind us, until long after midnight.

# Chapter 7

I woke gradually, drifting into consciousness like rising to the surface of a warm pool.

It was only my second morning waking in Abaddon Cottage. Blood loss and the shock of the first night had kept me in a state of anxious readiness. My body had been coiled, poised to fight or flee. Now that my anxiety had reduced from a constant rolling boil to a simmer, other feelings bubbled to the surface. The adrenaline rush of fright morphed into a different kind of arousal.

Sunlight wasn't yet peeking in through the window, but the dawn was making itself known by a kaleidoscope of colors reflected on the walls. I stayed in almost-dreams, not quite ready to face the day.

The sheets I'd found on the bed were old and scratchy, but the texture played against my skin, making me feel everywhere it touched my body. Awareness oozed slowly from my head down my torso into my fingers and toes. I curled them, feeling the mattress underneath shift as I stretched out.

I drifted my fingers idly across my thighs.

When was the last time I got off? Before I left home, obviously. With that girl Melissa? No. We were drunk, and when she left, I was too tired.

I rubbed my legs together. Desire was starting to build, and I inched my hands closer to my groin as I breathed in—old house and old, starchy sheets. The scent didn't exactly inspire.

Michigan, right. Abaddon Cottage.

Shit, Annabelle.

Was she here, in the walls somehow? She could have been watching me. But I was so stupidly horny. Maybe—

Nope.

I threw back the sheets. Time to start the day.

~

My phone vibrated so hard it almost fell off the table. I grabbed it but kept it face down while eating the delicious omelet Annabelle placed in front of me.

"Someone is surely *blowing up* your telephone," Annabelle said, curling her hands around her steaming mug of English breakfast tea. The mug had an outline of the state of Michigan and the phrase "Mitten smitten" on it. She couldn't drink it but she held it close to her face and inhaled the scent, seeming to glean satisfaction from the hot beverage anyway.

I narrowed my eyes. "How do you know the phrase 'blowing up' someone's phone?"

Annabelle set down her tea and gave me the coyest look I had ever seen on another person, living or dead. "I may be an old ghost but I do watch television, dear."

"That thing works?" The tiny set in the sitting room was built into a cabinet and looked like the last time it had been switched on was when Nixon resigned.

Annabelle smiled. "It does! Agatha and I became quite devoted to a program called *Passions*. We watched it every afternoon for eight years."

"My apologies." I ate the last piece of egg, scraping the plate with my fork to make sure I got all of it. "You're a regular urban dictionary."

Her eyebrows drew together at the unfamiliar phrase, and I felt a little bad for teasing but not so bad as to stop. Meanwhile, my phone buzzed again, this time in the short bursts that indicated a furious text message tirade. I sighed and turned it over.

In addition to a series of furious messages from my boss, I had several from Seymour Anderson, the real estate guy who advertised around the island. He also sent me four separate emails. I rolled my eyes and sent him a reply with basic info about the house and a few times I'd be available for a meeting.

Then it was time to deal with Babs.

I sighed and marked the texts as read without actually reading them. Then I logged into my work account on my phone for the first time since I left New York. Six different people had sent me meeting invites despite my explicit instructions not to and my out-of-office automatic reply. I didn't technically have time off since I was a contractor, not an employee. But in eight years, Babs hadn't found anyone else who a) could work with her and b) was willing to write rebranding copy for corporations that were guilty of crimes or had gotten away with them.

"Dammit, Babs, I told you I'm not working while I'm out here," I muttered. Then I gave in and requested a quote for a cable install on the house. Even if I only used it for a few weeks, it would be better than a spotty phone hotspot. And the new owners would be grateful, whoever they might be. The house was a money pit sitting on valuable real estate, so it probably wouldn't be too long before Seymour found me a buyer. Then I could fly back to Babs, the band, and normal life.

And Annabelle would have someone new to haunt. For some reason, the thought made my stomach churn.

"Babs is your . . ." Annabelle interrupted my thoughts, her eyebrows raised and her expression carefully neutral.

Was she jealous? Or did she have another reason for interrogating me about my life?

"Boss. Babs is my boss." I took a sip of coffee and studied Annabelle's face closely. "She's also my ex. We were disastrous in a relationship, but we're great as colleagues. Who knew."

"Oh, I see." Annabelle seemed to sigh in relief.

"Is that a . . . problem?" I asked cautiously. "That I date other women?"

"No!" Annabelle put her hands up and shook her head. She was clearly flustered, having gone invisible from the waist down. A shame, since her thighs were always nice to see. "In fact, it's . . ."

She didn't finish her thought, instead pensively looking out the kitchen window. Birds had gathered on the railing, and she smiled wistfully at them. "It's—"

The doorbell rang with a squawk that didn't sound like the correct sound for a doorbell.

"Hold that thought," I said.

As I walked through the hallway, the doorbell rang again but fizzled out by the end of the buzz. The person on the other side of the door tried it a few more times, but the only sound that escaped was a pathetic clink. Oh good, another thing to fix.

Opening the door, I said, "Yes?" in an unwelcoming tone.

"Are you Gibson Cartwright? Formerly known as Veronica

Cartwright?" The young woman at the door adjusted her glasses. They were thick-rimmed and black, but not in a fashionable way. The rest of her dress looked practical for traipsing to Mordor but not for spending the summer on an island. Her long, bushy skirt fell just above her ankles, exposing sensible brown laced boots.

"Yes?" I repeated.

"Good." The woman nodded. She was young but she looked like she might bite if you told her so. "My name is Yasmin," she said, sticking out her hand.

I shook it lightly, unsure why I felt the need to be polite to her. "Okay . . ."

"I'm Agatha Cartwright's grand-niece. This cottage rightfully belongs to me."

The woman leveled an impressive scowl at me that I returned with interest. She was carrying a briefcase under one arm and a trunk that looked like it contained at least a month's worth of clothes in the other. She set it down on the doorstep with a loud thunk. "I have papers from the family lawyer in my briefcase. Shall we review them?"

"Well, fuck," I said.

~

Annabelle went off to wherever she went when she was invisible without me having to ask.

Yasmin looked around the cottage with the look of an appraiser. She wore a serious expression. It looked like it might pain her to smile, and it made me fear I would have to relinquish my self-proclaimed title of biggest bitch in town.

I ushered Yasmin to the kitchen table. She opened her briefcase, then retrieved her birth certificate, Social Security card, family photos, and a handwritten letter from her mother. It was notarized. I dug out the paperwork I had from my lawyer. Then I plugged my external hard drive into my laptop and scrolled through pictures of my mom that I hadn't looked at in over a decade. There was no mistaking the resemblance between the two of us and the pictures of our mothers. Her mother was younger than mine by five years. But when she showed me a recent picture of her, smiling at the beach with long, dark hair and tan skin, my stomach did a flip. Mom had died before she could reach that age, but instinct told me she would've looked just like Yasmin's mother, Helena.

Together, we created a timeline. My mother and her sister, Yasmin's mother, were sent to stay with Agatha at Abaddon after *their* mother, Martha, died. Martha and Agatha were sisters with only a year of age between them. Yasmin had a photo of her mother as a girl in 1970s clothes standing in the backyard, along with one that showed Agatha working in the garden. I looked out the kitchen window at the backyard and held up the photo. It looked much better under Agatha's care.

My mother hadn't stayed with Agatha for long, and soon after, stopped contacting her own sister. Yasmin's mother moved to California and, from the letters and photos Yasmin showed me, stayed closely in touch with Agatha even as she moved and had children of her own. I didn't even try to unclench my jaw as we worked.

"See?" Yasmin said, getting up to stretch. "Agatha clearly made a mistake when she willed the house to you."

"Hmmm." I thought the same thing when I was notified of the inheritance. I thought the same thing when I arrived. Now I wasn't sure what to think.

The shadows on the garden outside the window grew as we

exchanged papers across the table, talking sparingly. We tried to look at Yasmin's legal paperwork, but after an hour of staring at documents, she started yawning. Then I started yawning. We agreed to postpone discussing the legalese until tomorrow. Only when I showed her to the second-floor bedroom with the rose wallpaper and cautioned her about using the wall socket did her hard veneer start to crack. She put her trunk down on the bed and stared out the window at the garden below.

"I didn't know it would be so beautiful," she said.

"It's . . . certainly something." I stood in the doorway awkwardly. "Get some rest, and we'll talk in the morning."

Yasmin nodded. "Thank you."

I patted the doorframe and then went downstairs but couldn't concentrate. The papers Yasmin brought seemed legit. It certainly looked like she was who she said she was. I sent an SOS email to my lawyer and then decided to go for an evening walk. Annabelle still wasn't around. I closed and locked the door behind me.

I tried to keep my mind blank as I wandered the island. It was too late to walk all the way to the fort. I had little interest in paying admission to see an old castle built by people who claimed this island by squatting on it and kicking everyone else out. The gazebo seemed too cheesy, and the fancy-schmancy Grand Hotel probably wouldn't let me in because I wouldn't adhere to the dress code. Instead, I wandered the path that circled the island.

I tried not to think of Dr. Johnson casually kissing her wife on the cheek yesterday like it was the easiest thing in the world. I tried not to think of the dead woman or the unwanted family waiting for me to return to Abaddon. But somehow, the people I had waiting for me back home in New York kept slipping away, their faces receding, replaced by thoughts of houses and relatives and ghosts.

Darkness surrounded me, but I didn't go back to Abaddon Cottage. I walked along the island's perimeter path, with no particular destination in mind. The pavement curved, hugging the limestone rock formations closely. Every now and then, a cyclist whooshed by. As the pink dusk became twilight, then dark, cyclists stopped coming. On the other side of the path, the still lake waters were pitch black. The edge of the path could've been a cliff dropping into an endless void.

Ahead of me and around a bend, there was a small pocket of rocky beach. Inky water crept up to meet shiny dark stones that glistened with slick foam. A thin line of vegetation was all that separated the path where I walked from the small beach made of slippery stones. A feeling of dread came over me as I approached the little cove, but I wasn't sure why.

I told myself I was done with the spooky stuff. Time to deal with *actual* problems instead of imaginary ones.

Jamming my hands in my pockets, I kept walking. The silence of the island was broken only by the whisper of water lapping at the rocks, endlessly grabbing at them like hands seeking something to hold on to.

I kept walking, feeling unsettled and angry for reasons I had a hard time pinpointing. I almost didn't recognize Annabelle standing on the rocks.

"Marley? What are you doing out here?"

She turned to face me slowly. Her feet were visible—white and bare on the jagged stones. I was reminded of clouds but wasn't sure why. She was wearing a long nightgown, the sort you might see on a BBC show. But the wind blew it across her figure, making the thin fabric hug her curves. Annabelle's body was solid, more solid than I'd ever seen her before. She also seemed to shine brightly from within, like a halo of light covering her entire body. As she turned to face me, her body and shoulders moved separately—like they'd been disconnected at the neck.

I sped up, but she was still a good fifty feet ahead of me on the rocks.

There was something wrong with Annabelle's eyes. They were too wide and too white.

"Marley!" I reached out, trying not to trip over my own suddenly-too-big feet.

Annabelle's ghostly body was still, but she raised an arm stiffly, struggling under the weight of it. She was dripping wet. Water streamed down her face from drooping tendrils of hair. Instead of its usual white-blonde, in the strange light her hair was a dark, mottled gray. A gash of moonlight ripped through dark clouds and threw strange shadows on her ghastly, beautiful face.

"Marley, I'm—" I wasn't sure what the end of that sentence would be. My walk turned into a jog as I sped up to reach her. I thought she couldn't leave the house?

Annabelle opened her mouth as if to reply, but when her lips parted, a dark gush of black water streamed down her chin. Her eyes were wide in horror as inky liquid and seaweed spilled from the gaping maw of her mouth.

I broke into a run.

My footsteps slapped loudly against the pavement. But when I reached the rocks, Annabelle had vanished.

~

Abaddon Cottage was dark.

"Annabelle?"

Nothing.

"Yasmin?"

No response. Only silence and the creaking of a front door I would need to grease. I stepped into the hall, not carrying anything but conscious of my hands, like a sense memory of everything I'd dropped onto this very floor, including myself.

"Marley? Are you here?"

Silence.

I sniffed the air, searching for a hint of her presence: freshly brewed tea; the smell of old books; the bright, fishy tang that followed her from room to room. But there was nothing.

Telling myself I wasn't searching for her but making sure the doors were locked, I went through every room on the main floor. The mugs in the sink were the same ones we'd used this morning. One with my coffee stains, one with remnants of Annabelle's unconsumed tea. I went out to the backyard and peered into the garden, softly calling "Marley?" and feeling like an idiot. The bushes didn't reply.

I told myself I wasn't disappointed. I also told myself I wasn't scared.

Listening at the door to the room Yasmin had taken, I was relieved to hear the soft sound of snoring from within.

Running up the rest of the stairs to my room, I closed the door gently and locked it. I tore off my clothes and threw myself down on the bed while my heart hammered. My body was taut, rigid with shock. With no sign of the ghost in the house and a growing sense of panic, I found myself staring at the ceiling, breathing hard. The house had become terrifying again now that the ghost who haunted it was gone.

What the fuck? What the actual fuck was that? And where is she now?

Willing myself to calm down, I tried to sleep, but my thoughts kept turning strange. Annabelle's frightful face kept appearing behind my eyelids. Then the contour of her body as her thin nightgown whipped in the wind. As I wrestled with my mind, fear morphed into a forbidden sense of desire. The sheets were rough, but every time I moved, I felt them against my skin and it drove me just a little mad. I needed to feel something other than unsettling, bone-deep dread.

My fingers moved south and I took a deep breath in, trying to focus, when I sensed her. She smelled like lake water and tea. I opened my eyes. The room was empty.

But I wasn't alone.

"I know you're there," I whispered.

Silence.

I arched my back, pressing into my fingers as I chased relief. The slick, wet sound was lewd in the silence of the room, but I didn't stop.

A light flickered from the corner. I looked over at the antique wooden chair, covered with a threadbare quilt full of homespun yarn and memories. On it sat Annabelle, with her ankles crossed behind a chair leg, wearing her house slippers. Her hands clenched on her thighs, knuckles white. Her mouth was set in a line, flat as the horizon. There was no smile for her to hide behind.

She met my gaze. Her expression smoldered with an intensity I'd never seen before. The heavy atmosphere of the room was silent but for my leaping heart and the sound of my movements. My pulse thundered in my ears. I sped up, gasping as I came closer. The sheets grabbed at my skin as I writhed on them, but I didn't look away from Annabelle's intense scrutiny.

Finally, I came, feeling waves of blissful release. I must have closed my eyes because when I returned to my senses, the chair in the corner of the room was empty.

# Chapter 8

Neither of us mentioned it the next morning. When Annabelle handed me my coffee, she did it with a sweet smile full of innocent, ghostly warmth. My cheeks warmed when my fingers brushed against her insubstantial ones around the cup. I looked away first, now unsure if I had really seen Annabelle as a 'normal' ghost on the rocks. I was also unsure if I should apologize for what I had done when I encountered her afterwards in my bedroom, especially since I wasn't sorry it had happened.

We drank our morning beverages in a comfortable silence. Well, I drank and Annabelle watched, inhaling and sighing every now and then.

Was this what it was like to live with someone you actually liked?

The thought came, and instead of immediately reproaching myself for it, I entertained the idea. What would it be like to wake up, come downstairs, and have a coffee with someone who knew me? Someone who had seen all sides of me and still smiled like I was an important part of her world? The thought filled me with an exhilaration that bordered on panic.

Footsteps sounded on the stairs.

"Oh, Marley, that's Yasmin, can you . . ."

Annabelle heaved a put-upon sigh, but before she disappeared, she gave me a cheeky wink.

Yasmin, on the other hand, pursed her lips and looked around the kitchen warily when she entered. Her long hair was braided, but so many strands escaped that the braid was barely intact. She was carrying a large book.

"Coffee or tea?" I got up to put the kettle on while my unknown-until-yesterday cousin sat at the table.

"Tea."

"I should have known."

"What does that mean?"

"It means you look like you're late for Harry Potter school, so of course you want tea."

Today she was wearing a similar outfit to yesterday's: swishy skirt and a blouse with long lace sleeves. I'd be damned if she managed to make it through the entire day without sweating through that shirt.

She sank down in Annabelle's chair and put her elbows on the table. She looked tired. That made two of us.

I put a tea bag in a mug that said "Four out of five Great Lakes prefer Michigan," feeling like an asshole. Yasmin ignored me and cracked open her gigantic tome.

"What's that?" I asked. When the water boiled, I poured it in the mug and handed it to her, then sat down at the table.

Yasmin looked at me like I was a child playing a prank by pretending not to know the colors or the alphabet. "You're kidding, right?"

I scooched my chair closer and peered over her shoulder

at the book. It was old and thick, with sections bound together and sewn into the spine with a kaleidoscope of colored thread. The worn cover had an intricate drawing of a tree that had faded over time. As Yasmin flipped through the pages, I saw a dizzying variety of handwriting and drawings, plus magical symbols that looked like they had been copied out of a video game. Some of the pages were lists of ingredients, complete with introductory text like you'd find on the internet.

"What's that?" I pointed to a diagram that looked like a pentagram with a snake coming out of one of the points.

"You seriously don't know? Don't you have one of these?"

"A freaky old book full of fruitcake recipes and demon exorcism diagrams? No. I do not have a freaky old book full of fruitcake recipes and demon exorcism diagrams."

Yasmin sighed. "There's no fruitcake." She chewed on the inside of her cheek for a moment. "Although I did find a recipe for scones from 1895 that rise better than Betty Crocker's."

She let me flip through the pages at random. Some of the entries were dated, but most weren't. They were clearly written and drawn by several different people, but the handwriting was similar, with pretty loops and swooping lines. One of the pages was taken up by a giant circle with a series of symbols drawn inside it and three points of the perimeter marked and labeled. Underneath it was a paragraph written in text that was too small for my tired eyes to decipher.

"This shit is wild."

Yasmin scoffed. "This 'shit' is my family legacy."

"What do you mean?"

She gave me a cold look. "I'm not sure I should tell you. If you were really a Cartwright woman, you would already know."

At that I rolled my eyes so hard it was almost painful. "Never been great at being either of those things. Whatever. Keep your secrets, see if I care."

Yasmin angrily turned the pages until she found one with a family tree. It looked like the one a teacher had made me fill out as an assignment in elementary school. On it, I spied Agatha's name, along with Yasmin's, her mother Helena's, and my mother's. My original name, Veronica, was nowhere to be found.

"See? The women in our family are connected by our books, which hold the practices handed down through generations. We all have these. The fact that you don't have one means you're not really a part of this family."

"Thanks." She clearly intended that as an insult, but I smiled sweetly, flattered to be cut off from the family I never wanted.

I pointed to a page that showed women doing various things, including stirring a big black pot and reading out of a book to a crowd of anxious people. The only thing missing was a broomstick. And a stake to burn them at. "Your family are witches?"

"Duh! This is the family business. Even if your mother didn't teach you anything, didn't you figure that out when you got here?"

I sat back in my chair and crossed my arms. "It's not like there was a cauldron sitting outside the front door, no. Besides, I don't believe in that crap. Spells and spirits aren't real. It's all bullshit that bored housewives put on throw pillows and sell on Etsy. Or multilevel marketing schemes."

Never mind that an actual, honest-to-god ghost saved my life.

"Believe it or not," Yasmin said, "but I can't believe you don't know your own family tree."

"I jumped off my family tree at the first opportunity," I shot back. "They wanted me to be radically different than I am, so I left as soon as I could." I turned the book over, revealing the cover with its worn, faded tree. I traced a finger down one of the branches until it ended. "The branch of my part of the family tree broke when my parents veered off the highway in a storm and wrapped their sedan around an *actual* fucking *tree*. No more branch, no more family. So, what do you want from me?"

"This house!"

"Well, you're not going to get it!"

"Why not?" Yasmin threw up her hands and sat back in her own chair—Annabelle's chair—and stared me down. "This house belongs to my mother. She made me come here as her representative, and I'm not leaving until I get an agreement from you that you'll concede it."

"That's not going to happen. Also, she didn't 'make you come here.' You're an adult, you get to make your own choices." I purposefully didn't dwell on the fact that I had similar thoughts about being stuck on the island when I first arrived.

"That's not the point. You have no connection to this house. You had no connection to Agatha; you didn't even know her!"

"Did you?"

"Well, no. My mom said she always meant to bring me here, but she never did."

"Aha!" I pumped my arm in the air, not actually sure what I had won but glad to see her angrily sticking her chin out. Arguing with Yasmin was annoying but also a little exhilarating. It felt like I could do it all day. "What would you do with the house, anyway?"

"I wouldn't sell it, that's for sure!" Yasmin crossed her arms angrily. "Agatha mentored my mother, and they built their spiritual bond in this house. It's meaningful to this family, and the fact that you don't know that means you don't deserve it."

"I don't even really want the house!" I heard the whine in my own voice too late to do anything about it. Like it or not, I was also an adult, older than Yasmin by a decade.

Then I shut my mouth and glanced around, hoping that Annabelle hadn't heard me say I didn't want the house. It was true, I didn't want the responsibility of owning a disaster house on a 1950s American fantasy island. But if I was being truly honest with myself, I liked being with *her.*

It didn't matter, though. It's not like I was going to stay here. This was a temporary reprieve from my usual life, which consisted of getting through the day so that I could play the night away, losing myself in the cacophony of a sound system and the smell of an audience sweating through leather. Punk music, the queer scene of the city, and being alone—that was my life, not this.

I took in a surreptitious breath, waiting for the smell that usually accompanied Annabelle, but I couldn't feel her. I hadn't offended my ghost, at least not yet.

"Then give the house back," Yasmin said, smiling as if the answer was really that simple.

"Give me two mil."

"No way in hell are you getting two mil for this house. Have you even been on Zillow?"

"Two and a half."

She huffed, then turned her head, not dignifying me with a response. I stared at her until she relented, unable to let me have the last word. "Even getting featured on HouseTok would not net you that much for this house the way it is." Yasmin folded her hands and looked at the table, taking a deep breath. "Gibson, you need to be realistic about this—"

Her tirade was interrupted by someone pounding loudly on

the door. The doorbell must've given up the ghost. So to speak.

"Hold that thought." As I left Yasmin to answer the frantic knocking at the door, I felt a sense of déjà vu. This time it was for an actual memory of mine—it was the third time in as many days that I'd said "hold that thought" to an unexpected person to go open the front door to my "new" house. I shook myself and opened the door.

An old man barged inside as soon as it was open wide enough to admit him.

"Where're yer boxes!" he bellowed into the hallway.

"Excuse me?"

"Fuse boxes! We haven't got all day." The pile-of-rags man from the bar the other night wandered into the living room and set a filthy toolbox on the bloodstained sofa. It was a metal square that looked as old as Annabelle.

A young man nervously stepped over the threshold after him. He was tall and broad, with sandy hair that flopped over his eyes in a way that made him look like he belonged on a TV show for teens. "Excuse us," he said, "we're the Switchfinder Army?"

"Is that a question?" I shut the door behind him and put my fists on my hips.

"Um, no." The young man radiated a nervous, harmless energy. Like a puppy or a third grader on a field trip. "We're the electricians? I'm Nate."

"Fuse boxes!" the older man shouted. "Oh, never mind, I'll find 'em myself." He stomped off through the hallway to the kitchen, grumbling the entire way.

Meanwhile, Yasmin passed him in the hallway, carrying her tea and looking confused. She stopped short when she saw me and the hunky assistant.

To Nate, I said, "I'm Gibson, this is Yasmin. Ignore her scowl and let me know if you need anything. If you need to destroy the house, start with the room upstairs with the rose wallpaper." I smiled sweetly at my cousin. Or whatever she was.

She gave me a withering look, but it didn't last long. Her eyes kept drifting toward Nate. She stood awkwardly next to him and said, "Um, do you want tea?"

Nate looked equally as awkward, putting his hands in his pockets, then removing them and folding them across his chest. He shook his head. "No, no, I couldn't take your tea."

"Oh." Yasmin looked down at her cup sadly.

Unable to bear the awkward heterosexual mating dance any longer, I said, "Well, I'm going to check on . . ."

"Old Pete. He doesn't mind if you call him that," Nate said, still staring anywhere except Yasmin's blushing face.

"Got it." I grinned at Yasmin's flustered expression. "You two carry on."

~

Old Pete and his bumbling assistant would need to work on the house for several days, according to the strange, brusque electrician. He showed me his quote for the work, handwritten on a stained yellow legal pad. It was much cheaper than I expected, so I let him be and took my laptop out on the deck to answer emails for as long as the battery would last.

Midway into editing a brain-numbingly boring white paper, my phone vibrated with a text. A picture was attached, and my eyebrows hit the top of my head when I saw it: Brooke wearing nothing but a string bikini and cowboy boots. She was holding a Corona and posing on a beach with some people I didn't know, making a kissy face. Her skin was bronze and shiny with sweat.

My eyes lingered on the little swell of sideboob sticking out the side of her barely there top. I was just starting to convince myself that the photo was meant for someone else when another text came through.

"miss u bitch, when coming bac?"

I licked my lips and set both my elbows on the table, holding the phone with both hands and swiping my thumb across the screen. Brooke would call me a boomer for that move, but it's not like she could see it. Unless I took off my own top and snapped a photo to send to her . . .

"Are you all right, Gibson?" Annabelle appeared at my elbow, causing me to fling the phone down on the table before she could see Brooke's photo.

"Of course!" My voice was too loud, but she didn't seem to notice.

"I heard you arguing with your cousin earlier . . ." She looked chagrined, casting her pretty eyes down.

Shit—maybe she heard me say I didn't want the house after all.

"It sounds like she's a very determined young lady," Annabelle said. She pulled out the other chair and sat beside me. "And did you say that your parents died in a vehicle accident? That's terrible."

I smiled, putting on my let's-not-talk-about-that expression. "It's fine, Marley, it was a long time ago."

"Hmmm." She didn't look convinced but didn't press the matter.

After a few moments of silence, I assumed she wasn't going to continue, so I turned my attention back to my computer. But then she said, "My father died before I was ready to let go of him."

She was also wearing a placid expression, one that didn't reveal much. It was almost a smile. If you didn't know Annabelle, you might think it was real, but I knew her now, and I could tell that she was hiding something. A deeper pain than she was willing to show me.

"He did?" I carefully closed my laptop and spoke softly, not wanting to disturb her. Annabelle was extremely reluctant to share, and I wasn't even sure how much she remembered of her past, so this felt special and rare.

"Yes. Shortly after we arrived on Mackinac. I was his only surviving child, and he was my entire world."

"What was he like? Do you remember?"

Annabelle's smile turned fond, but sad. "He was kind."

I had the urge to place my hand on hers but knew it would just go through it to the surface of the table.

"He wasn't alive for my wedding, and I know he would've wanted to be there. But sometimes I wish he could see me now instead."

Wedding? I snuck a quick glance at Annabelle's hand—surely I would've noticed if she wore a ring. Her hand was bare. I felt like the world had shifted a few degrees to the left, but I stayed quiet, hoping she would continue. The fact that Annabelle might've been married, or even had children, never occurred to me. I felt incredibly selfish all of a sudden.

"He wouldn't understand," she continued. "The world is a very different place. People are allowed to be different now. *I* might be allowed to . . ." She glanced down at herself, her body about three-quarters visible. "He might never understand me. But I like to think, perhaps, that he might *see me* more." Annabelle finally looked at me, her eyes full of yearning. What she was yearning for, though, I didn't know.

Old Pete slid open the door and stepped outside. He was out the door before I could ask Annabelle to disappear. He stomped across the back porch, not seeming to mind that he was interrupting an intimate conversation or the fact that there was an extra woman that wasn't completely visible.

"Shit, Marley—"

"It's okay. Hello, Pete," Annabelle said, waving cheerfully to the surly man. Her wistful mood had dissipated, her sunny mask back in place.

Pete waved her off, grumbling, "Away with you, spirit! I'm working."

I jerked my thumb at the electrician. "He knew?"

Annabelle nodded. "He doesn't like me very much." She shrugged, seeming unconcerned.

"Okay, I guess." I found it hard to believe that anyone wouldn't like Annabelle but didn't say that out loud. "Does everyone on this island know you live here? I'm beginning to think that literally everyone on this island knows who you are."

"Of course not, silly." Annabelle smiled broadly and made a motion as if she were slapping my shoulder. Her hand went right through me, but she made her point.

~

"No, Mom, she's not cooperating." Yasmin's voice drifted through the second-floor window. She must not have realized it was open. Or she did and she had more balls than I gave her credit for. "Yes, I showed her the letter!"

I chuckled, then shut my laptop. The internet would be installed as soon as my new pals Old Pete and his lap dog Nate were finished with the wiring. And Seymour Anderson would be showing up the day after tomorrow to "chat" about the property. Unfortunately, my lawyer responded to my distress call with bad news. Agatha's will was clear: I was the sole named inheritor of the property. However, she'd done several other big financial transactions around the same time, and it wasn't long after she was moved into a higher level of assisted care. In other words, since they may have benefited from the will before it was changed and Agatha may have been in an unstable mental state at the time she changed it, my annoying relatives might have a case. Or enough of one to fight me in court. That was the last thing I needed to deal with on top of sexy ghosts and a pack of ambitious punks in New York waiting to take my role in the band.

I sighed and pinched the bridge of my nose, listening to the drone of construction equipment from somewhere nearby. Annabelle had grown tired of watching me type and disappeared.

"I'm trying, Mom!" Now Yasmin sounded upset. Her voice pitched up, like she was a teenager trying to convince her parents to let her stay up past curfew.

I thought the sound of a young woman arguing with her mother might bring up painful emotions, but nothing came. All those feelings had burned out long ago. They were torn out of me through screaming fights with my mom, kicking and shouting until I was hoarse and the walls had holes. Not to mention ripping my clothes and cutting my hair and sneaking out to blast my brain cells on cheap beer and bad weed. But that was so, so long ago. Now there was a hollow feeling in my chest where I once used to rage. Playing guitar still brought the fire out of me. I used to play out my pain, now I played to find it again.

The back door creaked open, and I heard Yasmin's hesitant steps on the wooden floor. She plopped down in Annabelle's chair and sighed.

"Tough day at the stealing-other-people's-houses factory?" I said, feeling like an asshole for the second time that day and not letting that stop me from being one.

Yasmin had the book with her, as always. She flipped to a page that showed a woman with two smiling children. They were standing in front of Abaddon Cottage, which looked much better than it did now. A man stood next to the house with a hammer in his hand. Hovering in the garden was a figure in black. The person was only half facing the viewer, though, so it was impossible to make out their face. The drawing wasn't a professional rendering but it had been done by someone with talent and some artistic training. Yasmin pointed at the woman. "This is supposed to be me."

The page was dated 1954.

"How can it be you? You weren't even born yet."

She shook her head sadly. "When our family has visions, they're not wrong. I mean, sometimes they're not exactly *right*, but broadly speaking, they're not wrong. If I can't get this house back, I won't just be failing me, but my mother and my entire lineage both backwards and forwards."

I flipped the page. On the next one, there was a recipe for Dark Mother Bread and an advertisement for the Cartwright Women's Issues Mercantile and Apothecary circa 1899. I smiled at the snake-oil promises on the page.

"If your vision is so accurate, then why would Agatha leave the house to me, then?" I said, setting aside the book. "If she knew how much this house, and the continuation of whatever weird witchcraft thing you guys have going on, means to your side of the family, then why would she leave it to me? She wrote my name. Not just my birth name—my actual name. Gibson, not Veronica. How would she even know that name?"

"I don't know." Yasmin shrugged, but her voice was sincere.

"I think I may have an answer to that." Annabelle popped up out of nowhere, as visible as she was able to be, wringing her hands.

Yasmin's head snapped to the side and her jaw dropped.

I pointed at the ghost who'd appeared at my elbow. "Oh, and by the way, the house is haunted."

# Chapter 9

"Hello!" Annabelle waved at Yasmin, who stared at the sudden ghost, eyebrows folded into a tight V.

"Yasmin, Annabelle," I said, doing halfhearted introductions. "Annabelle, Yasmin."

Yasmin didn't yelp or fall on a sofa and insist she was dead, so she was already beating me in the reaction department. Instead, she adjusted her glasses on her nose and peered at Annabelle in close concentration. To my horror, she dug a pencil and notepad out of her skirt pocket and started taking notes.

"I have nine questions to start," she said.

"Stuff them for now, please." I turned to Annabelle. "Marley, you said you know why Agatha willed the house to me. Why?"

And why the hell didn't she tell me earlier?

She pursed her lips and wrung her hands, like she actually didn't want to tell me. "It might be easier if I show you what's in the shed."

Yasmin and I looked at each other, then at the shed in the

corner of the garden. It sat in the late afternoon sun, its siding and wooden trim innocuously rotting away with the passage of time.

"There's nothing in there, though." I opened my laptop and found the listing of Agatha's possessions from my lawyer. "I got a detailed list of what was in the house. The documents say the shed is empty. Agatha's inheritance included the house, the furniture in the house, the appliances, and her books."

Annabelle cleared her throat.

"Sorry, *Annabelle's* books."

"We have to open it, then." Yasmin bounded up from the table and across the deck, but didn't get very far. She stopped, probably realizing she wasn't the owner of this house and didn't have the keys.

I unhooked them from my belt loop and was getting up to join her when Nate the electrician stepped outside.

"Oh, I'm sorry to bother you, ladies." He pointed to the new electrical panel that he'd helped Pete install. It still had wires sticking out every which way and wasn't switched on yet. "Just need to check something."

He went to the panel, looked at one of the wires, then nodded to himself. Nate didn't seem to realize or was unfazed by the fact that one of the women wasn't quite as solid as the others.

"Right." I crossed the back deck, heading for the mysterious shed. Maybe, just maybe, whatever was in there would explain why Agatha chose me for her successor. Or maybe there was a rotting corpse. Or a pot of gold? Mature savings bonds? I tried not to get my hopes up. Whatever it was, I'd be happy if it convinced Yasmin that I was the rightful owner of the house so she would leave me alone. Then this whole thing—and all these people—could get out of my life for good.

"Ack!"

I turned to see Yasmin's foot had fallen straight through a plank on the deck.

She grabbed for the nearest thing to hold on to, which happened to be Nate's meaty shoulder. "Ow, ow, ow."

"Are you all right?" Nate held on to Yasmin's arm and helped her disentangle her foot from the rotten wood. Where she'd stepped was now a footlong hole.

"I'll be okay," Yasmin said. "It kind of wrenched my ankle, but I don't think it's broken. Maybe a little sprain." She carefully rotated her foot from side to side, still holding on to Nate. Then she gingerly put her weight on it, wincing slightly. "Mostly it scared the stuffing out of me."

Nate nodded. "You should really fix that hole. It's a hazard."

I rolled my eyes. "Yeah, clearly."

But my sarcasm and terrible attitude rolled off the burly electrician's apprentice like water off a duck's back. His expression was entirely earnest. "I can fix it for you. Just need a treated two-by-four. I might even have one in my bike pack. If not, I'll run down to the hardware store and get one. It'll be no trouble."

I opened my mouth to decline, not interested in having people in my haunted hazard house for longer than necessary. But Yasmin turned to me with an expression I could only describe as half pleading, half thirst. She silently communicated "Please, Gibson, I need to watch this man fix a deck, and I will hate you forever if you deny me the opportunity" with only her eyebrows and the set of her mouth.

Swallowing my stubborn distaste for good-natured people who wanted to help me, I said, "Sure. That would be excellent of you, Nate."

"Cool!" He helped Yasmin into a deck chair, keeping one

hand on her arm as she walked and carefully sat down. As soon as she was seated, she moved her ankle with no problem. Satisfied of her safety, Nate grinned. "I'll go get my tools!" He practically jogged around the side yard.

When he was out of sight, Yasmin exhaled. To me, she said, "Thank you."

I grinned. "Anything for you, cuz."

Yasmin's good cheer evaporated. "That was weird. Don't . . . don't call me that."

I chuckled, definitely planning to call her that.

~

Yasmin iced her ankle for a few minutes, but once Nate was assured that the injury wasn't lethal and she promised to stay off it as soon as we were out of the shed, we approached the innocuous building as a group. Annabelle hovered at the back, looking more nervous than I'd ever seen her, wringing her hands. She was so see-through that she was almost invisible. We crowded around the door to the shed, jostling into position like we were on a reality competition show about storage units.

I turned the key and heard the tumbler turn. But when I pushed on the door, it wouldn't budge. I shoved my shoulder against it, but nothing happened. "It's locked from the inside. Or blocked by something seriously heavy."

"How do we get in?" Yasmin said.

"I have a circular saw . . ." offered Nate.

Annabelle shouted, "No!" She waved her arms and jumped up and down to get our attention. "There's no need for that!"

She flowed past me and walked straight through the solid door.

"Whoa," said Nate. "Cool."

I smiled, feeling a sort of vicarious pride swell in my chest. "All right in there, Marley?"

"Just fine, dear!" came the response.

From inside the shed, there were several loud bangs. A moment of silence, then it sounded like a large piece of furniture was dragged across the ground. Something fell, shattering on the floor, and Annabelle said, "Oh, drat" in a soft voice. There were three metallic clanks as deadbolts were shoved open from the inside of the door. Then Annabelle reappeared, with dust covering her shoulders and her hair in a disarray.

"There," she said, "try it again, please."

I shoved the door, and this time it slid open with a groan. The air inside was stale and intensely humid, with the only circulation coming from an unmoving fan in an evaporative cooler unit mounted in the window on the back wall. The shed was wired, but Old Pete and Nate were still working on the power, so the only light that came streaming in was from the one window, and now, the door. If I wasn't 100 percent sure that Agatha was interred in the Mackinac Island Cemetery, I would have expected to find her here with spiders crawling on her decaying face.

"Spooky," Nate said, summarizing my thoughts nicely.

Yasmin turned on her phone's flashlight and held it over my shoulder, illuminating the contents. Inside, the shed looked like one that might appear on television, either as a tragic example of hoarding or a potential treasure trove of items worth millions at auction. With my luck, it would be the former. Spiderwebs happily spread all over the interior. The shed wasn't that large, but the walls were covered by tapestries with mysterious symbols, newspaper clippings, and maps with pins in places that seemed random. Bookshelves built into the walls held dozens of rotting books, making the place look and smell like a librarian's tomb.

"What is all this?" I said, not expecting an answer. I entered the shed, turning on my phone's flashlight and sweeping it over the eclectic collection of items.

Yasmin and Nate entered behind me. Nate had abandoned his electrician duties, finding treasure hunting in a garden shed with my attractive cousin more appealing.

"Oh my god," said Yasmin quietly, "this is amazing." She was standing next to a shelf that held a row of jars. Some were regular mason jars; some were old clay pots. Of the ones that had legible labels, I could recognize about only a quarter of the items inside. Things that looked like plants included adder's-tongue, coltsfoot, and jimsonweed, along with more disgusting items like eyelashes and toenails.

"Old Agatha really *was* a witch!" Nate had his hands on his hips, looking around in awe. "Cool. I always thought it was just a stereotype cuz she was an older woman living alone."

"She was definitely a witch," I said, pointing to a large book open on a small desk near the window. "And that's her book of spells."

Yasmin bustled over to see what I was pointing at, then gasped. "It's her grimoire." She reached out as if to touch the book, then withdrew her hand. "My mother assumed it was buried with Agatha since . . ." She glanced at me briefly. "Since it wasn't left in the will to her."

"*This* is what you really wanted?" I asked, incredulous. "A dusty old book?"

"It's more than a dusty old book! This is Agatha's true legacy." Yasmin looked around the shed in awe. "This, and the house, of course. I'll need time to catalog everything that she has here."

"You think it'll change the value of the estate? Oh, come on! I let you in here in good faith, even though you're suing me."

"I'm not suing you. That's not how any of this works. And besides . . ."

Yasmin kept talking, but her words were lost to the stuffy, unbearably hot and humid air of the shed. Everything else faded as I spied a familiar shape in the gloom. Sitting on top of a precarious stack of rotting magazines was a decrepit case. I carefully opened the clasps and found the most beautiful guitar I'd ever laid my eyes on.

# Chapter 10

The guitar was an acoustic Gibson Dove from the '70s, which meant it was either complete crap or a diamond in the rough. It had a few more cracks than I'd have liked, but the neck wasn't twisted. The fact that it was a little beaten up was better, somehow. Holding a guitar with a history felt better than holding a new one. This guitar had been played, then kept in a case in a shed full of occult whatnots. Someone had made music with this.

While Yasmin went gaga over the weird herbs and parchments with what could be recipes or serial killer notes on them, I ran my hands lovingly over the instrument.

"Whose was this?" I asked. "Agatha's?"

Annabelle nodded. "Quite a folk singer back in the day. She used to sing protest songs until the residents got mad at her and made her quit. They signed a petition, and eventually the city council passed a very specific noise ordinance."

While I examined my new obsession, Yasmin poured over the books on Agatha's shelf while Nate inspected the wires leading to a television mounted on the wall over her head.

"Ugh!" She slammed one of the books shut and rubbed her eyes.

"What's up?"

"I can't make heads or tails of this. Some of it is familiar Cartwright Coven lore, but a lot is hedge witchcraft with some plant magic thrown in. Hedge magic is inherently tied to the witch who develops it, so I'm never going to figure this out without the primary source—Agatha herself. I'm not strong in plant magic at all. It's not my discipline. My mother is a cosmic witch, but I'm still an apprentice. And the witchfluencers I follow are basically just putting Instagram aesthetics on classic New Age ideas, not actually coming up with untested rituals themselves."

I held up a hand. "I'm going to stop you right there." I got up from the trunk I'd been sitting on, wiping the dust off my butt. "I know nothing about that stuff, so don't bother trying to explain."

Yasmin pouted. She looked furious with herself, a feeling I was intimately familiar with. I imagined she felt exactly how I did when I was trying to learn to do barre chords consistently. But it's not like I could help. And why did I want to, anyway?

Then I had a thought.

"Actually . . ." I was wearing my favorite pair of black skinny jeans, one of three pairs I'd brought. This one had a thigh pocket that I sometimes put a knife in. But the first day I'd arrived, I'd received two business cards and stuck them in my knife pocket, then promptly forgot about them. I dug out Miranda's wrinkled card and handed it to Yasmin. "I bet I know someone who could help."

She did not look impressed. "Tarot readings? I was doing

tarot readings when I was six."

"Don't be an asshole," I said. "She can probably help you, and I'm going to call her."

Miranda picked up on the second ring and agreed to come over immediately without me even explaining why. I thought about warning Yasmin about Miranda's overeager friendliness, then decided to let her experience it firsthand.

It only took ten minutes for the older woman to arrive. She came in the door like a fresh breeze, kissing Pete on the cheek despite his grumbling, then waving a cheery hello to Nate.

"Oh!" she exclaimed when I took her back to the shed. "You were able to open it!"

I frowned, then asked, "Do you know why it was locked from the inside?"

Miranda cocked her head to the side. She was wearing light blue eyeshadow that extended all the way up to her eyebrows today, along with peach blush on her cheeks and matching peach lipstick. She wore a house dress that was far too fancy to wear while digging around in a dusty old shed. "There's only one person who could've unlocked that shed, Gibson. Agatha entrusted her most prized possessions to her."

With that, she nodded toward the far corner of the garden, then stepped inside the shed. She greeted Yasmin with a warm exclamation and then a series of murmurs as the witch and the medium got to work decoding whatever it was Agatha had been writing in her book.

I looked off to where Miranda had indicated, surprised to see Annabelle standing in the middle of one of the garden beds. Her feet were ensconced in the soil, as if they were roots and she had been planted in the bed along with a row of peas. I made plenty of noise as I approached so that I wouldn't scare her by appearing suddenly, which I thought was rather big of me, all things considered.

"You okay, Marley?"

She turned, and I had a moment of fear, wondering if I'd see a repeat of the ghoulish vision I'd had of her the previous night. But no black water streamed out of her face. She wore her usual placid smile, the one she used to hide behind. "Oh, hello, dear."

"Anything wrong?"

Annabelle licked her lips, considering her answer. Bugs buzzed around my head, tickling my ear. They went right through Annabelle while I was stuck swatting them in annoyance. She plucked at the lacy neck-tie that hung down from the collar of her shirt, seeming distracted.

"I never liked that shed. I was happy to see it locked up."

"You didn't have to open it for me, you know." I didn't mention that we probably would have taken Nate up on his circular saw offer if she hadn't.

"No, it's . . ." She wrung her hands, her face an unhappy war between a smile and whatever it was she was actually feeling. "Agatha and I were friends," she said at last. "We coexisted for a long time. But we didn't always agree on things."

"What things?"

Annabelle paused, then blurted out, "I didn't want her to do the spell! It wasn't good for her, and it wasn't necessary."

"What spell?"

She crossed her arms, then put them back at her side. "Near the end of her life, Agatha became obsessed with a ritual. She was convinced it would be her final act, one that would take great power to achieve. I think she found glory in it, to be honest. But she worked on it night and day, obsessing over it to the expense of everything else, including her health. Agatha locked herself away in that shed, day after day, sometimes not leaving it at all. And then when she knew she wasn't going to be able to do the ritual, the way she acted . . ."

"How did she act?" I needed to know—not just because it would help relieve Annabelle of whatever burden she was carrying about Agatha's death, but because if she was acting erratically prior to her death, Yasmin would have a stronger case against my inheritance.

"She was determined. Like she could make it happen, no matter what, even if it killed her."

I let silence fall between us as we processed Annabelle's words. Then, when it seemed like Annabelle had calmed down, I asked, "What was the ritual supposed to do?"

She shook her head. "I don't know. But it required three people. So, she wasn't able to perform it while she was alive."

"But she had you and Miranda?"

She shook her head again, vehemently this time. "Three *people*, Gibson. I don't count."

"You count, Marley."

"Not for this."

I didn't know what to say, so I didn't say anything. My fingers brushed against her insubstantial ones, causing me to shiver. "You didn't answer my question earlier. Why did Agatha leave the house to me when clearly Yasmin is a better fit?"

Annabelle shrugged. "Maybe she knew Yasmin would come anyway if she gave it to you. That gets the two of you here."

"And along with Miranda, we could do whatever magic thing she was working on? I guess she didn't realize I don't believe in all that stuff."

"It's just a theory, Gibson. Unless she specifically wrote it down, we can't really know what Agatha was thinking."

I nodded. If she did write her thoughts down in that big book of hers, Yasmin would find it sooner or later. "What do *you* want to happen to the house? Do you want Yasmin to have it?"

Annabelle turned to me with a surprised expression. "I don't know. I've never been . . . consulted on decisions like this before."

"Seems fair, don't you think?"

"I—no, I don't, actually." Her voice had been soft, hesitant. But she gained confidence as she pondered. "No. I had my time. And now it's up. This is . . . extra. I'm not sure why or how I came to have this afterlife, but it's not consequential. I cannot influence the state of the world like you can, nor should I."

"But—"

"It's not up to me. I'm merely an observer to whatever happens here." Annabelle's face shimmered in the afternoon sun like a heat mirage on an empty road. "It's how this has to be."

"It's a load of crap, is what it is."

"Excuse me?"

"Horse shit! What you just said is a bigger pile of nonsense than the one I stepped in the other day. There are some big piles of dung around here, Marley, you've seen these horses, and what you just said is bigger than—"

"I take your point, Gibson. No more manure, please."

"Good."

"But you don't understand. I'm dead. I *died*, Gibson. Over two hundred years ago. The actions of the dead cannot supersede those of the living. It's not—my actions don't have consequences. Yours do."

"Do I have to describe the horse shit to you again? Because I will." I raked a hand through my hair, surprised at how quickly my fingers ran through the short strands. It seemed like forever ago, but I'd only changed it two days ago. I wondered what else I'd end up changing about myself by the time I managed to leave this stupid island.

I paused, then said, "Eggs."

"What?"

"My head would be like that carton of eggs I dropped yesterday. Brains splattered across the hallway, just waiting for a sorcerer to divine the future in the pattern of my gray matter if it weren't for you."

Annabelle pursed her lips but didn't respond.

"I'd be dead, Marley. If you think you can't influence the world, you're wrong. Because if you were right, I'd be dead."

"I suppose," she said.

And there was clearly something here, something between us. Otherwise, I knew I wouldn't care so much. And I wouldn't have jerked off thinking about her while she watched me. What was that, anyway? I didn't know what it meant, but it wasn't nothing.

Annabelle stayed quiet beside me. I could feel the wheels turning in her barely visible head. The silence between us was as companionable as it ever had been, but it made me wonder what was supposed to come next. I didn't have a template for a relationship with a ghost.

"I'm going to get my new guitar restrung."

I left Annabelle in the garden, a frowning statue among overgrown weeds and decaying vegetables.

~

According to the poorly spelled advice from anonymous people on guitar forums, the island had one guy who sold and repaired musical instruments. He went by the name Big Mike.

The forum posters assured me that if I could find his shop, he could work wonders on my new-to-me guitar. However, all my searches led me downtown to a place called Big Mike's Mackinac Livery and Riding Stable. I dodged pedestrians carrying ice cream cones and cyclists weaving through them, making my way between the crush of hotels, restaurants, and gift shops that made up the island's downtown business district.

When I pushed open the door, an obnoxious bell rang. The teen at the counter seemed as annoyed by it as I was. Half their head was shaved, and the other half was dyed green. The kid was wearing an AC/DC T-shirt under a denim jacket in what I assumed was an ironic manner given their young age. On the jacket, they wore a little yellow, purple, and white enamel pin with they/them pronouns and a name tag that said Sage.

"How can I help you?" They made a valiant effort to not sound like they hated my guts for walking in the door.

"Yeah, I'm looking for Big Mike?"

The kid blew a bubble with their gum.

"To restring a guitar?" I held up the case, then added, "Please."

Luckily, a large man in a tight T-shirt entered from the back-room, saving me from further interactions with the surly teen.

"Hello!" He had a friendly voice and an instantly forgettable face. Despite his name, Big Mike was of average build, with only the slightest paunch that came as a matter of course in middle age.

I introduced myself and explained my situation, leaving out the ghosts, witches, and the fact that my own family was on the verge of suing me. Showing him the guitar, I asked if he could restring it. I'd already done what I could to clean the instrument but hadn't brought extra strings with me. Who knew if Amazon did free delivery all the way to this car-free island, strapping packages the saddles and tossing them into cottage gardens.

"It's a beauty!" He handled the guitar carefully but naturally, making me believe that he really might know what he was doing. "You play?"

Keeping my expression neutral, I said, "Uh, yeah. I've subbed in for a few big acts."

Mike grinned. "Nice! Anyone I know?"

"I doubt it." But I pulled up my Instagram anyway and showed him a quick video of me onstage with The Ent Wives Club. Only female members of that crossover thrash band were allowed to do solos. These were the only moments that slowed the pace of their set and they could go on for ages, but the band observed a hard cutoff rule—any solo ended when another member of the band yelled "Jerry."

Then I showed Mike a YouTube clip of me onstage with Call Me Kate Kane. We were at a shitty bar in Bushwick. The show had been raucous, with us in the middle of a long line-up of mostly women-led punk bands. At the end of the night, someone had been arrested for smuggling a baby goat into the venue. I couldn't help but smile at the memory of being onstage, drenched in sweat, watching Brooke writhe while she screamed the lyrics of songs she'd written on a napkin.

Moments like that almost convinced me I was a part of the family. But the most recent photos of the group included a rotating selection of random dudes on guitar instead of me.

"Oh shit, that's Call Me Kate," the teen named Sage said, grabbing my phone. I had a moment of panic, even though I didn't have anything lewd open.

"Kane," I said. "Call Me Kate *Kane*. Batwoman? Lesbian? Hot chick with red hair?"

"Right, whatever." Sage couldn't quite cover their embarrassment, and my cheeks warmed with shame for acting like an asshole to a teenager. I didn't know anything about this kid's life, and I had no right to make it harder.

Big Mike raised his eyebrows, impressed. "Well, if Sage knows your stuff, then I certainly won't." He chuckled, then looked down at the guitar. "It's even a Gibson. That's perfect!"

I frowned. "It's, like, forty years old, and Gibsons were crap in the '70s and '80s." There was an awkward silence, then I got it. "Oh, because of my name."

"Yeah." Mike scratched his forehead. "Well, we better get this one taken care of! Sage, you take the helm. The last tour won't be coming back till four."

Sage rolled their eyes, but it seemed like a fond, practiced maneuver. Then Big Mike waved me behind the counter and gestured for me to follow him out the back door.

~

Behind the office building where Sage was greeting a customer and answering questions about carriage rides, there was a series of small stables. As I approached slowly, Mike threw a saddle over the back of a patient brown horse. Next to it was a gigantic black one. The horse stamped, shaking its head. Although I'd grown up near a ranch, I knew very little about horses and intended to keep it that way. As a kid, they scared the shit out of me, and as an adult, they also scared the shit out of me.

"I don't think I can do this . . ." I raised my hands and backed away slowly.

"Well, it's a ten-minute ride to my place, or a forty-minute walk," Mike said. "Or I could find a bike, and you could split the difference." He looked at me expectantly but not unkindly.

"It's just . . . horses and I haven't gotten along." I gulped. "Historically speaking."

The black beast flared its nostrils and snorted, stamping the ground again. It was a beautiful animal, all sleek lines and power. The hair on the back of my neck stood on end just looking at it.

"That one isn't ready for a rider, anyway." Mike pointed to a much shorter horse that came trotting up next to his placid brown one. Compared to the black beast, this one looked like a toy. "How about we put you on Medium Sebastian here?"

"I have the feeling you're making fun of me, but . . . okay." I let Mike show me how to take the reins and give the little horse commands with my feet and the position of my body. It felt a little like a dream.

Ghosts, now horses. Instead of a quick trip to see a house and sell it, this trip had turned into a gauntlet of fears I had to face. Gee thanks, Aunt Agatha.

A terrifying ten minutes later, my entire body shook as I dismounted in front of Mike's house. It wasn't far from Abaddon, meaning I probably could've walked here directly and saved myself another near-death experience. Mike took the reins of Medium Sebastian from me, leading both his horse and mine. Indifferent to the entire experience, Sebastian accepted a baby carrot from Mike's pocket and trotted along happily, as if all of this was a perfectly normal afternoon. To him, it probably was.

Mike's house was tucked away from a private drive, hidden in a pocket of forest just like Abaddon. The peeling paint and old flowerboxes made it look lived-in and homey. We tied the horses to a post by the side of the garage. If this were a normal place instead of a carless island obsessed with charm, Mike's driveway probably would have been paved and filled with cars.

As we walked back toward the garage, a gang of kids emerged from the front door and picked up their bicycles from their resting places in the yard. One of them was the curly-haired kid who'd apologized for almost running me over my first night on the island. I raised my hand in a wave and he returned it, then rode off toward whatever summertime adventures awaited.

"Be good!" Mike yelled after them.

"Always!" the kid yelled back. His companions yelled variations on "Bye, Big Mike," and they were off.

"Your kids?"

Mike entered the combination to open the garage door and nodded. "Yep, but luckily only two of them. Adam there is eleven. And you met Sage earlier. Sage will be sixteen soon, though how that happened I have no idea."

I smiled politely and followed him inside.

"Welcome to my escape from Mackinac," Mike said. "Granted, it's . . . still on Mackinac. But this is my little slice of anywhere but here." He gestured proudly at the garage, which had been turned into a tiny music studio and hangout space. At the far end was a workbench. Concert posters competed for space on the walls with mounted instruments, along with tools and shelves. He had not only guitars, but keyboards, a drum kit, some basic recording and DJ equipment, and a crap ton of accessories. His power cords were neatly wound, with cable ties holding them in perfect loops, in contrast to the nest of snakes that made up the cords in my apartment back home.

I toured the space, checking out the guitars he had. A lot were bass, but he had a decent selection of electric and acoustic guitars. "Holy shit, you've got some great stuff."

"Thanks." He looked around proudly at his eclectic collection. "I had grand ambitions and even did some gigs in Traverse

City, but, well, life."

I nodded. "Life."

He chuckled. "Got divorced, moved back to the island I thought I left forever, took over Dad's business when he got cancer. You know, life."

"And now you run a stable slash music store on Mackinac."

"Indeed." He smiled ruefully, and I found myself smiling back. Mike's life wasn't similar to mine, but he was easy to talk to. Any minute now he'd ask me about the cottage, and I'd have to say "I'm going to sell it" for the millionth time. Instead, he set Agatha's guitar on the counter and opened the case.

While he looked over Agatha's guitar, I put my hands in my back pockets. Surprising myself, I said, "You're actually pretty close to my house. My great-aunt's house, I mean. I'm over at Abaddon."

"We're neighbors, then! My lot backs up to you. I would say sorry about the horse smell, but I mean, it comes with the territory." He chuckled again, an easy smile on his face. "Then Mrs. Montclair was on the other side. She just sold her property, though." His smile turned down. "I used to make Adam mow her lawn as punishment for getting in trouble and just to wear him out. Guess I'll have to find something else for him to do."

"I'm sure you'll find something."

He could paint the porch, I thought. Or pull weeds. I wondered if an eleven-year-old could replace a fence, then realized I was nuts. I wasn't keeping the house, so why did I care if there were weeds? All the horse manure had affected my brain.

Eager for something to do with my hands, I pointed at the Cherry Sunburst on the wall. "Can I?"

He hesitated for a second, but then said, "Sure."

I slung the strap around my neck, plugged it into a nearby

amp, and played a few notes. "My first real guitar wasn't a Gibson," I said. "My name wasn't even Gibson back then. I didn't know shit, but I saved up for *ages* to get a used Les Paul, then didn't have any idea how to play it. All I could get out of it was noise for the longest time, but I fucking loved that noise."

"And then you got a Gibson and became Gibson?" Mike asked.

I nodded. "Then I got a Gibson and learned to play it. It was a long time before I figured out who I was, but, eventually, I became Gibson."

I played a scale, picking up speed as I went. Seeing the Red Hot Chili Peppers poster on the wall, I launched into "Under the Bridge." I played the first verse and the chorus, then stopped, remembering where I was with a jolt.

Mike whistled. "Damn," he said, "you really do know your stuff!"

I smiled. "Yeah, I'm actually pretty good."

"You should join us at Helga's sometime!" He started rifling through tool cubbies mounted on the wall. They held all kinds of objects—instrument parts, garden tools, things I couldn't identify. At least they weren't likely to contain eye of newt or some other magic spell ingredient like the shelves in my shed.

"A few of us jam every week. We draw a decent crowd, too." Mike turned to face me, hands on his hips.

"I'm . . . not going to be here long," I said. I was grateful to him for fixing up my guitar, but that didn't mean we were going to be best friends. And I certainly wasn't going to join his sad dad jam band. They probably played a lot of Journey. "As soon as I sell the house, I'm going back to New York."

"Makes sense." He turned back to the guitar. "I think I have strings that'll make this sound decent, but they're in the house.

I'll go grab 'em and get you on your way. Feel free to hang out and play whatever you want. This won't take long."

I nodded, then wandered through his studio, picking up instruments and playing them for a few minutes before setting them back down. The Sunburst beckoned me back, so I picked it back up, marveling at the fact that this treasure trove of potential music was here, on this weird island, if only you knew where to find it. The strings felt right under my hands. Though it wasn't my guitar, it felt close enough to home to send a powerful wave of longing through me.

What was I even doing here? Repairing an old acoustic when I could be taking care of my shit and leaving? Unlike Agatha, I was not a fucking hippy folk singer.

Blowing out an angry breath, I played a few chords of "Black Me Out," then put the guitar aside. I turned to go outside and check my phone when a book of sheet music in the corner caught my eye: *Billboard Hits of the 1960s and 70s.*

When Mike returned with Agatha's guitar, I paid him as much as he would let me, then asked if I could buy the songbook, too. He shrugged and said, "Take it. And if you change your mind about jamming, you know where to find me."

# Chapter 11

When I got back to Abaddon, there was crackly music coming from Annabelle's alcove. The Everly Brothers crooning about dreams greeted me before Annabelle or Yasmin realized I'd opened the door. Yasmin was sitting on the carpeted floor, her skirt spread out around her legs, flipping through a stack of vinyl records. There were piles of them stacked all around the alcove, competing with Annabelle's books for space.

"Look, Gibson!" Annabelle exclaimed, hopping up and down happily. She was out of breath, somehow. "Pete fixed the electricity in here, and now the record player works!" She pointed to the Victrola in her alcove. It was old, but not so old that it had a hand crank.

"Vintage AF," Yasmin said, actually saying "AF" out loud, making me feel old. She inexpertly lifted the needle and replaced the album. It scratched, making all three of us wince, then Carole King's voice filled the room, wondering if her love would still be around tomorrow.

"Yas found a stack of records in her room—including

my favorite one!" Annabelle held an album to her chest and resumed dancing. She was terrible. Her elbows pointed out at weird angles, and if she wasn't able to float through objects, she would've knocked over her chair. I couldn't help the grin that spread over my face.

Yasmin was smiling too. She took the record from Annabelle's hands before she accidentally flung it across the room. It was *More of the Monkees*. "These guys are pretty good. Like maybe they influenced the Beatles or something."

"I don't . . . I can't even begin to tell you how wrong you are . . . Yas," I said, noting the nickname.

"Yas" shrugged. She wouldn't meet my eyes, but she had a small smile and her plump cheeks glowed with what looked like happiness to me. I didn't know what Yasmin's deal was, but I remembered growing up with a mother who ran my life like it belonged to her. If my mother's sister was similar, then I had an inkling of how lonely her childhood might have been.

I set the guitar down next to the bookcase and regarded the dancing ghost. She'd forgotten to stay anchored to the floor and was hovering about six inches above it.

"Oh! Shoot, the pasta is probably boiling by now!" Annabelle twirled in a full circle, then skipped back to the kitchen. She called out, "You two behave yourselves!"

"Always," I shouted back.

I sat down in Annabelle's chair while Yasmin put aside the records and stopped the music. Yasmin said, "So you've gone with appeasement, then?"

"What?"

"We haven't had a chance to talk without her." Yasmin nodded to the kitchen, where Annabelle was humming while she cooked. "There are several ways to deal with ghosts. One is appeasement. Give them what they want and hope they'll go away when they've got it." Her voice was matter-of-fact.

"No, that's not at all what I'm doing. At least not . . . consciously." How would I have known what Annabelle wanted? I didn't even know what I wanted.

Yasmin continued as if I hadn't responded. "It seems like an effective way to deal with this one, anyway. She's clearly not harmful, but I wonder what would happen if you tried to exor—"

"I'm not going to exorcize her!" I shouted, then lowered my voice, hoping Annabelle hadn't heard. The only sound coming from the kitchen was the lid of a pot clanging against the rim and the light tap-tap-tap of a knife against the cutting board. The smell of seafood wafted in the air.

Yasmin shrugged.

"She was here when I got here and she saved my life. Legally, the house is mine, but she has been here longer than any of us. Agatha, even. By all rights, the house is hers more than anyone else's."

"Yes, but a house can't belong to a ghost."

I sighed. "Granted. But for now, the ghost is making you dinner. So what the ghost wants, the ghost gets."

"Appeasement."

"Bah humbug!" I stuck out my tongue at my cousin, then went to help Annabelle in the kitchen.

~

Annabelle set a giant bowl of shrimp pasta on the table. "Ta-da! Oh, I didn't ask if you eat fish, Yas."

"I do," she said. "It smells delicious."

I set three places, even though Annabelle could only pretend.

While we ate, Annabelle and Yasmin chatted easily. Annabelle asked a million questions about Yasmin's childhood in California, her eyes growing wide when Yasmin described a trip through wine country. Then she made Yasmin recount her experiences in Disneyland several times and describe the theme park in great detail. It was hard to believe the house had once felt empty and sad. It was now filled by laughter and the clink of silverware.

In between bites, I asked, "But seriously, though, your side of the family . . . what? Owns a magic store that sells real magical stuff along with props? Like the guy on *Buffy*?"

Yasmin rolled her eyes. "Of course not." She looked down at her pasta, seeming to shrink a little. "My mom is an actress. She does magic on the side. It's like . . . she helps people who don't have anywhere else to go, or they've exhausted other options." Then she giggled. "And I made her set up an Etsy shop, but I run it."

"I knew it," I said, pumping my fist in the air triumphantly. "I *knew* there would be an Etsy shop involved somehow."

"Her spells work, though!" Yasmin insisted. "And even if they don't, they give people something to believe in."

It took an immense effort not to respond to that with unbridled cynicism. "And you're an actress, too?" I tried to picture Yasmin on stage waxing poetic or "yes, and"-ing with corny improvers.

"Ha!" Yasmin laughed, spilling pasta on her blouse as she did. "No, I'm a costume designer."

Annabelle sighed. "Helena always did have a flair for the dramatic. It makes sense that she'd be an actress."

Both Yasmin and I turned to her.

"You knew our moms?" I asked. I supposed that I shouldn't be surprised—she had been here the whole time, including the period of time when my mother and her sister stayed with their aunt Agatha. But somehow it never occurred to me to place my mother here. I thought of her on the windswept plateaus of New Mexico, not this breezy, flower-filled island.

Annabelle nodded. "They weren't here for very long after their mother died, so I didn't get to know Vivian very well." She looked at me sadly. "She was afraid of me."

I swallowed.

"They were so young. It was such a trauma for them . . . and to move to such a strange place . . . I can only imagine how difficult it would be to then be confronted with a ghost. Vivian was . . . resistant to the idea of me existing."

"That's not surprising," I said. "All she would ever tell me was that God saved her from the fate of her mother and sister. When she talked about them, it was like they were both dead, even though her sister was just two states over." I shook my head. "Vivian Cartwright went to church three times per week and once locked me in my room for a month because she caught me watching the TV show *Charmed*. She thought it was because I wanted to be a witch, not a lesbian. But it wouldn't have mattered either way. She was a zealot, Marley."

Annabelle set her hand gently on top of mine. It felt like a puff of cool air on my skin. I smiled my "it's okay" smile, and she returned it.

"I wonder . . ." Yasmin pushed the last string of pasta around her plate, not eating it. "It's just that my mom isn't like that. Obviously. She believes in the supernatural, and I've seen her spells do things that I can't otherwise explain. Her potions . legitimately heal people. But she didn't tell me the truth about

Abaddon. She told me the house was important to the family legacy, but . . ."

"She didn't mention me?" Annabelle asked. Her "it's okay" smile stayed on, but it was strained.

Yasmin shook her head. "No. I'm sorry, Annabelle."

"It's okay, dear. Your mother must've had a reason for not telling you. It's not your fault no matter what she did or didn't do."

"It was probably a test." Yasmin stabbed the little string of pasta with her fork, then set it down. "I'm always failing her tests. My potions never come out the same, and my horoscope readings don't align with hers."

It took less effort not to respond sarcastically this time since she seemed legitimately upset. My mother used to rap my knuckles when I made mistakes playing piano scales, then she'd give me an exasperated look. I knew exactly what it felt like to fail the daughter test.

"Well, I'm pretty glad she didn't tell you," I said, gathering Yasmin's dishes so she couldn't keep stabbing her pasta. "Because it gave me the chance to know something you didn't."

Yasmin laughed. The air between the three of us lightened.

It was amazing that I wasn't the one who wanted to stab something after talking about family, for once.

I brought our dishes to the sink and washed them while Annabelle read from one of her novels. Yasmin's face was buried in her phone instead of her big book of spells, for a change.

When I'd finished the dishes and returned to the table, Annabelle turned to me and whispered loudly, "Now it looks like someone is blowing up *Yas's* phone."

"Who're you texting?" I asked in a singsong voice that I was sure would annoy her.

Yasmin looked up, only a little annoyed. "Nobody. And nobody texts anymore. It's just DMs."

I raised my eyebrows. Annabelle put her elbows on the table and her chin in her hands, looking forward to an answer.

Yasmin blushed and looked away. "Okay, Nate. He and some friends are going to a distillery and he wants me to go but it's not like I'm going to."

"Why not?" I said bluntly. "Don't want a man to explain craft brewing to you?" Then I remembered how generous Nate had been with his time and how gently he'd treated Yasmin. "Okay, that was harsh. But still, why not?"

"I mean . . ." She paused, phone in hand, then seemed to retreat back into the armor she had when she arrived. "I'm not here to socialize. I'm here to get this house from you. And now that I know Agatha's grimoire is here, I need to decode and analyze it so that I can bring it back to my mom with answers."

I rolled my eyes. "You are the strangest person I've ever met."

Yasmin frowned.

"You're pretty. You're young. A guy you're obviously interested in is also interested in you." I pointed vaguely in the direction of the door. "Go out! Enjoy your life!"

"But—"

"Gibson is right, Yas," Annabelle said gently. "There's no harm in having a little fun."

I said, "Marley and I won't tell your mom that you went on a date even though you're twentysomething years old. Scout's honor."

On cue, Annabelle held up her hand in a salute.

Yas nodded, seeming more confident. "Okay. I'll go." Then she looked down at the pasta sauce she'd spilled on her blouse.

"Oh crap, what am I going to wear?"

"Want help picking an outfit?" I offered, only half joking.

"No offense, but from you? Absolutely not." Yasmin got up from the table. "Thanks for dinner, Annabelle."

The ghost smiled warmly. "You're welcome."

As she left the kitchen, Yasmin turned back to us with a sly look on her face. "Don't wait up."

~

We settled on the back deck, me drinking wine and Annabelle sitting with an empty glass in front of her, pretending. I'd bought a citronella candle from the general store after my interlude at Big Mike's, along with more food for Annabelle to cook for the two of us. Yasmin wasn't in a hurry to leave the house, and with Annabelle cooking, I'd eaten better in the last few days than I had in ages.

After a few minutes of comfortable silence, I said, "I have something to show you, by the way."

"Oh?" Annabelle clasped her hands around her empty glass.

I returned to the den to grab the guitar and songbook. When I got back to the table, I opened the book to a page I'd dog-eared, then held it open with the wine bottle. Running my hands over the page, I mumbled the song to myself as I figured out the rhythm, then started strumming.

Annabelle looked confused, then impressed.

I wagged my eyebrows at her as I got into a rhythm, and said, "Told you I could play."

She grinned. "I didn't doubt it for a second, dear." Annabelle watched, her entire body leaning toward me. "Though I'm sure your music is far more 'hip' than anything I'm familiar with."

"Nah, I think you'll know this one."

I couldn't meet her eyes and sing at the same time. If I did, I'd just get lost. So, I glanced down at the book and steeled myself. Doing my best to impersonate a '60s teen pop idol, I sang the song from *Shrek* about believing in love. It felt ridiculous.

But Annabelle's eyes went as round as saucers, and when she realized what song it was, she let out a quiet, "Oh." The intensity of her ghostly glow increased as she watched me and hummed along, terribly off-key.

I wasn't a great singer, but we flipped through the book of 1960s songs and I played a selection of bubblegum pop while Annabelle swayed and clapped beside me. She sang along and occasionally managed to harmonize with me, though not through any actual talent on her part. My throat would be sore tomorrow, but I sung the night away. Everything faded except the instrument in my hands, the ghost by my side, and the music we made together.

# Chapter 12

I barely saw Yasmin at all the next day. After grabbing a quick cup of tea from Annabelle, she retreated to the shed and spent hours in there doing who-knows-what with Agatha's magic book. Nate and Old Pete finished the electrical work around noon, and then Nate returned to the house to bring Yasmin a sandwich for lunch.

My own stomach was starting to growl when the doorbell rang. I stretched and closed my laptop, grateful for the break. When I reached the hallway, I realized that someone—Nate, most likely—had fixed the doorbell so that it no longer sounded like someone was stepping on a frog.

"What a lovely day for magic!" Miranda exclaimed when I opened the door. She was wearing maroon from head to toe today, including what looked like red velvet slippers. Her fingernails were painted to match. Under her arm, she held an old book—one that looked suspiciously familiar.

I let her in, then said, "You have a date with Yasmin, I assume?"

She nodded. "We're making great strides, Gibson."

"Great strides toward what, exactly?" I walked with her through the house and out to the back deck, where we looked at the messy garden.

But Miranda demurred. "Oh, I shouldn't say. It's still early stages, and . . . I think we'd best have that conversation together. The three of us."

"O-kay," I said, but she was already down the steps. She opened the shed door and hugged Yasmin enthusiastically. I could just barely see Yasmin's face as she greeted Miranda. Her eyes crinkled in a smile, and she laughed easily at something the older woman said.

"Weird sisters," I muttered, pulling the phrase from somewhere deep in my brain. "I think it's time I got the fuck out of this house . . . It's definitely time to stop talking to myself."

~

On my walk downtown, I passed the turnoff to Big Mike's just as Adam and his crew were speeding in the opposite direction. I raised my hand in a wave, and the four of them waved back. One honked a bike horn. They stopped before turning to go home.

"My dad says you're a wicked guitar player," Adam said. "Don't you have a bike?"

"Nah."

The kids looked at each other as if I'd just said I'd been abducted by aliens.

"Stay here!" Adam dismounted, letting his bike fall to the ground, and dashed down the lane that led to his house. "Make her stay!" he called over his shoulder.

His three friends, grubby from playing whatever games

they'd been playing in the forest, linked hands and formed a wall to prevent me from leaving. I put my hands up like I would if I was being apprehended. "What's going on?"

"You can't be here without a bike," one of the kids said. He was taller than the others, gangly and glasses-wearing. The others nodded.

"I think it's illegal," another one whispered.

I laughed, but the kids remained serious. A few moments later, Adam returned, riding a bigger bike than the one he'd left behind.

"Here." Adam dismounted and held the handlebars steady. "It's Sage's, but they have, like, two other ones, which is not fair, by the way."

"I can't take Sage's bike!" I said.

"Sure you can." Adam shrugged. "I'll tell them you borrowed it."

"But—"

Before I could protest further, Adam picked up his original bike from the ground, hopped on it, and the crew headed off. "Later!"

"I . . . Thank you!" I yelled at the kids. Then I stared down at the bike. I liked to think of myself as fearless but even I wasn't so brave as to ride a bike in New York City, so it had been literal decades since I'd ridden one. Was remembering how to ride a bike *actually* like remembering how to ride a bike?

After staring for a good thirty seconds, I summoned the courage to sling my leg over the center bar and try it.

~

Sweating and breathless but alive, I made it downtown. Biking was, regrettably, much faster than walking. But I'm sure I looked far less cool doing it with a white-knuckle grip on a set of wheels made for a teenager.

I had a turkey sandwich at a brewhouse called Mary's. The food was expensive but decent, and I finally found a beer that didn't taste like Pine-Sol cleaning solution. I sat by myself on the patio and watched the ferry come in. A light breeze tickled my cheek, but my hair was short enough not to fly in my eyes.

The experience was . . . not bad. One pleasant lunch wasn't going to convince me that this was the greatest place ever. But . . . not bad.

Reluctant to return to the house and work, I pedaled around the island, joined by throngs of tourists enjoying the last bit of their summer vacations before returning to real life. Slowly getting the hang of my borrowed ride, I biked through a neighborhood of flower-lined porches in front of mini-mansions and the expansive lawns of a resort before the path started to climb. As I passed a lookout called Lover's Leap, I resolutely looked ahead, not stopping. I was having a pleasant day and was not about to consider the possibility that Annabelle leaped to her death from this spot two hundred years ago.

Passing Arch Rock, I glanced up at the rocks and shrugged, then turned in toward the intense greenery of the island's interior following the signs to Fort Holmes.

The original British fort was located on the highest point on the island and surrounded by the dense forest of the state park. The sounds of birdcalls became louder as I got further from the tourists cycling the perimeter. To get to the fort, I had to hike my borrowed bike up a steep dirt road lined by trees on both sides. A few kids passed by on bicycles, but otherwise, I was left alone with my thoughts. When I reached the reconstructed building, I was breathless from the climb.

The sight of the fort itself was anticlimactic. It was nothing more than a dilapidated two-story wooden building behind a fence at the top of the hill, surrounded by a grassy field. I supposed it made sense that the American fort was far more imposing than the British one, given that it had been occupied for much longer.

I entered the building and gazed around the sparsely furnished room, skimming the informational plaques, not entirely sure what I was looking for.

While I was learning what a redoubt was, my phone buzzed.

Brooke sent a video of a rehearsal. I recognized the space, a tiny studio in the Village. The band was playing "He Knows You Want His Blood (So Don't Give It To Him)," but even through the terrible sound of the cell phone video, I could tell it wasn't right. Every member of the band was out of sync. After eight seconds of the song, the video cut to a selfie view of Brooke making a face that said, "Can you believe this shit?" Then she zoomed in on a guitar player I didn't recognize. He royally fucked the main intro chord progression, then left his cell phone on and stopped the rehearsal to answer it.

After the video, she sent a text saying, "u have got to come back Gibson I cant deal with this shit anymre"

Laughing, I sent a series of emojis in reply. She sent me back a GIF, and I responded with a kissy face. In the ten seconds it took her to like the text, I worried it'd been too much. Brooke and I weren't an item, but she flirted with me often enough that I knew she was interested. Before I left for Michigan, I would have grasped for every crumb from her like a drowning man grasping for a life raft.

I put my phone away and peered through the slatted window as if looking out for an impending American invasion. None of the signs mentioned anything about women at the fort, which was hardly surprising. I stood awkwardly in the center of the room, shoved my hands in my pockets, and exhaled.

"Yep," I said to no one. What was I looking for in this museum? A simple explanation on a sign about why I had an English ghost in my house? Come on.

My phone buzzed again.

Brooke said, "got a gig at The Crowbar on the 31st, some bigwig money bags are coming to see if they want to fund studio time for us." She added seven dollar sign emojis, then added, "u better be back by then cuz this guy sux"

My heart started pounding as fast as it had while hiking up the hill to get here. Studio time? The thirty-first? That was only a little more than a week away. I left her on read and walked outside the building, willing my heart to slow down.

Back in the sunshine, I looked at the reconstruction. It just looked like a sad, old wooden building where a bunch of English kids camped out through brutal Great Lakes winters.

I shook my head. I was being ridiculous. Why was I looking for remnants of a ghost when I should be rehearsing? Or actually trying to sell my house so I could return to real life?

Before I could convince myself not to, I sent a thumbs-up emoji in reply to Brooke. I could get back by the thirty-first. Somehow. Just needed to convince my cousin not to sue me and sell my house. No problem.

Exiting the fort, I spotted a sign that read "Post Cemetery Fort Mackinac." I hesitated. The afternoon was waning, and I still had work to do. I didn't need to repeat the list of things I should be doing instead of chasing ghosts. A chilly breeze sent goosebumps running down my arms.

And it felt wrong, somehow. What would Annabelle say if

she found out I went looking for her body?

I couldn't help but feel a pull, though. As if seeing a stone with her name on it might connect us. If she was buried here, I could touch the ground and feel something solid of hers beneath my fingers.

I turned back the way I came.

~

Yasmin and Miranda stayed in the shed until night fell. When Annabelle and I brought them dinner, both seemed legitimately surprised at how long they'd been working. In front of them were two open spell books and a stack of yellow legal notepads with scribbles. They had cleared a space above the desk and made it into a murder board of sorts, pinning notes and drawings to it. All they needed was a spool of red thread to connect whatever conspiracies they were uncovering.

"Bring these back," I said as I handed over the plates of food. "The last thing we need is mice out here."

Both women nodded, then turned back to their work. Annabelle and I shrugged, then went back to the main house to eat at the table.

All through dinner, Annabelle's smiles were flirtier than usual. She watched as I ate, making encouraging noises and asking me to describe the texture of the food. I tried but blushed under her scrutiny, stuttering until I made her giggle. When the dishes were done, she asked me to play her a song before bed. We sat in the living room, carefully avoiding the pink sofa, and I tuned the guitar while I thought about what to sing.

"Got it," I said at last. Annabelle sat across from me, hands on her lap, her feet tucked away and almost invisible.

I sang "Our Day Will Come," a song I knew from Amy

Winehouse's cover. I guessed that Annabelle might have a version of it on one of her records, too. This time, I had the courage to look at her as I sang.

Annabelle didn't join in. She just watched me, her full lips parted in rapt attention. Her eyes glistened in the low light of the not-quite-full moon. When the song ended, she didn't say anything. She just smiled at me like I'd parted the Red Sea. Or brought Lazarus back from the dead. I knew I was a good player, but she made me feel like my fingers worked miracles on the strings.

I cleared my throat, suddenly feeling my cheeks flush. I'd performed on stage hundreds of times, both solo and with a group, but I'd never felt like this. Like I was truly being *seen*.

When we said goodnight, she followed me up the stairs. At the third-floor landing, Annabelle remained visible for a few seconds longer, lingering in the periphery of my vision.

"Goodnight," she said softly.

"Goodnight, Marley."

I couldn't make myself go to sleep. The smile on Annabelle's face haunted me. The same kind of nervous energy thrummed through me that I felt before a show, especially one where I played a new song. The sort of *fuck-it* feeling that makes you do brave things. Or stupid things.

I put on a barely there bra and the best pair of panties I'd brought to Michigan. Then I sniffed under my arms. Could Annabelle smell me? She smelled her tea in the morning, so, yeah, she probably could. I splashed some water under my arms and wished I'd brought perfume, even though I normally never wore it.

Satisfied, I pulled Annabelle's chair closer to the bed. It was within arm's reach of the mattress now. If she showed up, there would be no question as to why.

I climbed into bed, pulled the sheet so that it barely covered my waist, and waited.

I didn't have to wait long.

The sense of her was intense. It hit me a split second before she appeared, prim as ever, standing in the corner. Something was different—I had just seen Annabelle not five minutes earlier on the landing, but in those five minutes, she'd changed her clothes. She was still wearing a gauzy, white blouse but of a different style. This one wasn't the high-necked number she always wore. It had notched lapels and was unbuttoned to her navel, showing her pale cleavage. If she usually wore a casual Marlene Dietrich look, this was the sultry version.

Looking down at my own tiny chest and then back up, I said, "See something you like, Marley?"

Suddenly, she was seated in the chair next to the bed. She hadn't bothered to walk the three paces it would've taken, as if she couldn't bear to waste a second. A rush of desire coursed through me.

"I think you know the answer to that, my dear," Annabelle whispered.

"Fuck," I whispered back. She actually wanted *me*.

I scooted back on the bed, pulling back the sheets and leaving enough room for another person—or ghost. Positioning my hand deliberately on my thigh, I said, "Do you want to join?"

Her gaze swept up and down my body, and she had the same hungry look in her eyes that she had when she watched me eat. But she shook her head. "I shouldn't."

"Why not?"

"It's not right."

I furrowed my eyebrows, the same cold bucket of water

crashing over me anytime someone talked about my sexual business being right or wrong. Even though she was two hundred years old, I thought Annabelle was different. "What do you mean?"

"I'm dead, Gibson. I can't . . ." Her glow dimmed. "I'm not real."

"Come here." I patted the spot next to me and smiled as she flowed into it. The edges of her didn't quite touch me, but I could feel the coolness of her. This was probably the closest we'd been since the very first night we met when she helped me fix my head.

I reached out my hand with my palm facing her. She held out her own hand, placing it carefully to mine. The familiar electric tingles went through my palm and down my arm, causing me to shiver in anticipation. She may be dead, but her touch made my whole body feel alive.

"I can see you," I said. "I can certainly hear you."

Annabelle smiled at that.

"I can smell you."

"You—"

I nodded. "Yeah, I can smell you, Marley." I moved my hand into hers, making her flow through me. Our hands joined as if they were one. "I can't touch you but I can feel you."

Annabelle exhaled. Her breath was cool against my face.

"Can't taste you, which is a damn shame."

She looked confused, which made me smile. My chest was bursting with the desire to . . . I wasn't even sure what I wanted; I just knew that I *wanted*. I moved my hand to her face and carefully cupped her cheek, wishing I could feel the softness of her skin.

"That's three out of five senses. You're pretty close to real.

But would you want someone like me? If you were alive?" I asked.

She chuckled. "Oh, my darling, I wouldn't be able to resist you. That's for sure."

*Darling.* I grinned, unable to stop the feelings from appearing on my face. Shifting, I lay back on the bed and kicked off the sheet. Undoing my bra, I threw it across the room, then slid my hand slowly down my chest. "Then come get me, Marley."

Suddenly, she was above me, hovering in the air. Her pale face was so close to mine, and every inch of my body felt alive with the almost-there contact. She felt like a thin fresh sheet draped lightly over my body, tickling where it made contact. "If I could, I would touch every inch of you."

"Yeah," I whispered, a new rush of desire coursing through me. I kicked off my underwear and parted my legs. I was intensely wet, and I couldn't help but moan when my fingers found the spot that drove me wild.

"I'm going to . . ."

"Yes, you are." Her voice was soft but firm. She was still hovering above me, whispering directly into my ear. Annabelle trailed her hand down my body until it joined with my own frantic movements. Her fingers were like shadows as they passed over and through mine, then pressed into the deepest parts of me.

"Come for me, darling," she said, pressing ghost kisses to my cheek and down my neck as I cried out, lost in bliss.

~

Breakfast the following morning was a solo affair. Yasmin showed up in rumpled clothes while I was still drinking my first cup of coffee. Her hair was sticking out from her head at even more angles than usual. Nate walked her to the front door, then waved at me sheepishly. As soon as her tea water boiled, she was out the back door, heading to the shed for more magical mystery homework.

Annabelle was nowhere to be found. I told myself that was fine. I wasn't very convincing.

The cable internet guy came and went, then the mailman delivered a mountain of Agatha's junk mail. I saved the weirdest newsletters for Yasmin and chucked the rest. The day passed slowly, with me in the living room or Annabelle's alcove working and the rest of my strange companions elsewhere. In between conference calls and working on documents, I Googled "were there lesbians in 1812" and "what did people in Mackinac do in the 1800s," then "how not to get rid of a ghost."

I played a selection of my favorite songs on my phone but soon grew tired of them. I took out Agatha's guitar and played a few Call Me Kate Kane songs to keep them in my head but couldn't find a connection to them. Playing felt rote, like I was just going through the motions. Then I flipped through Annabelle's records and found a Nina Simone album. I put it on the Victrola, and her version of "The House of the Rising Sun" filled the alcove. I struggled to concentrate; my thoughts scattered like the dust particles I could see drifting in the light of the afternoon sun.

Seymour Anderson arrived five minutes early to our meeting. He rang the doorbell, then knocked three times. When I opened the door, he grinned and said, "Hello!" somehow pronouncing the exclamation mark.

I let him in, and he let out a loud whistle.

"Been wanting to get inside this house for ages. How are you holding up out here? I heard you called the Doofus Army to do some work for you. Surprised they didn't burn down the place!"

"Hmm, yeah." I frowned, reluctant to insult Old Pete even though he'd been strange and off-putting. He'd never made my nose scrunch like I was smelling bad cheese though, and that was my reaction to Seymour.

I led him through the house, explaining what I remembered about the square footage and basic construction details from the paperwork I had read before I arrived. By now I had a spiel practically memorized about the house—one that left out the haunting and the witch in the shed. I hoped she stayed out there like she had been the past few nights. And I had to trust that Annabelle knew not to make a sudden appearance with a stranger in the house.

He grimaced at the bloodstained sofa and said, "Yikes. These furnishings would make for a great bonfire."

I smiled a tight-lipped smile but otherwise didn't respond.

When we'd toured all the rooms except Yasmin's, I led him back to the sitting room. I kept an eye on Annabelle's library alcove and tried to position him so that he faced away from it, just in case.

Seymour took notes on his phone, then said, "You could get two mil for this place." He added, "Maybe. Thereabouts."

I almost choked on nothing but spit and surprise. "Excuse me?"

He smiled that unnerving Cheshire-cat smile. "You couldn't be in a better location, after all. You know what they say about real estate!" He chuckled at his own joke.

"Wow." I didn't know what else to say. I considered telling him about Yasmin's challenge to the will but kept my mouth shut. She hadn't actually filed any paperwork yet, to my knowledge. I realized that meant she was freeloading and I was letting her.

Seymour continued. "I've got your email address to send the offer. Look it over, and we can haggle if we need to." He wagged his eyebrows as he said the word "haggle" like there wasn't anything he'd like more than to fight me over the details of a real estate transaction.

"Right."

"I'll give you time to decide, of course," he said, checking the calendar on his phone. "Let's say, sign by the end of the month, and close the fifteenth. That's a week for you to say yes to becoming a millionaire." He flashed me another Cheshire-cat grin, then added a thumbs-up.

"End of the month," I repeated. "Close on the fifteenth."

"Easy peasy. I'll be in touch." With a wave, he left, jogging up the lane that joined the main road.

I stood in the doorway, my brain struggling to catch up to the offer he'd just made. It would net me two million dollars if I agreed with Seymour's terms, whatever they were. I could leave and be back in New York just in time for the big show with Brooke. Then when I returned for the closing, it would be the last time I ever needed to see the Mackinac Bridge or smell the overpowering scent of flowers and horse shit ever again.

Or Annabelle.

Unable to stay in the house, I slammed the door behind me and walked downtown to find a place to drink. Alone.

# Chapter 13

U nsure of my ability to drink and ride a bike, I walked downtown as the sun started to descend on the Great Lakes. The crowds were heavy, with bikes zooming along the main road along with the occasional horse carriage. I spotted the group of women from my ferry ride here on one, squeezed into the carriage compartment like sausage in a casing. All of them but one was loudly laughing or taking a cell phone video. The woman squeezed into a tube top appeared about to vomit at any moment, but her companions were blind to her discomfort.

The Purple Stallion was busy, happy, and loud—not the vibe I wanted.

I passed two fudge shops, three T-shirt shops, and an overpriced steakhouse before arriving at Helga's as a band was setting up and tuning. With a groan, I sat down and watched as Big Mike plugged in his Larrivée Baker electric. Dr. Johnson, of all people, was at the mic. She adjusted the height of the microphone then tapped it a few times. Sage was barely visible behind the drum kit at the back. Two people I didn't know were also on stage, one at the keyboard and the other playing bass.

Into the mic, Dr. Johnson said, "Okay, folks we're going to be playing here in about ten minutes, so stay tuned and don't forget to tip your servers!"

"Woo!" The whoop came from Rebecca Johnson, seated at a table near the middle of the room. She was halfway into a pint. Seeing her in a different context was jarring. During my unexpected haircut, I hadn't noticed the little happy smile lines around her eyes or the way she wore chunky-but-tasteful jewelry. Tonight, she was wearing a dark blue high-waisted jumpsuit, and her hair was pulled into a knot high on her head the same way the bossy nurse from M*A*S*H wore hers. On Rebecca Johnson, the 'do was cute and just a tad sexy.

As a waitress took my order, Rebecca turned and spotted me.

Oh, shoot.

"Gibson!" She stood, knocking into the table and sloshing her drink but not spilling it. "Right? It's Gibson?"

I nodded, hoping she wouldn't approach. She did.

"Your hair looks great! I mean, I knew it would." She put a hand to her chest and put on an exaggerated expression of pride. "Since your stylist is perfect at everything she does."

I really tried not to smile.

"Seriously, though, I hope it's working for you."

"The hair? Yes," I said. "The hair is one thing in my life that is, actually, perfect." Surprisingly, I meant it. I had given very little thought to my hair in the last few days, which meant that it was perfect. There was no pulling it into a painful ponytail or burning my fingers to curl it and then not recognizing the person in the mirror with curled hair.

A few other people came into the bar, but it wasn't a packed house. Big Mike wandered over to the table, giving me a friendly wave. "How's the guitar?"

"It's, uh, also perfect," I said. I kept trying not to smile, but these people made it difficult to remember why I was upset when I arrived.

Dr. Johnson joined the party, throwing her arm around Rebecca. She was about three inches shorter than her wife even while wearing two-inch wedges, so she had to go up on her tiptoes. She was wearing a cute patterned wrap dress that accentuated her curves nicely.

"You remember Sara, right?" Rebecca said, seamlessly providing her wife's first name so I didn't have to keep thinking of her as Dr. Johnson.

We shook hands, and Rebecca told her I loved my haircut. Sara responded with a snort. "Of course Gibson loved her haircut! Her stylist is perfect in everything she does."

"Damn straight," said Rebecca with a smile.

"Hair aside, how are you?" Sara asked. "Your head must be just fine since you've come to see the best band on Mackinac. Also, the only band, but we try not to mention that part."

"I'm . . . . good. I, uh, got an offer, actually," I said with a grimace. "On the house."

I expected the mood to plummet as the trio realized I was betraying their little island of weirdos and fucking off back to the big city. But instead of frowning, Big Mike, Rebecca, and Sara all smiled.

"That's great!" Sara said.

Big Mike flagged down one of the waitresses, then pointed at me. "Do not let this woman pay for her drinks tonight. They're on me."

"Or me!" Rebecca said.

I held up my hands. "No, no, no. That's not necessary, really!"

"Of course it is!" Sara said. "Congrats on selling the house. It's what you wanted, right?"

"Umm . . ."

Rebecca leaned in to whisper, "And you will have to tell us how much you're getting. Like, ballpark."

Big Mike backed away. "I don't want to know! But I'm happy for you all the same, Gibson. Even if it means we're losing a potential bandmate."

"You play? Or sing?" Rebecca asked, her eyes wide.

"Guitar," I said, taking a sip of my beer and hoping to end the conversation there.

Big Mike clapped me on the back, graciously waiting until I'd swallowed first. "She's great! Way better than I am!"

"I mean—"

On stage, Sage had emerged from behind the drums. "Two-minute warning," they said into the mic. They gave me a small wave, but their neutral expression didn't change. For the performance, Sage looked much the same as they had when I saw them last—a band T-shirt and ripped jeans. They weren't wearing a jacket tonight and had swapped AC/DC for *Rick and Morty*.

"We gotta go, babe," Dr. Johnson said, pulling away from her wife's arms. "We're playing!"

"Fine." Rebecca let her go, checking out her ass as Sara weaved around the bar tables to the stage. Then she grabbed her purse and drink, moving them to the seat next to mine. "Break something!" she called to her wife.

"I won't!" the doctor said, blowing her a kiss before she returned to the stage.

~

Sage was amazing.

The rest of the band, not so much. Big Mike was a perfectly average guitar player, such that I hardly noticed his slips. There wasn't anything novel or interesting about the way he played, meaning that he had a level of skill that let him fade into the background while the mistakes of the rest of the players were loud and clear. The bass player appeared to be about eighty-five years old and half asleep. He missed half his chords and almost fell off his chair a few times. Sara's singing was the kind of singing you do in the shower or the car—not in front of people. I'd be damned if she didn't try, though.

But I couldn't take my eyes off the green-haired teenager. They played not only with technical acumen, but with the kind of heart you can't fake. The kid added flair to the simplest routines and even went off on a few solos that were just sophisticated enough to blend into the song without being showy. The kid had talent. Too bad they were stuck on this island full of tourists instead of living in a place with a scene.

Rebecca signaled for a waitress to bring us more beers and clinked her glass with mine when they were delivered. It was easy, somehow, to sit with her and watch these mediocre musicians. If Brooke or any of my other friends were here, they'd be making snide comments about the players' lack of skill and planning to head to the next bar. But as I watched Rebecca watching her wife on stage, I was humiliated to feel tears building behind my eyes. It felt like there was a gaping wound in my chest, one that should be bleeding all over this stupid bar high-top table and onto the sticky floor. Pressure built behind my sinuses, and I *hated* that I was getting emotional while a group of amateurs played "Wonderwall."

Why did they all have to be so fucking nice?

The song ended, and I gulped down half my pint in one go. While they played, people kept trickling in to the bar and filling the house. I looked around at the crowd. There were a few tourists in sundresses and khakis, but most wore jeans and T-shirts. These looked like locals, not the tourists who would flock to the bar, then go buy late-night fudge and a fifty-dollar Mackinac Island T-shirt.

Rebecca cheered louder than anyone else in the crowd, then whistled using her fingers. "Thanks, babe," Sara said into the mic.

It was so obvious how much they loved each other—disgusting, really. A goddamned little happy band family on this little happy island with their devoted groupie and kids who loaned bikes to strangers and . . .

I had to go.

The stage loomed over me, looking like a distortion from a movie special effect. I started sweating everywhere, including weird places like the dip of my collarbone under my black T-shirt. I recognized the feeling of an oncoming panic attack. If I didn't get out of this bar in the next five minutes, I would pass out.

I wanted what they had so bad it hurt.

As I bolted, Rebecca was belting out the beginning lines of "Don't Stop Believin.'" Luckily, I got out before the earworm became permanently lodged in my brain.

Leaving the bar, I gulped in the night air, and walked along the path circling the island. There wasn't a destination in my mind, but though I staved off an actual panic attack, I knew I couldn't return home just yet.

Home? Abaddon wasn't home. It was just a place to stay.

One that was going to make me a lot of money.

The moon was about a quarter full, bright enough that I didn't need to use my phone to walk along the path once my eyes adjusted. Buoys blinked at me from the dark waters of the lakes like red eyes winking from afar. I shivered at the brisk wind that came over Lake Huron. After walking for a good fifteen minutes, I'd left the bright lights of downtown behind. Ahead of me was darkness and a familiar bend in the path. It was the cove where I'd seen Annabelle that night.

I never figured out why she was here. At this cove—or in this world at all. I shivered again. Walking forward slowly, I watched the rocks for any sign of a beautiful ghost in a nightgown.

"Annabelle?" I whispered, my voice sounding louder than intended in the quiet, dark night. "Are you here?"

Nothing.

I walked to the little beach where I'd seen her, studying the features of the rocks. There was a mile marker on the side of the road, identifying this spot as mile three. But other than that, it was just a stretch of rock where the road curved to match the natural contour of the island. The dark rocks gleamed with spray from the gentle waves generated by the lake.

"Annabelle?" I called out, louder this time.

My voice was swallowed by the waves.

~

All the rooms in Abaddon Cottage were silent and dark when I returned.

The beer in my stomach sloshed around uncomfortably, pressing on my bladder and reminding me of my age. I trudged up the stairs to my room and readied myself for bed, but sleep eluded. I felt exhausted, worn like a rubber band stretched too tight. Before I could slip into unconsciousness, the scent of the lakes returned.

"Marley," I whispered, "are you here?"

My ghost appeared slowly, phasing into solidity like she was waking from an invisible sleep. Annabelle sat in her chair next to the bed, looking down on me with a sad, soft smile on her face.

"I'm here, dearest."

I closed my eyes and let myself fall apart. Instead of a gaping wound, now I felt like an overflowing bathtub. Too much feeling for one chest cavity to contain.

How could she call me "dearest?" What did I do to deserve that honor when I couldn't possibly be hers?

"Will you stay for a while? Read a book if you like." I reached out my hand, hovering it in the air between us, palm out, saying what I needed with the grasping of my fingers. "The light won't bother me. Just stay?"

Slowly, she reached out with her own ghostly hand. Our palms didn't touch. But I felt the shimmering, pulsing energy of her. When our hands finally overlapped, I felt the coolness of Annabelle's essence lightly kissing my skin.

"We've gotten ourselves into a predicament," Annabelle said softly. "Haven't we, Gibson?"

I curled my fingers, clinging to a hand that could never hold me back. "Yeah, I think maybe we have."

# Chapter 14

My head throbbed the next morning, reminding me how much of a lightweight I'd become. Though I tried to keep up with Brooke and the rest of the band, most nights I consumed half the alcohol they did.

Annabelle made me a pot of coffee, then sat at her usual place at the table. She was reading *The Canterville Ghost*, which I wanted to make fun of her for but couldn't summon the energy. Staying at the kitchen table, I read the *Town Crier* for a few peaceful moments in silence. The front page was full of details about the Mackinac Astronomical Society's plans for the super blood moon viewing party next week at the Somewhere in Time Gazebo.

"You look terrible," Yasmin said as she entered the kitchen.

I couldn't summon the energy to respond to that either, so I halfheartedly flipped her the bird.

"How about breakfast?" Annabelle asked. She flowed over to the refrigerator and hummed a tune while she considered what to make.

I got up to pour myself more coffee, then stayed at the counter, watching Annabelle pick things out of the fridge. Yasmin stood by the sink, filling the kettle. The too-full feeling came back to my chest, but it hurt less than it had the night before.

I knew I should tell them about Seymour's offer to buy the house.

I didn't tell them.

As Annabelle pulled milk from the fridge, a precarious stack of food items came crashing down. A carton of eggs wobbled for a moment on the tip of the shelf, then tumbled to the floor.

"Oh, drat!" Annabelle exclaimed.

"I'll get it." I pulled off a sheet of paper towels, making a mental note to buy a holder for them. At this rate, I was going to single-handedly buy out the entire island's supply of eggs.

Yasmin interrupted, yelling, "Wait!"

"What?"

She nudged me aside. Instead of answering, she knelt down by the spill. Two eggs had fallen out of the carton. Yasmin peered at the broken shells. Yellow and orange goo leaked out and spread onto the dingy linoleum floor. Absent-mindedly, I wondered how much it would cost to redo the floor in vinyl.

Yasmin muttered to herself for a moment, then sighed. "Nope. It's no use."

"What are you doing?" I asked. "Please don't say you're telling the future using broken eggs."

She stood up and shook her head. "My mom's better at scrying than I am."

Annabelle patted the vicinity of her shoulder in sympathy.

"Well, I mean, it's eggs," I said. "So don't beat yourself up." I dumped the gooey carton in the sink and cleaned up the mess on the floor while Yasmin finished making her tea. Then I turned back to the refrigerator. It was a yellow 1970s GE model that miraculously still worked. Though, like many things in this house, it made funny noises every now and then.

"Marley, I will buy you a new fridge," I said decisively. "This one is too small."

Annabelle said, "Oh, that's not necessary, Gibson, really." But she gazed thoughtfully at the old refrigerator as if mentally measuring for a new one. "Although it would be nice, since there are a few more people . . . staying here now." She very carefully didn't say "living here."

"I thought you were going to sell the house," Yasmin said, sipping her hot tea carefully. Her mug had a picture of a cat with sunglasses on it. "If you don't give it to me, that is."

"I'm not giving the house to you." She was right. I didn't say that she was right, though. She would have to pry the words "you're right, Yas" out of my clenched teeth.

"What's the point in buying a new fridge if you just sell the house? Why buy a new appliance for people you don't even know?"

Annabelle watched our exchange, her head swiveling between us like we were engaged in a tennis match.

But my head was throbbing, so instead of taking the bait—or telling them about Seymour's offer—I just sighed. "I'm not buying a new appliance for anyone except Annabelle. Okay?"

"And I appreciate it very much, Gibson," Annabelle said diplomatically. She didn't have to say, "And that's that—no more fighting."

The three of us gave up on breakfast and returned to our places around the kitchen table with our beverages. For her choice of smell, Annabelle boiled a cup of water and added a lemon to it. I went back to the newspaper, Annabelle read her novel, and Yasmin consulted Agatha's magic book.

"Actually, I need to run something by you," Yasmin said, suddenly. She bit her lip, looking shy.

I scoffed. "You? Run something by me? Who are you and what have you done with my cousin?"

"Ha ha." Yasmin stuck her tongue out at me, then faced Annabelle. "I meant Annabelle."

"Oh!" She looked up from her book, carefully placing a ribbon in the book to mark her place. "Yes? You really don't need to consult me on things, you know. But I'll help if I can."

"I wanted to have Nate over for dinner." Yasmin bit her lip and wouldn't look at me.

"That's a wonderful idea!" Annabelle clapped her hands together. In her excitement, she left her chair, floating a few inches above it for a moment before realizing and lowering herself back down. "Isn't it, Gibson?"

"Uh . . ."

"Isn't it, Gibson?" This time, her voice was syrupy sweet—daring me to disagree.

I faced Yasmin. "Yes, it's great. Have over your himbo."

"He's not—" Yasmin considered. "Thanks."

"I have recipe books in the den," said Annabelle. "I'll find a good one to make for all of us." She got up and flowed toward her library, then turned and said, "Gibson, I'll give you a list of items I'll need. Make sure you go before the store closes so you have enough time to shop."

"Why am I the one doing the shopping?" I protested. But she was already out of sight, still humming.

I shrugged and turned back to my newspaper.

"Also," Yasmin said, "you're going to meet us for lunch." It wasn't a question.

"Who's us?"

"Me and Miranda." Her face was deadly serious. Like, "someone dying" serious.

"Umm," I said.

"At the fish-and-chips place. One o'clock." She slammed her book shut and got up to leave.

"No. I cannot go to The Codfather. That place is ridiculous." My stomach growled, betraying its desire for food, even terrible fish and chips.

Yasmin rolled her eyes so hard I wondered how they stayed in her head. "You'll be fine. I'm going to Miranda's. Meet us at one o'clock." She left, swishing her skirt aggressively.

"Okay," I said out loud to no one. "I guess today is 'order Gibson around' day."

The house didn't answer, unsympathetic to my plight.

~

That morning, I emailed Babs with the last of my current client's deliverables. I sent her an instant message with the date of my return and asked not to receive any new work until I got back. She replied with happy face emojis, house emojis, and dollar signs. More importantly, she agreed not to send me any work and insisted we go out for drinks to celebrate when I got back.

True to his word, Seymour emailed me the offer paperwork. But when I opened it, the words swam in front of my eyes, and I just . . . couldn't make myself process the information. Instead, I researched the name of the music executive Brooke had mentioned. He seemed legit. The show on the thirty-first was listed on the venue's website and had gotten some advance hype.

I looked at return flights but couldn't make myself pick one.

None of the options were right. The time wasn't great, or they flew into JFK, or they wanted to charge me extra just for existing. I closed my laptop and walked into the garden.

Behind Yasmin's shed, I found a rack with rusting garden tools. There was also a plastic container with several pairs of gloves and hedge clippers that fared much better than the ones exposed to the elements.

As I hacked my way through a mess of shrubs, I discovered a ring of old stones deeply set in the ground. Dirt and weeds choked the middle of the fire pit, but the ring was intact and the stones were in fairly good shape.

What did you know? There was an actual place for a bonfire back here.

I snapped a picture of the pit, then a few of the back of the house from my vantage point at the fence, and sent them to Brooke with a fire emoji plus a marshmallow.

"wow what a dump" was her response.

"Haha yeah it's a little rough," I replied.

"maybe u should burn the house down and claim the insurance"

I winced as I read her texts. I should've expected her mocking tone, though. She sounded exactly like I did when I first got here.

"looks like the ending of Blair witch"

I laughed at that one, then responded with, "you don't even know."

"good for u tho, man, glad someone's gonna pay u 4 it!"

I swallowed past the lump that rose in my throat and sent a thumbs-up, wanting the conversation to end. Turning back to the fire pit, I managed to clear most of the debris and weeds out of the middle. I was sweating through my shirt, but the exertion felt good, like the stress leaked out through my skin and joined the humid morning air.

About ten minutes later, Brook sent another text. It said, "btw lemme know if u have thots on this... im not sure it'll be anything yet" This was followed by a screenshot of her Notes app, which showed a set of unfinished lyrics.

*hey girl hi*
*wanna come back down*
*hey girl hi*
*can we go downtown*

*my girl mine*
*wanna come back down*
*from that ledge*

*like Christmas in July*
*I watch my baby fly*
*come back down, yeah*
*come back down to me*

I saved the image to my phone. We had never written lyrics together. In fact, I'd never been much of a writer at all. But the idea of creating a song called to me, even if it was started by someone else.

Leaving the garden tools behind, I went back in the house and showered. Then I grabbed my guitar and a notebook, glad to have a new project to take my mind off the conversations I wasn't ready to have.

~

When I got to The Codfather, Yasmin spotted me immediately and waved me over. She was seated with Miranda in a booth at the back of the restaurant. The walls were lined with mobster movie posters, and the whole place smelled strongly of grease. When I sat down, Yasmin pushed a basket of fried cod and french fries at me.

"Here. We have a lot to go over." She wiped her hands on a napkin and added it to a large pile next to her plate.

I regarded the basket with suspicion. "You ordered for me?"

"We did." Miranda smiled sweetly.

They were both seated on one side of the booth, with me on the other.

"What is this? An interrogation?" I said warily. "Or an intervention? I don't smoke anymore and I had two beers last night, max. Not that it's any of your business."

"It's not an intervention," replied Yasmin. "Though your wardrobe could use one."

I looked down at my vintage Bikini Kill T-shirt and frowned. "What's wrong with my—never mind, you're changing the subject. Why did we have to meet here instead of talking at the house?"

"Privacy, dear," Miranda said. She picked up a french fry between two fake nail tips and daintily brought it to her lips.

It was the lunch rush, so the restaurant was packed with tourists. I raised my eyebrows skeptically.

"Eat," Yasmin ordered. "And we'll explain."

My stomach growled, and I relented, squeezing a lemon wedge over a fish filet. As I ate, Yasmin brought out her old book and set it next to Agatha's on the table.

Miranda gestured at the books. "These books make up the Cartwright Coven grimoire. Starting sometime in the 1600s, the book was passed down from mother to daughter, each generation adding to the knowledge contained within. At times, the book was copied—split to share between siblings who both inherited the gift of magic. This is what happened when Agatha and her sister Martha were born. Although Martha was the more powerful witch of the two of them, both sisters had a copy of the grimoire. When Martha died, hers was to be copied and split and passed to her daughters, Helena and Vivian."

At the mention of my mother's name, I put down the french fry I'd been eating, suddenly not hungry.

Miranda's face grew sad. "I wasn't on the island yet, but Agatha told me about the time she spent caring for her sister's children—your mothers. She tried her best but found it very challenging. The girls were traumatized by the death of their mother. Agatha didn't know how to raise any children, never mind emotionally fragile ones."

Miranda folded her hands on the table, looking down at her mostly full basket of food. "And Agatha was also a little lost, I think, after her sister's death."

We fell quiet for a moment, silently considering the passing of a woman none of us knew. But even though I struggled to understand my mother through most of my childhood and adolescence, I knew that the death of my grandmother Martha had a profound effect on her. She often blamed her death on spirits and threw herself even more fervently into her worship whenever something reminded her of her mother.

Miranda continued. "Since Vivian wanted nothing to do with Agatha, her sister, or witchcraft, instead of copying Martha's book, the original was passed to Helena. Then, to Yasmin."

Yasmin picked up the tale from there. "My mother added to her grimoire, in keeping with tradition." She flipped through her book until she got to a page almost at the end of the book. "When I left for Michigan, she entrusted it to me. I've been cross-referencing Agatha's book with my mom's to find out if

there's missing or complementary information in each volume."
She smiled, clearly proud of her work.

"Wait—" I pointed at Yasmin with a french fry. "She didn't
pass the book down to you until you left?"

Yasmin blinked.

"Why not? She didn't trust you with it until she sent you off
to do her dirty work for her?"

"I . . ." Yasmin's face fell.

"Let's not get sidetracked," said Miranda. "You've accomplished a great deal in the short time you've been here, Yas."

Yasmin shook her head. "You're right. Both of you." She
looked at me, unflinching. "My mother didn't trust me with her
grimoire, and she didn't tell me about Annabelle. When I see
her again, I . . . we're going to have a discussion about that. But I
think it's because she wanted me to figure this out on my own."

"And . . . what? I still don't see what any of this has to do
with me." I took a gulp of the soda they'd gotten me, slurping
loudly through the straw.

"I'm getting to that." Yasmin flipped through both books
until she got to a page with what looked like a long poem. Both
books had about the same length of text on the page, though
written in different handwriting. Yasmin turned the books
around to face me. "This is the ritual that we think Agatha was
working on before she died."

She pointed to the page in Agatha's book. "This page was
written in Agatha's grimoire by her grandmother long before
she was born." Then she pointed to the corresponding page in
hers. "And this page was written by Martha herself, sometime
shortly before her death. Each book has the instructions and
part of the ritual text."

I shrugged. "So? Two books with the same info. You said

yourself that they overlap." I waved my hands in the air sarcastically. "And that you have *psychic visions*."

She shook her head. "This ritual gains its power by numerology and the position of the moon. It's written in Sicilian tercet, and the whole thing is based on the number three. This means that Agatha only had one-third of the picture. She didn't know that my mother's book had the second part."

Miranda wiped her fingers daintily on a napkin, then rummaged in her purse. She brought out an old book and put it on the table. This one looked more like a dime-store romance paperback than a magic tome. "And I have the final third."

"But you're not a member of the family. No offense. How did *you* get a magic book?" I asked, before remembering that I didn't care about any of this.

With a smile, Miranda said, "It may not be a fancy handmade volume like yours, but this book called to me. I picked it up in an adult bookstore clearance bin in San Francisco in the '70s."

She pursed her lips, and I could tell there was a wealth of stories behind that sentence waiting to be told, if someone asked. But she shook her head. "When Agatha found out I had a copy of her family's heritage, she was beside herself. Nearly broke a hip laughing! It's a funny old world, isn't it?"

Yasmin sat up straight, squaring her shoulders. "This is what Agatha wanted to achieve before she died. According to her research, the ritual had to happen on a certain date, but she couldn't figure out what that date was. But *I* did. With this research, I proved myself worthy of the Cartwright grimoire."

"Congratulations," I said dryly.

She ignored my sarcasm and continued. "But the ritual must be performed on the date of the next blood moon."

I nodded. "Annabelle told me about Agatha becoming obsessed with a ritual before she died. But she said it required three people."

Yasmin and Miranda looked at each other, then at me.

"Oh, no," I said, holding up my hands. "I'm not going to help you cast a spell. I don't believe in any of this. If you two want to do some hocus pocus next week on the full moon, you can go right ahead. But leave me out of it."

Miranda dabbed her face with a napkin.

"You'll want to do this with us, Gibson." Yasmin looked like the cat that got the cream. Or the witch with the fastest broom.

"And why's that?"

"Because the spell summons Annabelle."

"You don't need a spell to summon her." I shrugged, letting my incredulity show in my voice. "Just walk in the door and say, 'Hey, Annabelle.' She'll come right out."

"Gibson, you're not listening." Yasmin leaned forward. Her sleeve pooled on the place mat, perilously close to a tub of ketchup.

"The ritual has to be done on the blood moon—the night of the thirty-first. If we perform it according to the instructions in all three grimoires, we can summon Annabelle, the *living person*. We can return her to her body."

# Chapter 15

My stomach dropped. The fries I'd eaten felt like heavy pieces of greasy garbage sitting in my belly, gathering stress.

"That's ridiculous," I choked out. "Annabelle is dead. She's not coming back."

"Maybe she can, Gibson," Miranda said.

"You believe in this, too?" I threw up my hands. "Come on, guys. I played along with your magic book and your witch stuff up until now, but this is just silly."

But Yasmin pressed on, leaning forward in the booth. She pushed the basket of fish and chips aside. "My mother knows this book backwards and forwards. She taught me that this page was a mistake, written by an incompetent witch suffering from malnutrition and untreated gonorrhea. Whenever anyone tried it, nothing happened."

"Because she didn't have the complete text," Miranda added.

"And because she wasn't supposed to do it alone," said Yasmin, seamlessly picking up again. The two of them were so in sync I wondered if they'd rehearsed this. "The ritual was meant for us. The three of us."

"There is no *us*." I shook my head. "I'm not a part of this. I'm not like you."

"Read this." Yasmin handed me a spiral-bound notebook. On it, she'd compiled the passages from Agatha's grimoire, her own volume, and Miranda's tawdry paperback. She had also scribbled notes all over the margins, drawing little hearts and flowers in several places. I tried very hard not to find them endearing.

> *When a fall breaks; no foresight enthralls*
> *Cut and sew and pace and stomp, look far then near*
> *Only love outlasts us all*
>
> *Sparks fly and sparks tame, a journey you'll hear*
> *The end of Caesar, thunder's day*
> *When three are one, they have no fear*
>
> *A Bell rings seldom but clear and gay*
> *Burn all burn one, burn thyself none*
> *Jack and Lil need a place to play*
>
> *Returned by the sea, while blood drips bright*
> *To the sea, with love, her home by night*

"Weird poem," I said, squinting at the handwriting. I put down the notebook and grabbed another fry, shaking off the vinegar to disguise the shaking of my hand. "But I guess it rhymes. Who are Jack and Lil?"

Yasmin shook her head. "I have no idea. There are parts I still don't understand and about five pages of instructions. But

'Returned by the sea' means Annabelle. What the sea took is Annabelle, because she drowned, obviously."

"Obviously." I sniffed, covering my surprise. I had my suspicions about Annabelle's death but never wanted to dwell on them. She rarely wanted to talk about her former life, so I'd been content to let the past be the past, even if somewhere deep down, I knew things were never that simple.

"'While blood drips bright' means that for the duration of the blood moon—the eclipse next week—she'll be returned. It's only one night, but it brings her here." Yasmin looked at me, totally serious. "This is your chance to be with her. I know you want to."

I met her eyes and lied through my teeth. "I don't know what you're talking about."

Yasmin sighed, leaning back in the booth.

Turning to Miranda, I asked, "Why do *you* want to do this?"

"Because when Agatha died, I lost my best friend," she said simply. Her normally cheerful face fell. "Doing this won't bring Agatha back, but it would honor her. It's what she would want me to do."

I swallowed. I kept thinking of Agatha in the abstract—even Annabelle was more real in my mind than Agatha was. But she'd been a living person, one with a best friend who cared about her. Agatha had been so obsessed with this magical nonsense that it consumed the last years of her life. And all Miranda could do was stand by and watch while her best friend declined.

What would Agatha's obsession do to the three of us? I remembered Annabelle's visceral reaction to the opening of the shed in the backyard. She said she didn't know what Agatha was working on. Had she lied?

I shook my head. "Even *if* you're both not insane and there's something to this, it isn't my decision. If there's a possibility that Annabelle can come back, *she* has to be the one to decide whether or not to try it."

Both Miranda and Yasmin nodded. "You're right," Yasmin said. "That's why you have to be the one to tell her."

"What? Why me?"

They shared another conspiratorial look.

"Because you care about her, dear," said Miranda gently.

"We all care about her," I countered. "She's been taking care of us since we arrived, and you called her your 'old friend.'"

"Yeah, but you *love* her," Yasmin said.

"I—" I sputtered but didn't deny it. "What makes you think Annabelle wants to come back? Especially since you're saying she would have to go back to being dead after one night!"

"Of course she wants to come back!" Yasmin said.

"How can you be so sure?" I pressed.

"Because she loves you too, you dork."

Her words hit me like I had jumped off a cliff and my body slammed into the water. I wasn't even sure exactly *what* I was feeling, but there was anger and shame and the very real fear that she might be right.

"This is ridiculous." I stacked my empty basket on top of Yasmin's and scooted out of the booth. "I'm leaving, anyway. The house is practically already sold. Seymour Anderson offered me two million dollars and I'm taking it. The paperwork is in my email, and once I sign it, this is all over."

"Gibson!" Yasmin raised her voice. Her eyes were shiny, and she sounded like she might actually cry, which just pissed me off even more.

I took the note with Annabelle's grocery list on it and slammed it down on the table. "You do the shopping."

I squeezed out of the booth and weaved in between sweaty tourists waiting for their orders. I shoved past them, wanting to run as fast as I could away from the women who dared to dangle hope in front of me like a lure.

~

As I biked back to the house, the wind took any tears that might have fallen on my face. I rushed inside.

Annabelle was reading in her wingback chair. She stuck her tongue out, concentrating, and marked her place with her finger. The afternoon light bathed her in a golden glow. If I didn't know better, I'd have called her an angel.

She looked up as I entered, and a smile lit up her face.

"I'm not here for long," I said. "Just grabbing my guitar." I didn't wait for her response. If I stayed, I wouldn't leave, and I needed time to think about what had just happened.

Was I actually considering doing a magic ritual? Seriously?

Of course I wasn't going to do it. Yasmin was just my batty cousin who was about to find the harsh truth about freeloading from relatives—it doesn't last forever. And Miranda was a crazy old lady who missed her friend.

But they could bring Annabelle back.

I shook myself to banish the conflicting thoughts. Then I grabbed my guitar and waved to Annabelle as I rushed back out the front door.

"Bye, Gibson," she called after me.

Wanting to be alone and unhappy, I walked through the maze of trails that made up the Mackinac Island State Park. I found a dark, secluded spot and flung myself down on the hard ground and pouted. There was no one to pout at, however, so after a few minutes, I sat back against a tree, wishing I'd brought a chair or a blanket on which to sulk.

I opened the case and put the guitar in my lap, then strummed absent-mindedly, letting my thoughts drift and my hands determine the rhythm. I propped my phone up on the guitar case in front of me and pulled up Brooke's notes. I would work on the song and I would not obsess over the absurd idea of bringing Annabelle back to life. It was already ridiculous enough that I seemed to have fallen for a ghost. Getting involved with magic spells was exactly the kind of behavior my mom was trying to prevent all throughout my childhood. What she could never seem to understand was that I never wanted to do magic, I just wanted to live my life.

Brooke's lyrics weren't terrible, but when I sang them, I couldn't hear anything but my own voice in my head. There was no soul behind it. I tried a few different chord progressions, but none of them sparked. Sitting back against the tree, I tried rearranging the chorus and adding some verses, but that didn't do much. When I thought about adding verses, they just sounded . . . shallow. The kind of nonsense you might hear on pop radio, which wasn't a bad thing, but it didn't mean anything to me.

Why did I think I could write a song? I wasn't a songwriter and I definitely wasn't a witch. I was just a useless guitarist from the desert pretending to be a big-city player.

I closed my eyes and remembered Annabelle's smile as I entered the house. It made warmth spread through my body— despite my insistence that I was a piece-of-shit impostor posing as a cool adult, I knew what she would say: "I think your songs are lovely, dear." Or "I'm sure it'll come to you when it's ready."

The Annabelle in my mind was right. I was punishing myself for no reason because I didn't want to think about the decisions I had made or the possibility Yasmin had presented to me.

Without opening my eyes, I strummed a basic rhythm and sang the first things that came to mind, forgetting Brooke's lyrics and making up my own.

*standing here, scissors and a match in my hand*
*so baby won't you fly-y to me*

*can't make it across, sometimes can't find you at all*
*baby, won't you come back down to me*

*gonna burn that bridge when I cross it*
*gonna burn that bridge*

*gonna burn that bridge as I cross it*
*gonna burn that bridge when I get to you*

"That's . . . crap," I said out loud. "But it's not the worst thing I've ever heard in my life."

I dropped my pick but kept strumming, singing my own lyrics and songs I knew by heart, until the tips of my fingers were numb and darkness started to fall. I jotted down a handful of lines that sounded decent in my Notes app. The brightness of my phone made inverted shadows against my eyelids when I focused on my surroundings.

With a groan, I heaved myself up from a sitting position and put the guitar back in its case. I slung it over my shoulder and shoved my phone in my back pocket. My butt ached from sitting on the hard ground for hours. But even though I didn't have a full song, I felt the shape of it. The finished piece might be a long way off, but I felt like the outline was in my grasp. Despite the damp warmth of late summer, a breeze rustled the leaves of the trees that surrounded me and I shivered, suddenly aware of how alone I was out here.

It was time to go home.

But where was home, anyway?

The trees seemed to close in on me as I walked, crowding me into the center of the path. It wasn't dark enough to need my phone flashlight yet, but the shadows were long and thin, like skeletons peeking out from the ground.

Behind me came the familiar clop-clop-clop of a lone horse. My breath caught for a moment as I pictured a headless rider swinging a scythe toward me. But I forced myself to turn around and saw Sage, approaching on the giant jet-black horse. I waved and stepped off the path to let them pass.

As they approached, they slowed, with Sage making soft whoa noises to the horse. To me, they said, "Do you want a ride?"

"On . . . that?" I pointed at the gigantic horse.

"Sure."

"I thought Mike said that horse wasn't ready for a rider." It lowered its head and snorted, but otherwise seemed calmer than it had when I saw it the other day. It was still a powerhouse of a horse, though, so I didn't trust it. I kept my eyes on its head and its sharp, powerful hooves.

Sage dismounted and rolled their eyes. They kept a hand on the horse's neck, petting and soothing it. "That's what he thinks. But Joan is perfectly happy to let me ride her. Aren't you Joan?"

The horse whinnied softly, seeming to actually understand the kid.

"This beast is named Joan?" I said. "Really?"

Sage smiled. "Yeah, Joan Jett the Blackhorse."

Despite myself, I laughed. "That's pretty good."

Sage unbuckled their helmet and offered it to me. As I looked off into the darkness of the forest, my stomach growled, making the decision for me. I hadn't accomplished much out here, but I felt more centered than I had when I left the restaurant. Yasmin's screwball spell idea wasn't going to change my decision to sell the house. Probably. But the idea that Annabelle might be a person again—a real one—didn't scare me as much as it had when I entered the forest.

I handed Sage my guitar while they helped me climb onto the back of the horse. Then they slung the case on their back, tightening it around their slim shoulders, and hopped on behind me. Sage's thin arms circled me. I felt a moment of sheer, blind panic when they made a clicking noise and the horse started to move.

"Easy," they said, and even though I knew they were talking to the horse, it helped calm me down, too.

Eventually, my heart stopped racing. We never went faster than a gentle walking pace, but I still gripped the saddle horn until my knuckles turned white. To their credit, Sage was as calm as a Zen master. Every now and then they made sounds with their mouth to communicate with the horse, but otherwise, they simply held me close, letting me adjust to the rocking motion.

"Say, Sage," I said, swallowing a lump of nerves. "If you had the chance to leave Mackinac, would you?"

"Like, to go to college?"

"Yeah, or . . . you're really good at the drums. You could play with an actual band."

"Maybe." There was a moment of silence, then I felt, rather than saw, them shrug. "My family is here, though, so I'm okay. Maybe I'll leave, maybe not. My dad doesn't care if I don't take over the stables, he's already said that a million times."

I smiled, remembering Mike's ambivalent attitude toward inheriting his father's business. The guitar player slash stable owner made his own choice to return home and take care of his family, but he wasn't going to foist any certain life on his kid.

We trotted past the turn to Big Mike's and went down the lane to Abaddon instead. Sage made soothing noises and said whoa to Joan as we approached. She slowed down and came to a gentle stop right outside the dilapidated fence that surrounded my cottage's yard.

"That wasn't nearly as bad as I thought it would be," I said. "Although I am going to need your help getting down."

"It was actually easier than I thought for me too," Sage admitted. They dismounted, then helped me awkwardly clamber off the horse. "I know I can handle Joan but I was a little nervous."

They handed me my guitar and said, "It's always easier when you're not alone."

With no warning and for the first time in nearly twenty years, I burst into tears. I couldn't stop the sob that burst from my chest. I didn't even feel sad, just tired, like a worn-out dishrag that had been squeezed so tightly it was dripping out every bit of moisture it held.

"Gibson? Are you okay?" Sage sounded panicked. They glanced from me to Joan and back, as if my emotional turmoil might spread to the horse.

I took a deep breath and wiped my eyes. "I will be. Thanks for the ride."

"Sure."

I unbuckled the helmet and handed it over as they climbed back into the saddle.

"Sage?" I said, struck by a thought.

"Yeah?"

"I might need your help. With a song I'm writing."

They grinned and gave me a thumbs-up. "Okay!"

I watched them carefully guide Joan back up the lane, waiting until the giant horse and its rider was out of sight before opening the gate.

From the Victrola in the alcove, Nancy Sinatra was singing "You Only Live Twice" when I opened the door. The kitchen light was on, and indistinct chatter from a trio of voices drifted through the hall. The smell of a delicious roasting chicken suffused the main level of the house. Nate's deep rumble joined Anabelle's high pitch and Yasmin's California accent. As the three of them erupted in laughter, I closed the front door, unable to stop the fond smile from appearing on my face.

"It's always easier when you're not alone," I repeated to myself as I took off my shoes and wiped my eyes, readying myself to face my family.

# Chapter 16

D inner was already on the table when I entered the kitch-en. I joined the meal in progress, shooting a quick glance at Yasmin. With my expression, I dared her to make a smart remark about my tardiness or our conversation at lunch.

"You've got to try this," Nate said. He filled my empty plate with pieces of chicken and piled it high with mashed potatoes. He handed me the plate and pointed to the wine bottle to ask if I wanted a glass. "Your roommate is an amazing cook."

I mouthed the word "roommate" to Annabelle, who wore an amused smirk. They'd pulled the table out from the wall so it could accommodate four people. Yasmin and Nate had already filled their glasses with wine, and I held mine out while Nate poured. Tonight, he was wearing a polo shirt and khaki pants. They were a little wrinkled, but he'd made the effort. His hair was even gelled in place.

"Gibson," Yasmin said meaningfully, "don't you have some-thing to tell Annabelle?" The sweet smile she wore had teeth of its own.

I cleared my throat and smiled right back. "Yes, I do." Turning to Annabelle, I said, "I'm writing a song."

"Really? That's wonderful, dear!"

Deciding to return fire on my cousin, I said, "Yas, did you want to tell Annabelle about your magical breakthrough?"

If she wasn't sitting all the way across the table, I think Yasmin might have kicked me.

"Did you make progress on what you were trying to figure out, Yas?" Annabelle asked innocently. Nate watched the three of us, looking completely oblivious to the layers of conversation happening between two cousins and a ghost.

"Yes, I did," Yasmin said. "I discovered the time frame for the ritual and that it requires angelica. I scoured the backyard for it but couldn't find any. Miranda is trying to track it down via sketchy sites on the internet."

"That's lovely, dear," said Annabelle, taking a pretend sip from her empty glass of wine.

Yasmin and I glared at each other until my stomach growled and I had to back down so I could take a bite. The food really was delicious. I told Annabelle so, and she accepted the compliment, seeming to glow even brighter. As I ate, she talked about the recipe she'd used and which book she found it in. Then she regaled us with a story of how she had almost burned down the house trying to teach Agatha to cook a turkey for Thanksgiving. Apparently, they'd had to call the Mackinac Island Fire Department, and then Miranda had flirted a little too hard with one of the firefighters and that led to a whole other story. By the end of it, all three of us were cracking up.

In the lull that followed, Nate asked, "So, Gibson, you live in New York? What's that like?"

"It's, uh, exactly like what people think living in New York is like," I said. "Rats. The best food in the world. Etc."

"Cool." Nate's eyes were wide. The man didn't have a sarcastic bone in his body. His earnest manner should've been infuriating, but it wasn't in the slightest. "And you like it there?"

"Don't even bother, babe," Yasmin cut in. "Gibson doesn't talk about herself."

"What are you talking about?" I protested. "I'm an open book!"

"You are not an open book," she shot back. "You're like . . . something happened to you and then you closed yourself off from literally everyone around you."

"That's not true at all." It was.

Nate carried on, unfazed. "Yasmin says you're a musician?"

"That's right." To prove my point about being an open book, I told them everything you could find out about me on a basic Google search. "I grew up in Los Alamos, New Mexico. I hated it, so when I turned eighteen, I hitchhiked to New York with a guitar, a dream, and a girlfriend who abandoned me when we hit St. Louis. I worked in shitty restaurants and played on the street until I met Babs. Now I rent a modest studio apartment and I have very little savings. I inherited an old house in Michigan and a crazy cousin. The end."

I glared at Yas, daring her to object. In the back of my mind, my own voice whispered, *This is not the end of my story.*

"Yeah, but that's just, like, facts," Yasmin said. She took another sip of wine.

"What else do you want to know?"

Yasmin pointed her glass at me accusingly. "Hopes? Fears? Dreams?"

"How about this," Nate said. "What did you want to be when you grew up?"

"Easy." I took a sip of my own wine and pointed it at him. "Debbie Harry."

"Who was your first crush?" he asked.

"Also Debbie Harry."

Nate considered for a moment. "Who was your most embarrassing crush?"

I winced, then admitted, "Posh Spice."

"No, no, that's legit." Nate nodded and gave me a fist bump.

Yasmin sputtered, "You can't be bonding with my boyfriend! That's not possible."

I raised an eyebrow at "boyfriend" but decided not to give her shit about it. Yet.

Nate continued, seeming to enjoy his role as inquisitor. "Do you have any siblings?"

"No. I think my parents tried after I was born, but no."

Yasmin nodded. "That explains a lot. My brothers would *not* let me act like you do."

"What?" I sat back in my chair. "Wait, you have brothers? You never mentioned brothers."

She shrugged. "Three. Daniel is a doctor, Eric is an accountant, and Dave is . . . Dave." She smiled fondly. "He's a screwball but he helps me with the Etsy shop."

"I can't believe you never mentioned them," I said.

"Are they witches too?" Annabelle asked.

She shook her head. "No. Daniel refuses to talk about Mom's practice, Eric thinks it's amusing, and Dave . . . tries to help but he's Dave."

My understanding of Yasmin shifted to allow for her as the only girl in a rowdy house of boys with their own lives and their own ideas about magic.

I asked Annabelle, "Did you have any siblings? When you

were . . . alive?"

Her eyes lit up. "Oh, yes! Two brothers." She also smiled fondly, fiddling with the fork next to her empty plate. "They fought and died in what you would call the Napoleonic Wars."

The three living humans fell silent, unable to formulate responses to that.

Then Nate said, "My sister moved to Cleveland."

After a pause, Annabelle, Yasmin, and I started chuckling, which then turned into all-out laughter. I had to wipe my eyes with a napkin.

"I did have a question about Annabelle, though," Nate said. He looked at Yasmin, first, silently asking for her permission. Yasmin shrugged.

"Go ahead," Annabelle said, her usual smile in place.

"Can you see the future?" he asked.

"She's a ghost, not a psychic!" Yasmin said.

But Annabelle answered gently, "I don't see the future, no. And I'm glad, too, because it's hard enough keeping two hundred years of memories in my head. So many things have happened in the world, I can't keep track of it all."

"Do you have slime?" Nate asked.

"Slime?" Yasmin and I said in unison.

"Yeah, like *Ghostbusters*!"

"Oh, goodness," Annabelle said, laughing. "I'm not sure. I suppose I've never tried to slime anyone!"

"Let's not slime anyone at the dinner table, please," I said. I gathered the empty dishes and brought them to the sink, then put away Annabelle's unused plate. Then I opened another bottle of wine.

Yasmin had brought out her magic book and was letting Nate browse through the pages when I returned to the table.

"Oh, this looks like the Michigan Dogman," Nate was saying, pointing to a page that did, indeed, look like a dog-like man.

"Don't tell me you believe in all this, too, Nate?" I said with a groan. "What kind of house did you grow up in where witches and ghosts are no big deal?"

He smiled. "My mom is a hippy. Always sending me crystals for my birthday." He scratched his stubbly chin, thinking. "She's really into essential oils right now, but they make me sneeze."

I squinted at him. "How are you real? It's like you were grown in a lab to be Yasmin's wholesome—" I stopped myself before I could say "boyfriend," but Nate just laughed.

"I guess I'm . . . open to possibilities." The look he shared with Yasmin was flirty as fuck. I averted my eyes.

They looked at the book for a while, heads together. Then Nate asked, "How come you're not a witch, Gibson? You didn't get the witch gene?"

"No," I said, "I most definitely did not. I don't believe in anything I can't see with my own eyes."

"How can you not believe in anything? You're sitting at a table with a literal ghost." With the addition of wine, Yasmin's words were bolder and louder than usual.

"Yeah, but the transitive property of spirits is not a thing." I gestured at Annabelle, who was calmly observing us, clearly amused. "Just because I acknowledge that Annabelle is a ghost who should have died two hundred years ago doesn't mean I also believe in the Easter bunny. Or leprechauns."

"Oh, leprechauns are definitely real." Yasmin nodded seriously. "You don't want to mess with those guys."

"Really?" Nate asked, eyes wide.

But Yasmin broke into a crude laugh. "No, I'm fucking with you."

"You're so ridiculous that I can't tell when you're joking!" I refilled my own glass and topped off Nate's. Annabelle had her hands curled around an empty glass so that she would feel included.

"Wait, babe," Nate said, "Can *you* see the future?"

Yasmin's expression went serious. She swayed a little and seemed to have trouble focusing on the book. "They're not . . . I'm not exactly sure what it is, honestly." She took the book from Nate and flipped through the pages until she found one. Pointing to a crude drawing, she said, "There. When I have visions, I see that."

"What is it?" Annabelle leaned closer to the book, but I grabbed it away from Yasmin, suddenly feeling completely sober and also like I might be sick.

"Where did you get this?" I flipped through the book and found several versions of the same picture. All the drawings were the same: black scribbles showing a nighttime scene. Some were in crayon, some in pen. But the darkness of the scene was always broken by a full moon and railroad tracks leading away from me. Just before the vanishing point, there was the light of an oncoming train. Some of the drawings were more detailed than others, but most were mere sketches of the scene, always from the same angle, always with the light of the full moon and the train. It never came nearer.

"I told you," said Yasmin. "I see it. Ever since I was little, I've had visions of this image. It happens often enough that I don't even bother drawing it anymore."

"What does it mean?" asked Annabelle. She'd flowed around Yasmin to stand behind me and look.

I held the drawings close to my chest so that she couldn't see them and abruptly stood. My entire body was flooded with adrenaline. There was ten times as much energy coursing through my body as there had been when I was on the giant horse. "Don't ever draw this again."

"But I can't control it—"

"Ever. Promise me you will *never* draw this again," I shouted. I stabbed a finger at Yasmin. My face was hot with a rage that, if I let it out, would flow directly at her.

Yasmin was too shocked to respond. I didn't give a damn.

"Gibson?" Annabelle said.

I yanked open the back door, taking the book and my wine with me. "Leave me alone, Marley."

~

Nate and Yasmin were doing the dishes and speaking in hushed tones. Then they went upstairs and turned the light on in Yasmin's second-floor bedroom. The window creaked as it closed, and I was relieved—I didn't want to hear their conversation any more than they wanted me to eavesdrop.

About thirty minutes went by before Annabelle appeared on the deck. I hadn't done anything but sit, wanting desperately to run somewhere and knowing there wasn't anywhere to go on this stupid island. Not only was there no subway to take, there were no cars to borrow and drive mindlessly out into the country, no motorcycle to hop on the back of—no way to speed away from my problems and my past. Instead, I had to sit with my stupid emotions and wonder how in the hell Yasmin would know about my darkest day.

"Are you all right?" Annabelle asked softly. She appeared in her chair as if she'd been sitting there the whole time.

"There was a day when I was seventeen," I said, not looking at her. "I stole my dad's car. It was a big ole Buick. Practically as big as a boat, with a leather interior that got stupid hot in the summer, and . . . never mind, you don't care about cars."

"I've never seen one except on television," she admitted. "There are a few on the island for emergencies, but I always found them too frightening to try and investigate."

"Anyway. I drove the car out in the desert. I wish I could show you the desert, Marley. It's like . . . it's huge, like the water is here, but so different. You know how the colors of the water and the sky are so vibrant, even though they're basically just shades of blue?"

She nodded.

"It's like that, but with orange and purple skies, plus green and brown and . . . I wish I could show you."

She placed her hand close enough to my arm for it to tingle and left it there.

"But, anyway, there was a day, when I was seventeen, when I stole my dad's car." I paused, not reliving the day but also not eager to talk about it. I didn't talk about it. Ever. And it was okay, not to talk about it. It really was. But it meant that putting the memory into words was new. That day lived in my brain for so long without words that I had never fit the experience into language before. It was a memory that only ever came out through my fingers on the strings, not words from my mouth.

Forcing myself to speak, I said, "I drove. And drove and drove. No destination, I just needed to escape. Finally, the sun came down, and I drove through a spectacular desert sunset. One of those sunsets that make you think maybe there is a God because it's just so damn beautiful. Then the sun went down, and I stopped at a railroad crossing."

I swallowed.

Annabelle was looking at me with infinite compassion in

the set of her mouth, but she didn't say anything. I remembered her sitting here telling me about her father, and how fragile that moment had seemed. I imagine she felt something like that now.

I shook my head, not wanting to worry her. "It's fine. Everything worked out, and it's fine, I promise."

"Gibson . . ."

She moved her fingers so that her hand was resting in the same space as my arm. It felt zingy, like pop rocks on my skin.

"It's fine now, Marley. But it wasn't, not then. It was too hard, to be young and angry. So I drove and I stopped on the tracks and for a while, I thought I might let it—"

"No," she whispered.

"But then I looked and I saw the train coming. Yasmin's stupid drawing . . ." I shook my head. "It's exactly what I saw that night."

The words weren't nearly as difficult to pull out of me as I thought they might be. Time had dislodged them from where they stuck in my chest, and somehow Annabelle coaxed them the rest of the way.

"I don't know how it's possible, but that drawing is an image I've had in my head for over twenty years. When I see it, I'm reminded of the feeling I had when I hit the gas pedal and moved off the tracks. That I wasn't ready for the end."

Annabelle brought her other hand to mine, trying to grab on to me with both but she couldn't. She slid right through.

"It's fine, Marley." It wasn't. Yasmin kept trying to tell me that we were connected, and I kept refusing to believe her. The fact that she'd been drawing that image proved she was right. Somehow, as crazy as it sounded, we were linked.

And if Yasmin could see into my life, maybe that meant she could bring Annabelle back.

"I believe you, my dear," Annabelle said quietly. "Because you're here with me."

We sat quietly, listening to insects buzzing around the porch light. There wasn't any music in the back of my head. But for once in my life, that was okay. I sat with the silence and the image of the train, but it never came any closer. And it was fine.

"If you could come back," I asked, trying to sound casual, "what would you do?"

"What do you mean?"

"I mean, if you could be . . . real again, what would you want to do? I'm just curious. If all of Mackinac Island was yours to roam for a day, what would you want to do?"

"Oh," she said, looking thoughtfully beyond the garden. "I'd like to have high tea."

"At the Grand Hotel?"

Annabelle nodded. "I'd like to go shopping. And play the candy game."

"Candy game?"

She held out her hand as if she was holding a cell phone, then mimicked touching the screen with her fingers.

I laughed. "Candy Crush? Okay, yeah, you can play Candy Crush all you like. But be careful whose money you spend. Then what?"

"Then I'd like to visit my father's grave." She turned to me, her smile sad but fond. "Pay my respects. And then . . ."

"Then what?"

She shook her head. "I don't know. Dinner, I suppose. And I'd like to dance. With someone, I mean."

I nodded. "Sounds like a nice day."

"It would be, wouldn't it?" Annabelle giggled. "Not terrifically exciting, though."

"Well," I said, "exciting is in the eye of the beholder."

"Indeed." Annabelle clinked her empty glass to mine, and we traded smiles. I turned back to the garden, but suddenly, it looked completely different.

It was like there was another layer of reality on top of the one I was currently seeing. The decaying vegetables and empty fire pit were still there, and the weeds were omnipresent. But I could also see a roaring fire, with children standing around it holding sticks with marshmallows at the end. The night was dark, but it also wasn't. I saw strings of fairy lights extending from the house out to the end of the porch and lamps strategically placed throughout the garden, filling the whole place with soft, magical light. The garden beds were full of colorful tomatoes and other plants I couldn't identify. There were bicycles leaning against Yasmin's shed and a horseshoe pit off to the side of the yard.

Tears welled behind my eyes, and instead of fighting, I let them fall. I heard people murmuring, glasses clinking, and from somewhere behind me, a song that I half recognized.

"Gibson?" Annabelle said, "are you all right?"

I blinked. The vision disappeared but the feeling didn't. I looked at Annabelle's beautiful face, shining with concern, and said, "I'm great, actually. I think . . . I'm home."

# Chapter 17

The next morning, I woke up in the third-floor bedroom to the sound of construction from next door, feeling like a different human being. I was a little hungover. But I hadn't realized there was a hollowness in my chest until it wasn't there. I woke up in the room that had belonged to my great-aunt and I didn't feel like a stranger anymore.

I padded downstairs before Yasmin and Nate woke up and quietly made myself a coffee and watched for any signs of Annabelle. Apparently, my ghost was sleeping in. I poured the fragrant, dark liquid into a travel cup that had a pair of baby goats on it along with the words "Here's looking at you, kid!" Then I put my guitar on my back and slipped out the front door. There was no reason I would have needed to explain my plans to my cousin, her boyfriend, or the ghost who haunted my house, but I was glad they weren't around regardless.

The first ferry off Mackinac Island was in the early morning. I was first in line.

Sea spray pelted me from the side of the large boat and the wind stung my eyes, but I turned my face up to greet the rising sun. I didn't hate any of this. By the time we arrived back on the lower hand of Michigan, I was sweating through my bra, but I hopped off the boat and stretched my legs, grateful for the fresh air and change in scenery.

I checked my phone directions and pointed my feet toward the public library. It was a twenty-minute walk on roads that were built for cars, not horses. The sounds of real life were jarring after a week spent on the horse poop-filled bicycle graveyard that was Mackinac Island.

If I could prove that Annabelle was a real person—if she actually lived and died on the island like she said she did, then I would go through with Yasmin's stupid spell and see if I could bring her back. What did I have to lose? Dignity? Time? Seymour Anderson could wait another day for his high-value land with my creaky old house on it. I'd been so wrapped up in the stress of it all that I seemed to have forgotten that *I* was the one with the valuable asset to sell to him—not the other way around.

At the entrance to the public library, I started to lose my nerve. Was I really about to try to research a ghost? But then I remembered the vision I'd had the night before. Somehow, Yasmin had seen into a painful memory of mine and drawn it in her prophetic book. And somehow, I'd gotten a glimpse of what the house could be—full of life and happiness and music.

Preparing myself to look stupid in front of a librarian, I went inside.

The library looked and smelled exactly like I expected a public library in Michigan to look and smell. Old, damp books and the smell of the general public. It didn't smell all that different from Annabelle's alcove, actually. I approached the reference desk, which was staffed by an older Black lady with white hair wearing a purple floral shirt, and asked about the local history archives.

"Do you have an appointment?" she asked.

"Oh, um, no." I hadn't even considered the possibility that I would need one, thinking the hardest part about this journey would be summoning the courage to go and not the bureaucracy that might be involved. "I'm sorry. I just wanted to see if I could find someone."

"Well, I'm not supposed to do this if you don't have an appointment because it takes me away from the desk. But, seeing as this is a bustling metropolis full of citizens requesting library materials . . ." She gestured at the stacks, which were completely empty except for a white-haired lady browsing the gardening section and a man napping on a chair with a paperback on his chest. "I think I can pencil you in."

With a wink, she gestured for me to follow her to the Michigan room of the library, which was filled with local memorabilia and framed photos of the Great Lakes from various times in history.

She told me her name was Linda and directed me to sit at the table in the center of the room. Then she asked, "Who are you looking for?"

"A woman who was on Mackinac Island in the early 1800s." I set my guitar case down, resting it against the table. "She was British but stayed there after the Americans got it back."

"Hmmm. Well, that might be going back a bit far, but we can try. Do you know the year she was born? Or died?"

"She died in 1816," I replied, somehow pulling that piece of Annabelle trivia out of my brain. Then I unlocked my phone and brought up the notes I'd cobbled together on Annabelle. I scrolled past the ones that said things like "great cleavage" and "how can she change her clothes?"

Linda scratched her chin, then pulled a handful of boxes from the wall. She opened one carefully, pulling out a binder. Each page was encased in a sleeve.

"That time period might prove difficult," she said. "There's a project at the university to translate documents from the French colonies around Mackinac, but the French were driven out by the British in the 1780s, so I doubt you'll have much luck there. And the earliest photos weren't quite that early."

Together we looked through the files from the transition of Mackinac from white British colonizers to American ones. I could barely read the faded ink script in the documents, but Linda described the documents to me, pointing out their importance. She had little reading glasses that she put on the tip of her nose as she worked. Linda was patient and kind as I asked basic questions about the fort, the geography of the region in general, and the documents we looked at.

After looking at over a hundred pages of property deeds and municipal tax records, I took a break to wipe my eyes. Then I blew out a breath and said, "It's wild to think about how the island is now when it started like this. I mean this in a nice way, but . . . it's such a weird place."

She hummed in agreement. "Nice to visit. Full of rich white people and horses, but a nice place to visit."

"But it's like . . ." I wasn't sure what I was trying to say. My first impression of Mackinac was exactly that—gentrification to the max, and horse shit. But then I saw how much people loved living there and how devoted the community was to staying. And yet, there were just so many rich tourists and almost everyone who vacationed there was white.

"Visitors pretend their problems don't exist out there cuz there aren't any cars and it reminds 'em of what they think the past was like." Linda shook her head. "But that's not what the past was *actually* like. In the past, it was hard just to live. Eating fudge, not seeing any poor people, and not driving a car for a week doesn't make going to Mackinac experiencing the past— just Mackinac." She looked down, her glasses slipping almost off her nose. "And by poor people, I mean brown people."

"Yeah, it's . . . strange? Like . . ."

"It costs a million dollars to buy a garden shed on the island. That ain't strange—that's America."

"Two."

"What?"

"Two million." Sheepish, I admitted, "I'm out here because I inherited my great-aunt's house. The 'as is' offer I got for it was two million." I grimaced, but Linda threw her head back in laughter. Her glasses slipped off her nose and fell onto her ample chest, caught by the beaded chain around her neck.

"Good for you, girl," she said, wiping her eyes. "Good for you."

Somehow, several hours passed while I looked at municipal drawings, handwritten letters I could barely read, and flowery poems written by people other than Annabelle. Linda went back to the reference desk when she was satisfied that I could handle the sensitive documents carefully enough not to damage them. She showed me how to put them back in their special boxes in the right order, then returned to her post at the library's entrance.

My stomach growled, so I raided the library's vending machine for lunch. I ate in the hallway while Linda kept a careful eye on me to make sure I didn't bring crumbs back into the reference room.

After my improvised lunch, I went back to my old records. I had just pulled out a stack of photos that were too late to be related to Annabelle but that I thought were neat when a teenager flounced down on the seat next to me.

"Hi," she said.

Linda approached the table. "This is my granddaughter, Tanesha." To the girl, she said, "Behave yourself and get your homework done." Then she went back to the reference desk, leaving us alone in the stale air of the Michigan room.

"Hi," I said to the girl.

"What are you looking for?" She pulled out an expandable file and a pencil case with unicorns on it from her backpack.

"A . . . friend of mine." I realized how insane that sounded as I said it, but the girl just started on her homework and didn't comment. "She lived on Mackinac Island when the British were there a long time ago."

"Slay."

I snuck a peek at her notebook, which was full of math equations and doodles. Seeing the innocent rose patterns and fancy S's made my Grinch heart grow a size.

The girl pointed at my guitar case, which I'd set down next to my chair. "What's that?"

"My guitar," I said, realizing I'd started thinking of it as mine instead of Agatha's. "I'm writing a song and was going to go to a special place to work on it after this." I sighed. "But this is taking longer than I expected. Do you come here all the time after school?"

"Only when I don't have plays." She made a dramatic gesture with her arms to showcase her thespian sensibilities. "Or choir. I'm a singer."

"Nice."

"Do you know this song?" Tanesha said, showing me her phone. It was a thirty-second clip of a teen in her basement, singing Fleetwood Mac's "Dreams" into a sneaker and pretending it was a microphone. She was pretty good.

I smiled. "I mean, yeah. That's a classic. Don't ask if I can do the dance, though."

Slapping the table lightly, Tanesha said, "We should do a concert!"

"What?"

"I'll sing and you can play for me."

"You can't . . . sing in a public library?" I protested. "You're supposed to be quiet in a library."

But she waved aside my concerns. "It's okay, my grandma will let us. Besides, this is a cool library."

Before I could stop her, Tanesha hopped up and ran out of the room. I followed her to Linda's station at the desk, where Tanesha begged with her grandmother to let us put on a show in the middle of the afternoon.

Linda hesitated, then sighed. "I can give you one hour in the conference room."

"Yes!" Tanesha literally jumped for joy, then ran ahead of her grandmother down the hall to a room marked Conference 1. I didn't see a Conference 2.

Linda let us into the room while Tanesha started rearranging chairs. I watched while Linda directed the teenager, who was a tornado of activity. This was clearly not the first impromptu performance the girl had insisted on putting on. I smiled watching them, a little surprised not to feel any resentment or jealousy toward the duo, who clearly adored each other. This was not at all how I expected to spend my afternoon, but I reveled in the warm fuzzies I got from watching Tanesha rush around making the library's conference room into a miniature Madison Square Garden.

After a harried twenty minutes of intense preparation that included printing a promo poster with the library's computer and taping copies of it to the front door, reference desk, and water fountain, then heated discussions about a possible set list, Tanesha prepared our entrances. Since we didn't have the option for a costume change, she insisted that we do what we could using our attitude and intro songs played on her phone speakers. Hers was "Juice" by Lizzo, which was an excellent, if somewhat racy, choice. Mine was "Cherry Bomb" by The Runaways.

Tanesha evaluated my entry, and I smirked at her surprise. Yes, I was physically capable of werkin' it. I'd roomed with enough queens over the years to have learned a few things by osmosis. And while I hadn't ever played drag shows, I'd attended enough to know how to enter a room.

Our audience consisted of Linda, Janice (who was the lady who'd been browsing the gardening books earlier), a man who wandered in looking for the restroom, and Bernard, the man we'd woken up from his nap. Linda had provided a microphone for Tanesha and a chair for me. We warmed up for a few minutes, then launched into our agreed-upon routine.

Tanesha wasn't a virtuoso, but the girl could sing. It didn't take long for me to get into the rhythm of performing with her, though, being a teenager, she had more energy than most of the people I'd played with in the last decade. I smiled as she put her own spin on top-forty songs by Rihanna, Destiny's Child, and Alicia Keys. Improvising with her, playing songs I didn't really know but could fake, and making things up on the spot was . . .

fun.

The rush of joy I felt when she and I shared the microphone during our rendition of "Independent Women Part 1" almost knocked me over. I genuinely couldn't remember the last time I had this much fun. With other musicians, I enjoyed joining them but never felt at home. To me, it was a job, a stepping stone on the way to something else. Even during shows with Call Me Kate Kane, there was an undertone of anger. At the world, at each other for some petty remark said backstage, or even just the bitterness I felt at not being a permanent member of the band. But here, in a library conference room playing with a teenager in front of four people, I remembered why I loved being on stage in the first place.

We concluded our last song, then I asked if I could play one that we hadn't agreed on ahead of time.

Tanesha nodded. She was sweating and breathing hard, but she couldn't stop smiling. The metal braces on her teeth glinted in the fluorescent lighting. "I'll sing if I know it."

"You might," I said. "Have you seen *Shrek*?"

Her eyes went wide. "Oh. My. God."

Launching into Annabelle's favorite song, I pictured her, sitting in the back of the audience clapping and swaying along with the music. Tanesha, Linda, and the gardening lady all joined in, and we blew the roof off the public library with a cheesy song about believing in love. Bernard recorded our performance on Linda's phone.

"Thank you!" we both said when we finished the song.

Tanesha bowed several times, then gestured at me to stand and take a bow. Our audience stood and clapped enthusiastically while I set my instrument aside and bowed.

While we put the chairs and tables back in their original positions, Tanesha asked, "Why did you start playing the guitar?"

I snorted. "Because my mom wanted me to play the piano."

Linda laughed at that. "Mmhmm."

"My mom was an opera singer," I said. "I learned the basics of a couple of languages from the songs she sang, and my entire house was one big stage."

Tanesha had gotten distracted on her phone, but she put it away. "No way."

I nodded. "Way. She wanted me to be a musician like her or an engineer like my dad. But I'm terrible at math, so I studied music."

"Word," said Tanesha. Linda shook her head.

"I didn't want to play the piano," I continued. "I thought it was too stuffy, too controlled. Just like her. We fought all the time because she wanted me to be . . . somebody other than what I was."

I stole a quick look at Linda, who had taken a break in one of the chairs. I didn't know what the history was between Linda, her daughter, and her granddaughter. The last thing I should do was trauma dump on complete strangers. But Tanesha had asked, and somehow on this trip, I had gotten used to telling people the truth.

"My parents agreed that I could learn guitar instead of piano, so of course I wanted to play the loudest, most annoying electric guitar I could find." I smiled, remembering the sheer power I felt when I strummed my fingers down the strings for the first time. The electric squeal it produced was nothing but a wall of noise and I loved every single second of it.

"That's rad," Tanesha said.

"Rad," the gardening lady agreed. She had stayed behind to help us move the furniture.

"But I guess," I started, unsure what I was about to say, but feeling like something needed to come out. "I was so angry at the time, and I poured my emotions into music. But I never really stopped to consider that my mom was doing that, too. She played out her pain through a different instrument, so I couldn't see it."

The car crash that killed my parents happened at the height of her career. When I was a child, she'd dress me in an elegant gown and sit me on the piano. Then we'd play duets for an audience of adults that her and my father knew. I hated those parties, but remembered my mother, sweating through the armpits of her dress while she played. She was such an accomplished player that I struggled to keep up, to not embarrass her. Even when she sang directly to me, I was so distracted by other things that I didn't hear the love that must've been behind it.

"We both loved to create music, but we were singing past each other. I couldn't understand or appreciate what she brought to it," I said. "She died before I could go back home and try to get her to understand what I was bringing to my own music."

As I said this, I wondered what I would play her, if given the chance. My own song was only half finished. And somehow, I couldn't imagine my uptight, Christian mother would appreciate an acoustic punk song. But a voice in the back of my head that sounded suspiciously like Annabelle's said, "*You never know, Gibson, only love outlasts us all.*"

There was a moment of silence in the little room, which I broke by scraping a chair leg against the floor. "Whoops."

When we finished, Linda said, "Did you find your mystery person, Gibson?"

I shook my head. "No luck. Annabelle doesn't seem to want to be found, I'm afraid."

Tanesha cocked her head to the side. "Annabelle?"

"Yeah, my friend's name is—was—Annabelle Williams."

Tanesha turned to the garden-section lady, who was loading her books into a public radio-themed tote bag. "Hey, Janice, does that name sound familiar?" To me, Tanesha said, "Janice has the best memory of anybody here. She helps me sometimes during the summers, and we digitize the collections."

Janice pondered for a moment, then said, "I don't recall an Annabelle. But A. W. might be who you're looking for."

"A. W.? Who's that?" I asked. How likely was it that A. W. stood for Annabelle Williams?

"Oh my gawd, I cannot believe you are looking for A. W.!" Tanesha said, drawing out almost every word she said for emphasis.

Janice nodded. "She's a favorite around here."

"Sounds promising?" I smiled. Leave it to Annabelle to be a local favorite. Everyone who knew Annabelle, even only via records in a library, loved her.

Heaving herself off her chair, Linda said, "It'll take me a minute to find those films. T, you need to work on your homework while I set Miss Gibson up."

"Yes, ma'am!"

~

I had a brief flashback to high school as Linda loaded a sheet of microfiche onto its plate. She showed me how to use the dials to zoom and move around between the little pictures on the screen. Tanesha settled down in the chair next to me. She had her homework open on the table but clearly wasn't paying much attention to it.

Linda explained, "These letters were included with the

estate of a gentleman by the name of Grant Williams. His an-
cestors lived on the island, and he kept a bundle of their corre-
spondence. The earliest was named Timothy Williams."

My eyebrows rose at the name Williams. Could these actually be Annabelle's letters? I wasn't sure if I was excited to find
her or afraid of what I might find.

"There was also a set of letters from A. W., but who she
was is unclear. Timothy's wife was named Jane, but in their cor-
respondence, he does make mention of an earlier marriage in
which his wife—"

"Drowned," I said, finishing for her.

Linda frowned. "We don't know how she died." She pointed
to the screen and said, "I've loaded the first sheet, and here are
the others. I'll be back to check on you."

"Thank you." I zoomed in on the handwritten pages, trying
to decipher the old, faded cursive script. ·

Each letter was addressed not to a person, but "To The
Other Side." They varied in length, but all were addressed sim-
ilarly and all were signed with the initials "A. W." The first few
were hesitant, filled with mundane details about her life. She
filled pages of letters with details about the weather and the
birds she'd seen that day, but rarely talked about herself. That
was consistent with Annabelle, at least from the few days I'd
spent with her. In the letters, she wrote about her fascination
with the indigenous fisherman and fur traders who came to
camp and her love of walking in the forest that surrounded the
quarters where she lived. She wrote a poem about a butterfly
and described her joy at witnessing the migration of birds that
arrived with the onset of June.

Yet, at other times, she seemed desperately sad. A. W.'s father was a Royal Army Chaplain who arrived at the new Fort

George with his daughter, then promptly died. After her father's death, she remained on the island alone, staying with a friendly local farmer and his wife. Though she still addressed her letters "To The Other Side," the phrase took on a melancholy note as A. W. wrote about the oncoming of a brutal winter.

She wrote, "The first snow has yet to abate and though this is not my first winter here, it's the first one I face alone. Without my father or a sense of home, I walk through the forest as if a spirit not entirely bound to this world. The silence presses me. Though I'm only being nipped by the teeth of winter and not yet living in its belly, I feel forever and irrevocably cold."

Was this Annabelle? I remembered her wrapping her hands around a mug each morning, even though the August days were hot and sticky. I assumed she, as a ghost, didn't feel the temperature of the world, but she seemed to gravitate toward the comforts of life, including warmth. I read on.

"To The Other Side; I am overcome with emotion today and know not how much I'll be able to write. Not only has Timothy asked to marry me despite my many flaws (of which I will spare you the recounting), but his gift to me is a treasure that brings tears to my eyes even now, several hours after I first encountered it. He has brought me a teapoy. How he managed it, I cannot imagine! And though it stands empty until his savings are replenished, the thought of blending tea in a house of my own fills me with such an intense longing for a home I never really knew. I could scarcely thank him through my tears. Though I'm loath to stay on this island, having no attachment to it now, Timothy has been a dear friend and a comfort to me. I've agreed to the marriage."

I took a deep breath and read on. Annabelle only mentioned her husband once, but she hadn't seemed traumatized by her marriage, just wistful. Of her wedding day, A. W. simply wrote, "It was a nice day. Many people attended."

Skimming through the next few entries, which mostly talked about how difficult it was to figure out what quantities of lard to purchase, I stopped when I came across a recipe for tea. Half the page was made up of doodles of leaves and teacup patterns, and the other half was a particular ratio of Earl Grey black tea leaves, vanilla, botanical lavender, and a small pinch of white tip.

"Oh my god," I whispered. This was Annabelle. No doubt about it. The writing sounded like her, and I'd seen her make a rapturous face over the steam from that exact blend of tea. My ghost was real. I'd found her.

But there weren't many letters left.

She wrote of one day, "Mr. H allowed me on the boat again today. Timothy was cross when he found out how far we'd gone." Several times after that, she mentioned badgering Mr. H to let her borrow his fishing boat. She described taking long walks along the shore and occasionally wading out to her waist, before the icy water drove her, shivering, back to the beach.

As I reread the earlier letters and finished the later ones, I noticed several themes emerging. Annabelle was clearly lonely. She often mentioned being sad, despondent that her father had died and left her on the island. She also longed to leave. Timothy never explicitly forbade her from leaving the island, but he worried about her being on the water by herself. Then, one day, she met someone new.

"My heart has found a new reason to beat. It's as if spring has come early, though the ice is still thick and the days still brief. But Lucy is like a beam of light on the darkest of days. Her voice is like a bell, and truthfully, hearing her singing is the only reason I desire to leave my room."

Lucy was the wife of the new chaplain. Prior to this, Annabelle only mentioned going to church in the sort of perfunctory way she might mention visiting a relative she didn't really want to see. Lucy's husband belonged to the same denomination as Annabell's father—one that required absolute piety and left very little room for frivolities like special blends of tea or reading novels. Although Annabelle had clearly loved her father, I wondered how often he caused her to suppress her enjoyment of life's pleasures. But now that Lucy had arrived, Annabelle made regular attendance at church service, despite her earlier indifference.

I felt a flush coming over my face as I read about Annabelle's feelings toward her friend.

"Yo, she had a crush on Lucy, don't you think?" said Tanesha, interrupting my thoughts. She was reading over my shoulder, scrunching up her face to read the text. Linda had rejoined us and put up a sign on the reference desk to tell patrons where she was. Keeping one eye on us, with the other, she silently read a thriller novel.

Tanesha said, "When Janice and I first scanned these, she didn't believe me, but it's super obvious."

"Umm," I said. "It's certainly possible." This was ridiculous—I couldn't be jealous of a woman who'd known Annabelle two hundred years ago. I shook my head.

Tanesha doodled on the margins of her notebook absently. Her folders were brightly colored, with photos of dogs wearing glam collars on them. "I don't get why she didn't just write about it. I write about my crushes all the time," Tanesha said. On my other side, I could feel Linda radiating disapproval at the thought of young Tanesha having crushes, but she didn't say anything.

"Maybe she didn't know," I said, mostly to myself.

"What?"

"I just mean that, back then, she probably didn't have access to people who thought differently. Even now, it's hard enough to figure out how to live, but in her time, without the internet? Without books? I mean, how would you know what you felt was love if you didn't have any frame of reference for it? If you weren't a dude, you wouldn't have had much choice on—"

"A white dude," Linda said, eyebrows raised.

I nodded. "If you're weren't a white dude, you wouldn't have had much choice on how you got to live. That's . . ."

"Tragic as shit," finished Tanesha.

Linda murmured, "Language."

Tanesha rolled her eyes. "But it is! Sometimes, I write stories where Timothy dies and Lucy's husband, the reverend, dies. Then A. W. and Lucy get together and they live in a nice little cottage."

Linda looked scandalized. She rested her open paperback on her chest and gave Tanesha the stink eye. "You do know that Timothy is the reason you have these letters, right?"

"I don't make him die horribly! Just earlier." Tanesha shrugged. "I want her to get a happily ever after."

"So do I," I said. "So do I."

# Chapter 18

On the ferry back to Mackinac, I took pictures of the bridge from several angles. Then I was harassed by a bird, and before it flew off, I took a video to show Annabelle. She liked it when I showed her videos on my phone. She got quiet and contemplative when I scrolled through videos of places she read about in her books. But cute animal videos were her favorite.

Before I left the library, Tanesha had given me her social media handles—several were on apps I'd never even heard of. But she posted a video of us on TikTok and sent me the link. The sound of the wind and the ferry's engines was too loud for me to hear the video, but I watched us playing together and was amazed at how young I looked. I shared the post with Brooke and put my phone away, turning my face to the sun.

I grabbed a hot dog at Windermere Point and decided to walk home via the perimeter path instead of taking a shortcut through the residential neighborhood.

Without realizing it, I walked past the particular curve in the rocks that I'd started thinking of as Annabelle's cove. It looked unremarkable in the daytime. I walked right by it initially but doubled back when I passed the familiar mile marker. Standing at the spot where the road curved just enough to create a little cove, I watched people in kayaks and sailboats in the jewel-green waters of Lake Huron. The afternoon was warm and the air was thick. Gulls screamed overhead, and as I stood thinking, bikes whizzed by me on the carless road.

There were no ghosts in the water. Feeling lighter than I had in days, I removed my guitar from my sweaty back.

I'd done it. I found her. And I was going to try and bring her home.

I stepped off the path and set my phone against a rock, then started the video recorder. It wouldn't be a good recording at all—the soft susurrus of the lake in the background competed with my voice and the guitar. But it would remind me of this moment, when I looked out on a giant lake and felt something just as big. Something important and good. Something that made me feel like I could be a whole person, if I tried.

While the water lapped at the rocks and the wind caressed my face, I sang a song to the other side.

~

Annabelle was in her alcove in the cottage, holding a steaming cup of tea in both hands and balancing a book on her lap. She looked up and smiled brightly when I entered.

"Welcome back," she said.

"Hey, Marley," I said, suddenly unsure how to start this. Honest conversations and I had never been very well acquainted. "Can we talk? Maybe outside?"

"Of course." She set her cup aside on the end table, which already held three mugs with varying levels of brown sludgy tea in them.

"Where's Yasmin?" I put my guitar down in the front room. I was having a hard time looking at her.

"She's with Nate, I believe." Annabelle looped her fingers around the mug handles, carefully carrying them with her to the kitchen sink.

I followed Annabelle outside. But before I started my spiel, I texted Yasmin and asked her not to come back to the house for about an hour.

She texted back, "r u askin her?????"

Even though the answer was yes, I didn't respond. I looked out at the garden, trying to summon the vision I'd had the other day. Happy people, string lights, a bonfire in the corner, someone playing music and everyone singing along.

I cleared my throat. "I found out what Agatha's spell was supposed to do."

It was only for a second, but a look of panic crossed Annabelle's face. She had sat at the table, but I was too nervous to sit, so I paced in front of her.

"Oh?" She folded her hands in her lap and didn't quite frown, but her usual smile didn't appear. Annabelle crossed her ankles and sat up straight, the very picture of an English lady. She was mostly visible, but her edges blurred a little.

"I know it sounds crazy, but Agatha thought she could bring you back."

Annabelle didn't respond. Her face was a mask, not of indifference but intense concentration. For perhaps the first time since I met her, I had no idea what she was thinking or feeling.

"According to Agatha, there's something special about the three of us. Me, Yasmin, and Miranda. And the blood moon. It's coming up soon, and, supposedly, if we chant some things and burn candles or whatever, we can bring you back for as long as the blood moon lasts." I raked my hand through hair that was too short, realizing I didn't know anything about the details of the ritual. I still only half believed it would work, so I hadn't bothered to know about the herbs we would need or if we'd draw a pentagram on the floor. All that stuff was Yasmin's domain. "Anyway, I'm not explaining this very well, but Agatha said—"

"Agatha said a great many things, dear," Annabelle said gently.

"Yeah, okay. But even if it's crazy . . . you could come back!" I finally stopped pacing and faced her. I had no idea what my face was doing, but my heart was racing. As if instead of taking the ferry back to the island, I swam.

Slowly, Annabelle stood. Her face was still inscrutable. A slight breeze blew the curly strands of blond hair at her shoulder.

"You could come back," I repeated. My arms ached with the lack of her. "Marley, we're connected. Even if it's not physical, exactly, there's something between us, and we could—"

"No." She shook her head. "I'm sorry, dear, but we're not. We can't be. I am not a part of this world. You are."

"It doesn't matter—"

"Yes, it does!"

We were both shouting now, our voices taking on an edge of desperation.

Annabelle closed her eyes and bowed her head, almost as if she were praying, though I knew from her letters that her sense of faith was, like mine, tenuous at best. "No, Gibson. I told Agatha no, and I'm telling you the same."

"So, you knew what Agatha was trying to do all along?"

We faced each other.

"Of course I knew!" There was a haughty note of scorn in her voice now. A mocking tone I'd never heard before. "But I didn't want to come back! Why would I want to come back?"

I sputtered. "Why wouldn't you?"

"For one day? What would happen to me after that? Would I die permanently? Or go back to being like *this*?" She grabbed at me, sending cool shivers down my arms where her insubstantial hands clawed at my flesh.

Then, to prove her point, she walked right through me.

I had a moment of full-body revulsion. She did it without warning and without consent, making me step backward to try to get away from her. I grabbed at the railing behind me.

Annabelle retreated. She rounded her shoulders and looked down sadly, seeming to regret what she'd done. "Why would I go back to the world of the living for one day? As it is, I can read in my nook and make myself cups of tea that I can smell but not taste. What I have is enough. I don't want anything more."

I shook my head. "You're wrong."

She crossed her arms, but I didn't back down. I stepped toward her, pushing my reluctant body in her direction, ignoring the fear that she'd try to push through me again.

"You wanted more," I said. "I know you did because I read your letters. You wrote to the other side! To a future you couldn't have! You wanted more from life and you never got it. But now you have the chance to live like you wanted to all those years ago."

Annabelle's eyes went wide, and for a moment, I remembered the apparition of her I'd seen on the cove. She'd been a true ghost, then, more spirit than human.

"You read my—"

"Yeah, Marley," I said firmly. I hadn't meant to tell her

about my trip to the library, but I couldn't take it back now. Not if this was what convinced her to go through with the ritual. "I found your letters and I read what you wrote. You were alone. Your husband was kind, but you didn't love him. And you never got to experience life, not really. You didn't get to have garden parties, or, or . . . I don't know, play Candy Crush and see the stupid gazebo." I ran a hand through my hair, again forgetting that it was too short for it to feel satisfying. "I know it wasn't there when you were alive, but you know what I mean! You never got to live, Marley. Or . . . Or love. And now you can."

Silence fell between us, but instead of a smile lighting up her face, all she did was grimace and look away.

"And you know all about living, do you?"

"What?"

She turned to me, her expression hard. "You have no right to lecture me about life. Not four hours after you arrived here, you almost threw yours away. You know nothing, Gibson." She spat the words at me now, and her edges flickered, like a failing projection or a hologram in a movie.

As she stepped toward me with her hands balled in fists, I felt another stab of fear. Her voice was dark, dripping with anger.

I'd learned not to be afraid of her almost immediately, but now I tensed. Although she couldn't touch me, if she wanted to, Annabelle could cause me harm. There were plenty of rusty garden tools and other heavy objects lying around the house. I had to sleep, but she didn't.

She stopped, inches from my face. "You can't tell me about enjoying life or being with a person you love because *you* don't love anyone. You keep yourself alone, terrified that someone might catch you having a feeling or getting close."

I hadn't realized tears were spilling down my face until one caught on the tip of my nose. I wiped it away and scrubbed my face, unable to believe how wrong everything had gone.

"No, Gibson, you have no right to ask me to do this. And I won't." She shook her head sadly and started to fade.

"Fine!" I yelled, a sudden flare of anger rising in my belly. "Seymour offered me two million dollars for this house, and I'm taking it. He'll strip it and sell it to some politician to use as a summer house."

I let my voice get low and nasty, savoring the taste of quiet rage. "I hope you're happy smelling your tea and reading your books forever. See if I care."

Annabelle took a shaky breath, then disappeared.

# Chapter 19

"Fuck," I whispered to the empty air.

A bird trilled back. Behind me, the empty house seemed to loom, mocking my desperate words and beating heart. The little patch where Yasmin had fallen through the deck stood out like a black eye. The window in the shed with all of Agatha's secrets, including the one that just blew up the one good thing that had happened to me here, seemed to wink at me. The empty fire pit beckoned, its mouth open wide.

Of all the ways I expected our conversation to go, the possibility that Annabelle would say no, and be cruel about it, had never crossed my mind.

How had this gone so wrong? My heart was still beating rapidly, and my face was burning.

I shouted "FUCK" at the house. That helped, but not much. My first instinct was to run. To get away from this decrepit house and its ghost, who would rather stay dead than be with me.

Balling my fists so tightly my nails dug into my palms, I stalked back into the house, through the kitchen, and into the hallway. I paused under the chandelier that had almost been my downfall when I arrived. This fucking thing had almost killed me. It was what made Annabelle reveal herself and started me down this path of magic books, spells, blood moons, and insanity.

My blood was still boiling. I still wanted to run as fast as I could away from this house. But there was nowhere to run.

The fugly pink sofa, still stained with blood from my head wound, sat in the front parlor. I stared at it, focusing every bit of rage I felt at being rejected. Tendrils of anger clawed at my throat. I was alone in a cursed house, having opened myself up to the ridiculous possibility that I could be loved, completely and honestly, by a ghost. How fucking stupid. Now I was cleaning up the messes of a family I never wanted in the first place instead of living the life I worked so fucking hard to build for myself with no one's help.

This wasn't supposed to be my life, anyway. I came here to get my millions and fuck everybody else. Staring at the sofa, I remembered Seymour, who had made one very helpful suggestion: burn the ugly pink couch.

"We could have a bonfire," I said to the house, smiling widely. It felt like my insides were too big for my body. "Let's burn some bridges, shall we?"

I shoved matches from the kitchen in my back pocket and grabbed today's edition of the *Town Crier* for kindling. There was nothing but garden tools behind the shed, but at the side of the house was a wood pile. Leaning against it, perfectly placed and only a little rusty, was an axe. I was already sweating as I grabbed as much wood as I could hold under one arm and slung the axe over my shoulder. I placed the newspapers in the pit and stacked the wood in a pile next to it.

"What's next," I said to the wind.

"The sofa" was its answer.

It took much more effort than I expected to hack the sofa to pieces. The upholstery didn't want to come apart, and I didn't have my knife to cut it. I managed to rip it into three uneven pieces and hacked off the legs. Breathing hard, I hauled them out to the garden, leaving deep gouges in the hardwood floor as I dragged it behind me.

The newspapers and a few small pieces of wood ignited easily.

When the fire was about a foot high, I threw on one of the sofa legs, then another. The sculpted wooden shapes looked like bones. With both hands, I lifted one of the bulky pieces of the sofa's frame and tossed it in the fire. The stained pink fabric sizzled as it burned. A terrible smell emanated from the pit.

I whispered, "To the other fucking side you go."

The fire made a satisfying crackling sound and the flames danced beautifully in the deepening shadows of the late afternoon. I stood watching the bloody sofa burn, feeling the heat on my face.

Entering the shed, I spotted Agatha's book sitting innocently on her workbench. I picked it up and stuffed it under my arm, then returned to my fire.

"Bye, Aunt Agatha," I said, and threw the book into the fire. Flames curled around the edges like hot orange fingers, clasping the book and pulling it into the inferno.

"Gibson!" Yasmin yelled, throwing open the door and running across the deck. "What are you doing?"

She lost one of her chunky sandals on the stairs, and she kicked the other one off before picking her way carefully barefoot across the yard.

"Oh, hi," I said. "Want a s'more? No marshmallows, though."

When she saw the black, curling pages of Agatha's grimoire, she screamed, "No!" Her voice cracked.

I threw back my head and laughed, becoming the cackling witch I had accused her of being.

"The book!" Yasmin shrieked. She rushed at me and tried to reach past me into the fire. I blocked her, grabbing at her arms before she could thrust them into the flames. She fought me, trying to reach the burning book.

"Yaz!" Nate had followed her into the backyard and scooped up her shoes. He dropped them and grabbed her around the waist.

"No!" she yelled. It turned into a sob as the three of us watched the fire consume Agatha's life's work. Yasmin stopped fighting and sank to her knees, defeated. She was breathing hard. A sheen of sweat was visible where her gauzy blue blouse clung to her neck.

Pieces of wood and hunks of the pink sofa littered the yard around the fire, which was starting to burn down. I put my hands in my pockets and turned my back on it, heading back into the house.

Yasmin caught up to me in the kitchen.

I had already thrown Annabelle's angel wings mug on the floor, though infuriatingly, it didn't break. I chose a mug that said "Tea Sluts Gotta Have It Every Day" to smash next.

"What are you doing? Are you insane?" she said, staring at the ceramic shards on the floor.

"No, actually, I think I'm quite sane now. My ghost problems are over." I had to stand on my tiptoes to reach Annabelle's tea blends. Her English breakfast went down the sink first. I needed the stepladder to reach her custom blend, which was situated at the back of the cabinet, so I let it be.

"Where's Annabelle?" she asked. Nate was still in the back-yard, watching the fire. I could see him through the window, stealing glances at the house every now and then.

"Annabelle, where are you?" Yasmin looked around as if the ghost might appear on the ceiling or walk through one of the walls.

I scoffed. "She's gone. She's not doing your stupid ritual. And the book is gone. You can take your stuff and leave."

"What do you mean, she's gone?"

I got into Yasmin's face, invading her space until she shrank back. "She. Is. Gone." Still running on adrenaline, I could smell the burned upholstery and paper wafting off my clothes and hair. "She said no. She's gone."

Yasmin's face went through a series of emotions, all of them variations on sad.

Unable to look at them, I stomped through the broken mugs down the hallway and into Annabelle's library.

"Do you think any of these books are first editions? Might be worth something."

I picked titles at random, looking at the spine as if I knew anything about old books, then throwing them on the floor.

Yasmin followed me, and the door opened and closed, meaning Nate had come back inside. Drifting over to the Vic-trola, I considered Annabelle's record collection. "Now these might be worth something. Just gotta find the right person on eBay."

"Gibson, stop!" Yasmin stood at the stairs. Her whiny voice was grating to my ears. "What did she say? Why won't you talk to me?"

"I'm done talking." Sitting on Annabelle's side table was the songbook I'd found at Mike's. I opened it and ripped the book in half, expecting my heart to rip in two as well. But there wasn't anything left in me to tear.

Behind me, Nate said softly, "Let's go, babe. Give her some space."

"Nate's right," I said. "Go."

Yasmin was crying now. "No."

I spun around and demanded, "What happens after?"

"What?" She wiped her eyes.

"The ritual. You said Annabelle could come back for one day. Then what?"

Yasmin shook her head. "I don't know. Agatha didn't—"

"Of course not! There's so much you don't know, but you and Agatha were more than willing to do this anyway because it means fulfilling some family tradition or whatever. Because *you* don't risk anything! If Annabelle disappears after the moon sets, then who cares, right? You get to move on with your life."

"Of course I care! Gibson—"

I grabbed one of Annabelle's larger books and took it to the front door. Swinging it wide open, I used the book as a doorstop and pointed. "Get out of my house."

Yasmin stood by the stairs, looking hurt and confused. "But I can't—"

"Yes, you can." Pointing again at the front porch and gesturing at the wider world beyond Mackinac, I said, "You can go home! To your family, where you can ask your mother why she sent you here and you can apologize to her for anything you need to apologize for, and you can try to understand why she sent you here."

"But—" She wiped her nose with the back of her hand and

then wiped her hand on her skirt. Nate was standing behind her, bracing her shoulders gently. His expression was infuriatingly kind.

"No buts." I crossed my arms and stayed at the open door. "Your family is alive, and you can get the answers you need from them. Mine isn't. I will never get to try again. I will never know if they would've accepted me as I am, and I'll never get to try. Because you were right about me. I put up a wall and I kept everyone out, including and especially them. Maybe that was wrong. It can't have been easy to love me. I know that. But it's too late! They will never get to see that I've grown up to be . . ." I pulled in a shaky breath, losing steam and unsure what the end of that sentence was.

Yasmin's eyes filled with fresh tears. She stared at me, her lip wobbling, unable to speak.

I shook my head and lowered my voice. "You need to leave."

Nate touched Yasmin's arm. "You can stay at my place, babe."

I pointed to the stairs. "Pack your shit. Go to Nate's and then go home to your family and leave me the fuck alone."

Yasmin sobbed once, then twirled dramatically and ran up the stairs. She stomped her feet as she went, then threw open the door so hard it banged against the wall. Nate watched her go, then turned back to me, hesitating.

I sighed. "Help her pack, please."

He nodded.

Before I could stop the words, I added, "Thank you."

~

Eventually, the silence in the house got to me. I called to her a few times, but Annabelle never reappeared. She really was gone. All through my confrontation with Yasmin, I'd wondered if she might reappear and chide me for my childish behavior, but she stayed away. I wasn't sure if she could see us but decided it didn't matter anyway.

With broken cups littering the kitchen floor that I couldn't look at without feeling a fresh wave of spite and no one to cook dinner, I left.

At dinner, I ignored messages from Brooke about the library video and the upcoming show. I ordered a burger at the distillery where Nate and Yasmin had their first date. It tasted like nothing. I drank three in-house craft beers that were so light I couldn't feel anything until halfway into the third. Using the distillery's Wi-Fi, I purchased a plane ticket back to New York and sent an email agreeing to all of Seymour's terms. I told him to bring the paperwork and a notary to the house on the thirty-first so I could sign everything and be done with it. My mouth tasted sour with sadness and Michigan craft beer.

As I walked back to Abaddon on the cycling path, I stopped at a particular patch of darkness, somehow knowing that I'd stopped at Annabelle's cove.

It was just a place.

I didn't believe that, though. The night was breezy and bright with moonlight. I felt incredibly alone. The nightlife downtown was in full swing, with many of the island's tourists and locals filling the bars and restaurants or walking from fudge shop to fudge shop. I stood in the spot where I was convinced Annabelle had died, feeling the hole in my chest growing again. After the unfamiliar heaviness of a full heart, its reemergence felt refreshingly familiar.

I was alone again. So, what? It's how this was always going to end. I was kidding myself by thinking I could have more.

The moon was half full, so I walked further onto the rocky beach than I had before, using its light for a guide.

Annabelle's letters hadn't offered any clues about her death. They simply stopped. On the last day, she wrote about going to the market to find ingredients for a new recipe. There wasn't any final letter announcing her intentions. Linda had cautioned me not to jump to conclusions, saying that we couldn't know how—or why—she stopped writing. But I knew. Annabelle had come to this cove, alive. Then she returned, bound to the island forever, as a spirit.

I ached for her, but she didn't feel strongly enough about me to cross over the divide between us. She would remain tethered to the house no matter what I did or how much I cared. I turned to go. With my back to the lake, I picked my way back to the path, but something made me turn.

Annabelle stood in the lake, a shining beacon of white submerged in the dark water. She faced away from me, looking out toward the bridge with the water up to her waist. Like before, she wore a thin white gown. It was long, floating on the surface around her body while she was as still as a lighthouse, shining and immobile.

Seeing her here, when she wouldn't appear at home, plunged a knife into my heart. It felt wrong. I was seeing the hidden parts of Annabelle, the past she kept hidden behind a smile, when what I wanted was *all* of her.

I rushed forward as she stepped further into the water.

"Annabelle!"

I scrambled as far as I could go on the black rocks of the shoreline, trying not to slip and fall. I was wearing boots with rubber soles, but they were fashionable boots meant for being seen, not clamoring on a beach full of jagged rocks and the icy cold water of the Great Lakes.

Now in the water up to her chest, she turned.

Annabelle's face was drawn and sad, the thin line of her mouth holding no hint of a curve. The laughing, teasing, plump lips that I longed to see lift into a smile were instead pressed together, painfully tight. They were as white as her face and hair. Her usually joyful face instead held the haunted look of a tortured soul.

"Annabelle!" I shouted, plunging into the water. The shock of the cold registered distantly in my mind, but I pushed it aside.

But the ghost didn't seem to see or hear me.

"Can you hear me? Marley!"

I splashed forward, my shoes filling with water and weighing me down, like I was wearing sand-filled socks on my feet. The water was up to my knees now. My feet slipped over the algae-covered rocks. Throwing my arms up for balance, I wildly flapped them in the cool night air.

Ahead of me, Annabelle silently walked further into the lake.

"Annabelle!" I yelled again. What was she doing out here? Was it really her? "Marley!"

The tails of her white gown floated on the lake's surface, dragging behind her like a sodden wedding train. Annabelle sank deeper into the dark water, and I knew I wouldn't be able to reach her before her white-blond curls went under.

"Marley!" My voice broke. It became a grinding, desperate thing, clawing at my throat. "I need you. Stop!"

She kept going, disappearing into the freezing black water, unmoved by my shouts, which dissolved into the whisper of waves lapping at the shore.

I stood in shock while the sting of the cold night air pricked my skin.

"Marley," I whispered one last time, knowing I'd receive no answer. She was gone.

When the numbness in my feet turned into pain, I carefully waded back to the rocks. I stood for one last moment on the shore, looking out at the empty water.

There was no sign of Annabelle.

No ghostly white gown swirling around her body. No pale blue eyes staring at me in horror. No open mouth, gasping. Just the dark lake and the bright disc of the moon.

# Chapter 20

I woke up knowing I was alone. It was so much worse than knowing I was sleeping with a ghost in my house.

"Marley?" I whispered anyway. "Are you here?"

The house swallowed my words and gave nothing in return.

Hungover and drained, I nudged the ceramic shards in the kitchen aside with my foot so I could make coffee. I didn't dump any more of Annabelle's special tea but I closed the cabinet so I didn't have to look at it. Like I had so many times before I got here, I unlocked my phone and scrolled through meaningless bullshit while I waited for caffeine to make me into a human. It didn't. It felt like I lost something yesterday.

I scrolled up to the beginning of the unread messages from Brooke and read her responses to the video of me and Tanesha. She reacted exactly the way I thought she would, saying, "Ummm? Are you singing in a prison???" But she liked the version of the video that I reshared on my own account.

"It's a long story," I texted back, adding a chagrined smiling face. "I messed around w/ ur song."

It felt strange to send the video I'd recorded at Annabelle's cove to someone else. Like I was sharing a secret that didn't belong to me. But I uploaded it to a shared drive and sent the link to Brooke anyway. I said, "Let me know what u think, sorry sound is crap."

Little dots appeared on the bottom of the screen to tell me she was typing, but I didn't stay and wait for her text. The song reminded me of Annabelle and so did the tea and the old refrigerator I'd promised to replace. The house felt haunted again, and I needed to get out. Annabelle had made her point—she wasn't coming back.

I'd been ghosted by a literal ghost. At least she hadn't thrown anything at me, written ominous messages in the mirror, or tried to smother me in my sleep. But I still didn't want to be in the house without her. She was what made the house feel livable in the first place.

~

I decided to return Sage's bike. Even though I would have a few days left until Seymour brought the paperwork that would free me from this island, I didn't intend to spend the time enjoying myself. Without Annabelle at home waiting to hear about my adventures, what would be the point in having them?

I wheeled Sage's bike out from the side of the house, then mounted it and rode up the lane, standing up to pedal. The skill had come back to me slowly, like, well, riding a bike.

Instead of turning toward Big Mike's property, I went the other way, curious about my former neighbor, Mrs. Montclair. I expected to see a private lane leading from the road down to the house, similar to the ones that led to Abaddon and Big Mike's. But the way was blocked by a temporary plastic fence.

The sign forbade entry and warned of penalties for trespassing. Attached to it was a notice of rezoning and change in occupancy rules, but I didn't read it. Another sign with a logo for Compact Development advertised future luxury condos.

Past the barricade, many of the trees had been cleared to level the ground where Mrs. Montclair's house had once stood. There wasn't a house anymore. The foundation was still visible, but dirt and construction equipment replaced the walls, doors, and everything else that made Mrs. Montclair's house a home. Dimly, I recalled hearing construction noises the past few days but hadn't stopped to think about where the noises might be coming from.

A mixture of feelings competed for my attention, then canceled each other out, leaving me numb. I wondered how much Mrs. Montclair had gotten for her house. Then remembered Miranda saying that she'd regretted her choice. Did she know her home would be replaced with boxy generic-looking units? What would it be like for the future occupants of Abaddon to live next to high-end vacation rentals? And why did I care?

I shook my head and turned my—Sage's—bike around.

At Big Mike's, two horses were tied to the fence out front. I recognized Joan Jett the Blackhorse, but the other was a medium-sized dappled gray one I hadn't seen before. They watched me with placid eyes, swishing their tails as I approached the front door.

Before I could knock, the door opened and Sage stepped out.

"Oh, hey," I said, feeling unmoored. I held on to the handlebars of Sage's bike to keep me grounded. "I brought your bike back."

Sage looked down at the bike. "K. Thanks."

We stared at each other awkwardly.

I said, "So, um . . ."

A toothy smile spread over Sage's face. For the first time, I noticed that they still wore braces. Seems they were getting used to dealing with an adult who was every bit as awkward as a teenager. They pointed at the garage. "This way. We can put the bike in the garage."

As we walked over and Sage entered the code to open the garage door, I asked, "Did you know that the house on the other side of Abaddon was being demolished?"

"Yeah. There's new stuff being built all over, so I don't really pay much attention." Sage shrugged. "I liked Mrs. Montclair. She was old, though, so I'm sure Florida will be nicer."

"That's true."

"Some guy approached my dad a few times about selling our house and the stables. Dad thinks he's trying to get all the properties in this area to make a new complex and compete with the resorts. But he was so obnoxious my dad chased him off." Sage had a proud smile on their face. "I thought Dad was going to punch him right in the face."

I chuckled, then froze. I had been incredibly stupid. "Do you remember the guy's name?"

"Seymour something-or-other. Adam called him See-More Buttcrack."

Absently, I said, "Anderson. Seymour Anderson."

I pictured Seymour in the house, laughing at all the things wrong with it. He'd been humoring me. The developer had no interest in buying Abaddon to resell the house to another family. He wouldn't renovate it to make it a home for new year-rounders. It wouldn't be a summer house for a rich family to use while they showed their kids what they imagined life was like a century ago. Seymour wouldn't tear strips of rose wallpaper off the walls in Yas's room to replace them with something more modern. He wouldn't buy a new fridge to entice buyers, telling them how the electrical panel had been recently redone to accommodate modern appliances. Compact Development had no interest in the backyard where I'd pictured fairy lights and sang to Annabelle. They would demolish the garden, which was lying fallow, waiting for a new pair of hands to raise it back to life.

They would remove everything that had ever meant something to the people who'd lived there. Seymour would raze Abaddon to the ground.

What would happen to Annabelle if the house was destroyed?

I pictured her standing in the house as it lost its layers. Would she start to fade gradually? Would her edges dim as the pieces of the house were removed? In my mind, Annabelle stood in her alcove, gradually becoming invisible as a bulldozer's giant claw came closer and closer to her beloved bookcase. She flickered as the bric-a-brac was cleared and made into rubble.

If the bare walls of the house were an empty skeleton in a dark meadow, Annabelle was its fading heart. As Abaddon lost its foundation, she disappeared altogether.

"Gibson?" Sage waved a hand in front of my face, and I realized I'd been zoning out for who-knows-how long.

"Sorry, I'm a little distracted. I . . . I think I was dumped yesterday, and it's been messing with my mind."

"You *think* you were dumped?"

I winced. "I thought I had something special with someone here, but she didn't feel the same way."

I could see the wheels turning in Sage's brain. As they processed, Adam came through the garage and said, "Hey, Gibson."

"Hey, Adam." I waved. In my back pocket, my phone buzzed with a new series of texts from Brooke.

Seeing the name of the contact on the screen, Sage said, "I can't believe you're friends with a famous rock star."

"Fuck buddies, yes. These days I'm not so sure about friends," I said before I could stop the words "fuck buddies" from coming out of my mouth in front of an eleven-year-old. "Oh, fuck. I said 'fuck.' Twice."

Adam held up three fingers. "Three times."

Sage couldn't stop laughing. But my phone kept buzzing—Brooke was calling now.

"Sorry, guys." I turned away from the garage and answered. "Hey, what's up?"

There was a burst of static from her end. "I can't talk, but . . . wanted you to . . . before you saw it online . . ."

"Brooke? I can barely hear you."

"Just want you to know . . . hard decision . . . we'll talk when you get home. The band just needed someone reliable."

"What?" I took the phone from my ear and stared at it as if I could somehow make the reception get better by willing it. "Brooke?"

"It's not personal, Gibson! I gotta go." The call disconnected.

"Not personal?" I muttered. "Someone reliable . . . Oh, fuck, no. They didn't."

They did. On the band's Instagram page, Stephani With One E was smiling and holding her prissy pink guitar next to Ivan and his bass. The caption read: "welcome @stephan1 to Call Me Kate! we're dropping the Kane and a new song on Thursday! come check out the show! ticket info in bio"

"Shit. Fuck." My stomach dropped. "Shit. They really replaced me." The kids stared at me, and I realized I was still swearing up a storm in front of them. "I'm so sorry. You didn't hear any of those words from me."

Sage made a zipper motion across their lips.

Adam raised his eyebrows in the most withering look I'd ever seen on a kid. "I'm eleven. I hear worse every single day."

I scrubbed my face, suddenly tired even though it wasn't yet noon. "Well, none of this is your problem, but I just got dumped again. For sure this time. So, I'll let you get on with your ride."

Adam and Sage looked at one another, then at me.

"Do you want to come with?" Adam asked. "I'll ride on Joan with Sage, and you can take Brian." He nodded to the gray-and-white horse standing next to Joan.

I considered my options. There was overpriced lunch somewhere on the island, followed by wandering around places filled with happy, annoying tourists. I'd spend the entire time stewing with rage about being passed up by the band. Then I would go back to an empty house and try not to talk to a ghost that I'd scared off with my feelings.

Nope. At that point, even a ride on horseback sounded more appealing. "I'd love to ride with you."

"Yes!" Adam pumped his arm in the air. "I'll go get you a helmet. Be right back!" He raced into the garage, then into the house, slamming the door behind him.

Sage and I walked over to the horses, and they showed me how to treat the unfamiliar one. Mirroring the teen's actions, I carefully approached from the front to make sure the horse could see me and extended my hand. Sage whispered calming words to Joan.

"Brian and Joan . . . Who names your horses, anyway?" I asked.

Sage chuckled. "Me and Dad name most of them, but Medium Sebastian is Adam's. This is Dr. Brian Mare. Despite his name, he's a boy."

I groaned, but couldn't help the smile that came with it. "Pleasure to meet you, Dr. Mare," I said, stroking the horse's nose gently. "I'm a big fan."

~

Riding a horse did not come back as easily as riding a bike. The two times I'd ridden since I arrived on Mackinac had left me with sore buttocks and no increased horse-riding abilities. I followed behind Adam and Sage, who rode together on the back of Joan Jett the Blackhorse. They insisted that Brian would do 99 percent of the work and to relax so that the horse didn't get mixed signals from my body, but it was extremely difficult to relax while perched atop a gigantic animal with nothing to hold on to but a flimsy piece of rope.

Sage and Adam led me out the back of their property and into the forest. I tried to use my core to stabilize myself and regretted never going to Pilates. While we rode, I focused on the clip-clop of the horses and the sound of birds playfully calling in the trees. Sweat was making my shirt stick to my back, and even though I wasn't really exercising yet, I was breathing hard.

Instead of fading away or becoming transformed into positivity by the magic of horses and sunshine, doomy thoughts crowded my skull. I kept picturing Annabelle's face as she mocked me for wanting her to come back and inhabit a body. Or Stephani onstage with Brooke, their faces mashed together like Bruce Springsteen and Clarence Clemons.

I kept expecting a rush of anger to make my face hot and my fists clench. But all I felt was a sort of hopeless, numb nothingness. Mackinac Island was supposed to be my cash cow, my ticket to financial security and a future with the band I thought I loved. Somehow while here I'd fallen in love and become consumed by it, only to have the whole thing go up in flames. And finally realized the band I loved didn't love me back.

I had less than I did when I arrived. Nothing. That's all I had and it's all I amounted to.

The horse underneath me tossed its head, shaking me out of my reverie and throwing me off balance.

Despite the fact that it was about noon, the forest was so dense that it was dark underneath the canopy of trees. Sunlight drifted in through the gaps, sending beams through the dark, shadowy trees toward the ground. I shaded my eyes and looked around; Sage and Adam were a few horse-lengths ahead of me, going around a curve in the trail.

Willing myself to relax, I closed my eyes for a moment and felt my heart pounding against my ribs. I kept hearing Annabelle saying "Why would I want to come back?" and seeing her face split in two, with black horrors spilling from her mouth. When I opened my eyes again, the forest was dark, completely dark, not just shadowy and green. The trail ahead of me cut diagonally through the darkness, only it wasn't a trail anymore, it was railroad tracks. And in the distance, the light of a train.

*No!*

I shook my head, physically shaking myself out of the vision that had plagued me since adolescence. My legs and thighs tightened around the horse as I struggled to regain my sense of place, and Brian Mare kicked forward, thinking I was telling him to gallop.

Adrenaline spiked in my veins, like a shot of battery acid pumping through my body. I gripped the reins tighter, but this only urged the horse on.

He surged forward, throwing me back in the saddle. I tried to compensate by shifting my weight, but it wasn't enough. I felt my thighs sliding, felt the force of the horse's motion pushing me out of the saddle like I weighed nothing at all. Before I tipped over completely, I shook my foot to wrench it from the stirrup. A blaze of pain flared from my ankle. I threw my body forcefully away from the sweating, stinking mass of the horse.

A rush of adrenaline coursed through me. My arms flailed. It happened so fast, but before I hit the ground, something deep within me rebelled. I was only in the air for half a second but I had time to rail against the unfairness of it.

*This is not the end of my story.*

When I hit the ground, I gasped at the overwhelming force of the impact on my right shoulder, then felt nothing at all.

# Chapter 21

The hospital smelled clean and sterile, but with a slight hint of horse. Even here, the horse scent lingered. Reassuring beeps and boops from the adjoining rooms filled my hearing.

"Oh, thank god," Mike said when I opened my eyes.

"Thank *someone*," I replied, but it felt like I had a bag of sand in my mouth and a balloon in my brain, so I'm not sure what it sounded like.

"I'm going to get the doctor," said Mike. "Do not move!"

To Sage, he said, "Keep her here and do not let her die."

"I don't think I'm going to—"

Mike waved his arms. "You don't get a vote!" He rushed out of the room, going one way down the hall, before turning and going the other way. His flannel shirt was tucked into his jeans, but only on one side, and his shoelaces were untied.

"What happened?" I asked Sage.

There was a series of triumphant beeps from the corner of the room and then a very sad-sounding series of beeps. Adam punched a button on his game console, then set it on his lap and looked up. "You almost died!"

Sage put their arms out. "No, you didn't. You just fell off Brian." Sage's face was sweaty and their hair was messy in a way that didn't look planned. Grimy green strands fell over one of their eyes, and they pushed it back, then crossed their arms. "It was an accident. And . . ." They bit their lip, making the metal braces on their teeth dig into the flesh. "I'm really sorry, Gibson. I didn't mean for you to get hurt."

My heart ached for so many reasons, both literally and metaphorically—what was one more?

"This isn't your fault, Sage, it's mine," I said. "It's me who should be sorry. Clearly, I wasn't ready to ride by myself."

"Clearly," Adam added.

"Ouch. Accurate, but ouch." To Sage, I said, "Tell me some more horse names, please, I could use a laugh."

Sage cleared their throat and said, "Um, well, there's Britney Spurs and Marvin Gelding."

It hurt but I laughed anyway.

"Dad loves Sir Paul McHorseney. We had to sell Bayonce, unfortunately. And The Horse Formerly Known as Prince, but his name was too long to say and hard to abbreviate anyway."

I closed my eyes. The smile stayed on my face. "Those are perfect names. Fifteen out of ten, no notes."

I had almost faded back into hazy, drug-assisted sleep when Mike returned. With him were Rebecca and Sara Johnson. Rebecca was wearing a low-cut black tank top and lime green high-waisted pants, the kind that would be extremely difficult to pull off but that looked fabulous on her. For some reason, she looked happy to see me. Dr. Johnson was wearing sky-blue scrubs and a professional, bland expression. There was no trace of the Sara Johnson who'd belted out Journey songs in front of the drunken audience at Helga's.

Dr. Johnson smiled warmly. "Well, Gibson, you are going to be in an absolute world of hurt tomorrow, but you'll live." She checked my heart with her stethoscope and shined a bright light into my eyes. "Most minor head injuries don't need additional treatment, but we'll need to keep you overnight for observation since you don't have anyone to monitor you for signs of a worsening condition."

I sighed. "My insurance will definitely not cover that. Are you seriously going to make me stay here even though you know I'll be fine?"

She frowned. "I don't know that you'll be fine. And I do not trust you to be alone. It's barely been a week since your last head injury. Not allowing patients with head injuries to go home with serious painkillers is covered on day three of med school." Dr. Johnson clicked her pen and put it in her scrubs pocket. "Days one and two are when they show you how to make balloon animals with your gloves and pass out rubber noses."

"I'm not—" I was going to say that I wasn't alone, but I was. If I went back to Abaddon, there would be no one waiting.

"You get off in an hour, right, babe?" Rebecca said. "Could Gibson stay with us?"

I shook my head, then had to close my eyes to stave off a wave of dizziness. "You don't need to do that. Everyone on this island needs to stop being so nice to me, I swear to god."

Mike said, "That's a good idea." He was hovering anxiously on the other side of the bed, keeping one eye on me and one eye on Adam, who had returned to his video games. "I'm not being nice," he added. "I don't want you to sue me. Or my idiot kids."

"Hey!" Adam said.

At the same time, Sage said, "Fair."

"Mike, I'm not going to sue you or your kids."

"Let's not talk about litigation in the hospital. I have enough paperwork in my life as it is." Dr. Johnson checked her watch. "I do get off soon, and I could be comfortable discharging you if you stayed with a responsible adult."

"We'll have a sleepover!" Rebecca said, clapping her hands and sounding way too excited about bringing a damaged person home.

At the confused looks she received from Mike and Sara, she said, "Hey, I need to take the excitement where I can get it. You guys have your band to spice up your life, and I have the Gibson Cartwright reality show in my living room."

To me, she said, "You're basically my *Survivor* until the new season comes on."

"Glad to be of service," I said.

The Johnsons left to arrange my escape from the hospital, and there was a flurry of instructions, paperwork, and waiting for people to type things into computers. Finally, Mike wheeled me out of the hospital and through the streets of Mackinac to the Johnson house. Tourists stared at me and my little entourage. I giggled, not feeling foolish even though the not-drugged Gibson of yesterday would have.

When we reached the barbershop slash family home, Rebecca led me up the stairs, holding me up by the waist and keeping me balanced. "You can rest in Tyler's bedroom."

"I don't need to rest."

"Okay." She led me down the hall and opened the door, scooting me inside gently.

"I don't need to . . ." I sat down on the bed. My limbs were as heavy as rocks. My eyes closed and everything went still and dark.

~

Posters covered every inch of every wall. I stared at the shapes and colors in the dim light drifting in from the hallway and the moonlight filtering through half-open blinds. Without context, my brain couldn't turn the images into meaningful patterns. The room smelled like feet and adolescence. The moon was high in the sky, meaning that somehow, I'd slept deeply for several hours.

"Is this hell?" I asked no one. "Is hell a teenager's bedroom?"

The room didn't answer.

Everything hurt. I wiggled my toes, then my fingers. I drew in a deep breath, then winced at the pain in my chest. I could move all my limbs, but it wasn't easy or pleasant. What the fuck had happened? I remembered the smell of a horse, the damp forest, a light through the trees, then nothing. A lump formed in my throat as my memories rewound.

Brooke had called me. "It's not personal," she had said.

The band couldn't wait for me—I lost my chance at success. If I had ever really had one. My chance at truly belonging with them was gone. I had been playing fill-in gigs for over two decades, including two years with Call Me Kate Kane, and yet no one on the scene wanted me as a permanent member. Pressure built behind my eyes as I realized what a fool I'd been. Ever since I arrived in Michigan, I'd been sending Brooke snippets of my life and she hadn't cared, not really. She was committed to the band, not me. I could understand, but it hurt.

Going back even further, I remembered setting the sofa on fire in Agatha's backyard. I closed my eyes and sighed, recalling how I'd yelled at Yasmin and forced her out of the house. She was my family, and I'd turned her out on her ass.

Annabelle's mocking voice filled my ears. She had said, "And you know all about living, do you?"

How stupid I had been to hope that she would want to come back—for *me*.

Agatha had lived in the house for decades with Annabelle. They were friends who watched soap operas together. If she couldn't convince Annabelle to come back, why did I think I could? We had known each other for, what? A week? This place was making me crazy. Even if I didn't have much of a home to go back to in New York, that's where I had made myself into the person I was today. It was where I could lose myself in music and a crowd, and it was time for me to go back.

I groaned as I forced myself out of a bed that was too small for me. My legs were covered by a Spider-Man blanket. When I felt steady enough to stand, I smoothed the sheets back as best I could before creeping down the hall. The hallway was dark, but the flickering light of a television filtered up from the ground floor. I made my way carefully down the stairs and had to stop at the bottom to catch my breath. My left ankle felt like it was three sizes too big, and my right hip didn't want to move right. It felt like everything, even the inside of my nose, was bruised.

To my right was the empty barbershop room. To my left, a dark living room lit by the flickering of a screen. I recognized the scene with the bridge made of marigolds from Coco.

"Well, hello there," said a voice from the couch. Rebecca and Sara Johnson were cuddled together under a large blanket. Sitting in an armchair off to the side was a preteen engrossed in his phone. I vaguely recognized him as one of the kids who'd run around with Adam and figured he was Tyler—the kid whose bedroom I'd commandeered. Sitting on the floor at his feet was Adam. Big Mike and Sage also sat on the floor with their legs squished under a coffee table. The room was way too small for this many people. The front room of my house was three times this size, although Agatha's old television was way too small.

Everyone looked up as I came down the stairs.

"How are you feeling?" asked Rebecca. She paused the movie.

"Like I fell off a horse," I said. "Did I fall off a horse?"

Rebecca chuckled. "You did. Let Sara take a look at you."

Sara stood, stretching her back. She said, "Full disclosure, I already took a look at you when you were unconscious. Didn't really want to have a dead visitor in my son's bedroom and I was the one who discharged you, so I had to make sure you weren't permanently broken."

"Uh, thanks." I stood behind the couch and let her poke and prod at me until she was satisfied that I wouldn't keel over on her watch.

When Sara was done, she sat back down on the couch. "Why don't you join us? Tyler can sit on the floor." Tyler looked up from his phone but didn't move.

"I should . . ."

"They're not going to let you leave and go back to that old house," Mike said. He had a bowl of popcorn in his lap. "This is a mandatory family movie night."

"Family . . . oh, shit. There's someone I need to call." I patted my sweatpants, looking for my phone. Apparently, I was wearing sweatpants—they must have belonged to Rebecca. She wasn't as tall as me but had a similar boyish figure. Sara, on the other hand, was very short and all curves.

Rebecca, Sara, and Mike all looked at one another as if they were deciding whether to believe me.

"I do have someone—my cousin. She's pissed at me right now, but I need to let her know I'm here. Yeah, I know, I should've said something earlier, but my head was kind of in the clouds."

Rebecca got up from the couch. "Your phone is in my purse." She led me into the hallway and rummaged around in a purse hanging from the coatrack mounted on the wall. It held a variety of kids' jackets, hats, and cloth grocery bags. From the purse, she produced my phone. The screen was cracked, but it still turned on.

I dialed Yasmin, wondering if she would pick up.

"What do you want?" she said, answering after the third ring.

I let out the breath I'd been holding until she picked up. Rebecca had returned to the living room, but they hadn't resumed the movie. No one was looking at me, but they were clearly all listening. I cleared my throat. "Hey, so, uh—"

"If you're calling to apologize, I do not accept, Gibson. It was extremely rude of you to kick me out, and you *know* I don't even have keys to the house. Annabelle had to let me back in to get my curling iron."

"You use a curling iron? I thought your hair was just like that."

"That's not the point! Where are you?"

"I had an . . . accident." There was silence from the other end, then a rustling. "I'm okay, but I kind of . . . fell off a horse." I winced, picturing Yasmin's pinched face.

"You fell off a—"

"Gibson!" Annabelle's beautiful, worried voice cut in. "What happened? Are you all right?"

Despite myself, I smiled at the sound of her voice. "I'm

fine, Marley, just a little banged up. I'm at the Johnsons' house. They're . . . I'll send Yasmin the location." Putting them on speaker phone, I swiped over to my maps app and sent the location of Burn Your Bridges Barbershop to Yasmin via text.

"I'll be right there," Annabelle said.

"Wait, Annabelle—" There was another rustling sound from the other end of the phone, and then Yasmin repeated, "Annabelle?"

I frowned. "What's going on?"

"She just disappeared," said Yasmin. "I don't know . . ."

I didn't hear the rest of Yasmin's sentence because suddenly, the ghost I'd been longing to see was standing in the hallway of the Johnsons' house. She flickered a few times before settling into her usual not-quite-there self. Annabelle looked around the hallway and reached out a hand to the wall to steady herself.

"Marley, how are you here?" I stepped forward, forgetting that my ankle was fucked and grimacing at the pain. I had never seen her outside the house, except for when she appeared at the cove. And those times she hadn't seemed aware of her surroundings. "Are you here? I thought you couldn't leave the house."

"I'm not sure. I've never done something like this before." Her body was now only visible from her knees up, and the rest of her legs were fading fast. "I'm not sure how long I can be away." Then she looked past my head at something only she could see, crinkling her forehead and frowning. "The darkness is calling."

"Then go back home!" I waved my arms in a panic, then carefully lowered my right one when pain ricocheted through my shoulder. "Don't go to the darkness, that sounds very, very bad."

Annabelle turned back to me. She tried to hold on to me, but her hands went through my arms. On the third try, she managed to put her arms approximately on my shoulders. "But are you okay? You said there was an accident." She peered at my face, scrutinizing my bruises.

"I'm fine." I let her examine me, turning my head as she requested with gestures. "You don't need to worry about me."

"But I *do*, Gibson."

I took a deep breath, which hurt my ribs. But I didn't have anything to say that wouldn't also be painful.

"You need to stop falling, my dear," she said, keeping her cold, insubstantial hand next to my cheek. It felt nice.

I held her gaze. "Yeah. In more ways than one."

She brought her other hand to my face and held me gently. A tear fell down her cheek, and I longed to brush it away.

Someone in the living room cleared their throat.

Annabelle turned to face the stunned group, seeming to notice them for the first time since she'd appeared in the hallway.

"Oh, hello, everyone," she said with a little wave. "I'm Annabelle."

# Chapter 22

After a moment of charged silence, there was a flash. It lit up the dim hallway and made me close my eyes. When I opened them again, I had to blink a few times.

Adam said, "Cool, she doesn't show up in the picture." He leaned over to show Tyler, who tried to take another picture with his own phone. I covered my eyes at the flash and so did Annabelle. Her waist was invisible now.

Sara swatted at Tyler's phone, saying, "Stop that." Then everyone started talking at once. Adam and Tyler kept trying to take pictures of Annabelle, trying different filters. Sage suggested that maybe a video would work. Big Mike stood up and put his hands on his hips, frowning at the appearance of a ghost in the hall as if he didn't approve. Rebecca rushed over to Annabelle, cooing and gasping like a kid who caught Santa Claus in the act. Sara hadn't gotten up from the couch. She looked tired.

"Excuse me, everyone! Please calm down," Annabelle said, raising her voice and commanding the room. The sound of it sent involuntary shivers down my spine. I'd never heard her speak in quite that tone before. I gulped, realizing I was eager to hear it again—in a different context, definitely in private.

To Adam and Tyler, she said, "I assure you that I will not show up in those no matter how many you take."

Reluctantly, the preteens put down their phones. They didn't put them away, though, preferring to hold on to the devices, just in case.

"I'm sorry for appearing suddenly like this," Annabelle said. "I'm sure it's frightening, but—"

Sage broke in, saying, "It's fucking cool."

"Language," murmured Mike.

To me, Adam said, "You didn't tell us you were dumped by a ghost!"

"Would you have believed me?"

Annabelle cleared her throat and turned away so I couldn't see her reaction to Adam saying she'd dumped me. She was still disappearing, but more slowly now. She looked around the house, admiring the family photos on the walls and the homey decor. A smile lit up her face as she noticed a piece of framed artwork showing a nude woman reclining on a divan. "What a lovely house."

"Thank you," Rebecca said. "Who are you, by the way?"

"Well, you see—"

Annabelle was interrupted by a loud knocking at the door. Rebecca opened it and admitted a harried-looking Yasmin. Her hair was sticking out of a side ponytail, and she was out of breath. "Excuse me, but is there an asshole named Gibson here? And maybe a—"

Annabelle waved at Yasmin. "Hi."

"There you are!" Yasmin rushed into the hallway, sounding relieved. She turned to me, and her vibe instantly turned sour.

"And there *you* are."

I sighed. "Rebecca, this is Yasmin. She's my cousin and she wants to take my house." I gestured at the group in the living room. "Yasmin, this is . . . everybody."

Everyone started talking over one another again, but I tuned them out because Annabelle was still disappearing. I could only see her lovely bust, shoulders, and head. Her arms were still attached, though. The effect was both unnerving and a little silly. Like a special effect from a movie.

"You need to go, Marley."

She nodded. "Gibson—"

I shook my head, pointing at the door even though she wouldn't be using it. "Go. We'll talk when I get home."

"You'll come home?"

I held out my hand, palm up. She held her palm to mine, her ghostly energy just barely touching my flesh.

"I promise."

~

Everyone took the ghost explanation differently. Rebecca nodded, accepting every word of Yasmin's like she'd been waiting her whole life to receive concrete proof of the existence of ghosts. Adam and Tyler asked so many questions that Sara ordered them to bed just to get them to stop talking, and Mike harrumphed the entire time Yasmin talked, crossing and uncrossing his arms.

After a debate that I didn't really listen to, Mike rolled me back to Abaddon while Yasmin and Sara walked behind us talking about medical instructions. I overheard Yasmin trying to explain Annabelle and my family's history of witchcraft, again, to the skeptical doctor. My eyelids were drooping, even though Mike hit every rock on the roads that led to the house, jolting me in the chair and sending new waves of pain through my body.

Yasmin hopped up the steps and opened the front door, which she hadn't locked. Mike and Sara helped me out of the chair and across the porch, then finally inside, where Annabelle was waiting. She was wearing her white house slippers and a worried smile. Her hands fluttered nervously, but all of her body was as visible as she ever had been.

After taking me up to the third-floor bedroom and leaving me with Annabelle, Mike and Sara stuck around for a few minutes. I heard them talking with Yasmin, their indistinct voices drifting upstairs.

Just as they left, Miranda arrived. She helped me into the bathroom so that I could improvise a shower, and she helped me scrub in places I couldn't reach. It hurt too much to extend my right arm. She held my T-shirt sleeves patiently while Annabelle stood by and watched, biting her lip. Then she helped me to bed, tucking in the covers and helping me arrange my aching limbs.

Annabelle fussed. She hovered by the side of the bed, drifting here and there, adjusting blankets that didn't need adjusting and wringing her hands.

"Why don't I get you a cup of tea?"

"I don't—" Behind her, Miranda nodded vigorously, telling me to let Annabelle make me tea. "That would be great, Marley, thanks."

"I'll be right back!" She disappeared with a little poof of energy instead of leaving via the open door.

Miranda chuckled. "She'll feel better with something to do. She was the same way with Agatha toward the end." She perched on the edge of the bed. Miranda smelled like old-lady perfume and sugar cookies. Her face was perfectly painted as usual, with scarlet lips and smokey eyes. "Do you actually need anything, though? Other than tea?"

I shook my head. "I'm sorry," I said.

"For what, dear?"

"Everything." I swallowed, tasting the chalky pill I'd just taken. "I promise I wasn't always such a mess. Well, okay, I've been a mess a few times. But not like this. It's like the moment I got here, I just fell apart."

She smiled kindly. "Oh honey, that's okay. Sometimes you need to fall apart so you can put yourself back together. And maybe you've been holding yourself together too long. You needed to fall apart but didn't have a place to do it safely until you got here."

Miranda handed me a tissue. I blew my nose, loudly discharging a giant wad of snot, then took a deep, painful breath. "Now I'm sorry for blowing my nose right at the end of your really nice speech."

She threw her head back and laughed. "I wish you could've met Agatha; I really do. You remind me of her." She wiped her eyes, smearing her mascara. "She was much worse to take care of, though."

"Somehow that doesn't surprise me."

Patting the edge of the bed, Miranda rose and said, "Just when I thought I was through with taking care of stubborn Cartwright women, you showed up."

"I'm—"

She shook her head. "No, dear, I'm glad you did." Miranda looked out the window at the almost-full moon. "Your auntie was a royal pain in my rear for over twenty years, and I wouldn't trade a second of it. Even when I had to help her wipe her rear."

That made me smile. "Why did Agatha really give me this house? She had a Gibson guitar sitting in the shed like it was waiting for me to find it. Why?"

She cocked her head to the side, then shrugged. "I don't know. Maybe she just wanted to see what would happen."

"But she's dead."

Miranda winked. "That doesn't mean she can't see us, love."

# Chapter 23

When I woke the next morning, there were three mugs on the bedside table next to me. Annabelle had dragged a table upstairs from one of the spare bedrooms. Each mug was a different color and held a different variety of tea that I had no interest in drinking. One had the phrase "Uff da" on it. I sipped from each, trying to keep my face from showing how much I hated the taste. Annabelle hovered by the bed, literally unable to keep her feet anchored to the floor.

I managed to get to the bathroom under my own power, then accepted a piece of toast from Annabelle and notified Yasmin that I wasn't dead via text. Finally, I settled back down in bed, exhausted after being awake and moving for only an hour.

"Sit down, Marley," I said, patting the empty stretch of bed next to me.

After fretting for a few more seconds, she sat down carefully on the bed, then lay down and faced me. I carefully turned onto my uninjured side and reached out my hand. Annabelle reached back, holding her hand above mine. Our palms were ships passing each other by, sharing the same water but never meeting.

My eyelids dropped. With her cool, ghostly energy next to me, I felt safe and tired enough to sleep for days.

"What if I stayed?" I said, only half aware of what I was saying.

"What do you mean?"

"What if I didn't go back to New York?" I didn't say "back home." My apartment was nice. My pothos plant would probably miss me eventually. But it wasn't home. It was just the place I went to in between stints on stage. As long as I was playing music, I was home. Or so I thought. For a while, I thought Abaddon could be home, as long as Annabelle was here. Now I wasn't sure where home was anymore.

"I could stay here. With you."

"If you stayed here," Annabelle said slowly, her voice barely more than a whisper, like she didn't want to wake me, "you'd need to make an actual apology to Yasmin. And I'd hold you to your promise to buy me a new fridge."

I smiled but didn't have the energy to laugh.

"And you'd finish your song," she continued. "You'd record it and put it on the internet Tubes, then make a million dollars off it."

I chuckled at that. "Don't make me laugh, Marley, it hurts."

She smiled, tucking the hand that wasn't holding mine under her cheek. "Fine. You would sing to me, and I would be the best audience of one."

"That's much more likely."

"I would make dinner for you. We would pretend to have tea together. And you would get bored."

"I wouldn't—"

"You would. I would tell you to travel, and when you got back, you'd tell me all about the places you'd seen. And you'd bring me souvenirs and buy me more books. I'd read to you at night and watch you sleep."

I must've made a face, because she added, "Not in a creepy way."

"Sounds nice," I murmured.

"It would be," she whispered. "You'd grow older. There's nothing either of us could do about that. And if you got sick or sad, I couldn't hold you or comfort you. If you fell from another ladder or another stupid horse, I couldn't fix you. I could only watch as you slipped further away from me. And then one day, I would be alone again."

There was no sound in the room but my raspy breathing and the beating of my heart. Eventually, I blinked and shook my head, trying to come to my senses through a thick fog of painkillers but not quite getting there.

"Nuh uh," I said.

"What?"

"That's horseshit. A great big pile of—"

"Oh, not again, please."

"Nuh uh," I repeated. "You're just scared."

"I beg your pardon?"

"You're not scared of *me* eventually dying. If I left, you wouldn't have to risk being alive again. You're scared of being alive again because *you're* scared of dying. But it's okay, Marley, it's normal to be scared of dying. Even if you're a ghost."

"Oh darling," she said, and I realized that Annabelle was crying softly. Her tears fell from her face but dissipated into nothing before they reached the pillowcase. "That's not at all what I'm afraid of."

"Then what?"

"I'm afraid of only being able to love you for one day." She wiped her eyes, then held my hand again. I expected it to feel wet, but it didn't, just cold and tingly. "What if I came back, but all I had was one day with you? I couldn't bear it, knowing that we might've had a lifetime. It would break my heart to see you live your life to the end, but I would rather have that than only one day."

I put both my hands out, about a foot apart. I gestured to one, then the other. "Rock. Hard place."

She passed her hand through both of mine. "I go through them both."

"You're right, Marley," I said, closing my eyes. I was exhausted even though I'd only been awake for a short time. "I didn't have the right to ask you to choose. Those are both shitty options. But I still wish you would choose to come back and be with me."

I must've fallen asleep again, because the next thing I knew, my room was full of daylight and my ghost was gone.

~

Dr. Johnson had been right. The day after the fall—and the day after that—I was in an absolute world of hurt. I slept most of the next day in a painkiller haze, then moved downstairs. My bruises got darker and uglier while my joints screamed at me every time I moved.

While I recovered, Sage, Adam, and Tyler became permanent fixtures in the house. Tyler delivered casseroles from his moms and sent back reports on my health to Sara. He and Adam followed Annabelle around the house, relentlessly prodding her with questions and asking her to walk through walls. Every attempt at filming the result failed, but they recorded at least a dozen tries, dissolving into laughter each time they witnessed Annabelle float or stick her arm through a wall. She laughed along with them, rediscovering some of the joy of her current form as the boys found her mundane life in the cottage worthy of a dozen failed TikToks.

My right arm was still too sore to comfortably hold my guitar, but I sat on the intact sofa in the sitting room and watched Sage play, giving them pointers. Sage was a natural musician, and watching them improve after just a few hours of instruction did something funny to my insides.

When Nate appeared at the front door holding Yasmin's trunk in his beefy arms, Annabelle let him in. He gingerly stepped toward me and kept his voice in a whisper. "Hi, Gibson."

"I'm not in a coma, Nate, you can talk normally."

He looked relieved but still stood at a distance like he was afraid I might bite him. "Okay, then. I'll just . . ." He pointed to the stairs. Yasmin had moved her things back into the rose-wallpaper room for the time being. Our ceasefire was holding, but Yasmin and I hadn't really talked since she brought me home from the Johnsons.

"Yeah." I chewed the inside of my cheek. I settled in Annabelle's chair in her alcove, trying not to move in ways that hurt, which meant mostly not moving.

Annabelle gave me a disapproving look that said "You need to talk to her" with her eyebrows.

I cleared my throat. "Nate, can you ask Yasmin to come downstairs? I'd like to talk."

"Sure." He continued up the stairs with her bag, and gently opened and closed the door to her room.

"How about some tea to help you with this conversation?" Annabelle asked, even though I already had a half-full mug at my elbow. Her manic insistence on making tea as a way of repairing the damage done by our argument and my fall made me even more fond of her.

"Sure, Marley." I got up with a groan and followed her into the kitchen, watching as Annabelle busied herself at the sink. When Yasmin came downstairs, Annabelle set two cups on the table and then vanished, giving me a thumbs-up before she faded completely.

"Do you want this? I literally can't drink any more tea but I will never tell Annabelle that." I pointed to my mug. It was yellow and was labeled "Tears of Ohio fans."

Yasmin sat down in what had become her usual spot at the table. She sniffed her mug and then mine. She shrugged and accepted both.

I began, "So, uh—"

At the same time, she said, "I guess we—"

We both paused, then I said, "Look, I'm sorry for what I said the other day."

She played with the lacy hem of her sleeve. She was wearing a blouse that wouldn't look out of place at the Renaissance fair.

"I was mad at Annabelle for rejecting me and I took it out on you. Even though you were basically squatting here without paying rent or utilities, it was immature of me and it wasn't fair to you."

"Thank you for apologizing." She directed her words to the mug in front of her instead of me. "I don't know what went down, but clearly it really hurt you and I'm sorry for that. We both probably could've handled this better."

"Maybe." Sitting across from her, I felt attached to my weird cousin all of a sudden. "But we're Cartwright women, so maybe that's expecting a bit much."

She laughed. "Facts."

We sat comfortably while awkward guitar chords drifted in from the alcove. Sage was trying to learn "Because the Night" on my guitar, but their progress was slow.

"We can still do it, you know," Yasmin said quietly. "The ritual."

I frowned. "But I burned the book."

She rolled her eyes. "Do you honestly think I didn't copy that entire book? I scanned it and hand copied the diagrams. They are backed up to three different types of drives. The Cartwright family grimoire is fully digital now."

"You are something else, you know that?" I said. She frowned, and I added, "I mean that as a compliment."

Yasmin finished one mug of tea and started on the other. "She really didn't want to come back?"

I shook my head.

"I guess it doesn't matter, then."

Annabelle appeared suddenly, seated in the chair between us. Both Yasmin and I jumped, startled, and Yasmin's empty mug knocked over.

Annabelle righted the mug and said, "Let's do it." She looked at Yasmin, then at me, a serious expression on her face. "I'll do the ritual. Just tell me what I need to do."

# Chapter 24

The days in between my fall and the ritual passed in a blur of activity. Yasmin rushed around gathering materials and practicing her magic chants like she was rehearsing for a play. She had a notebook full of scribbles that she consulted, adjusting her glasses and squinting at her own handwriting. She tore off a page and told me to memorize the lines on it. "Can you do that?" she asked. "It has to be perfect."

I scoffed and reminded her of all the lyrics and chords I kept in my brain. Learning a magical chant was nothing compared to the list of places in "I've Been Everywhere."

On the morning of the ritual, Nate, Sage, Adam, and Tyler helped move the furniture in the sitting room out of the way, then rolled up the large rug that had covered the floor. The rug wasn't horribly ugly, but it had at least a decade's worth of stains and dust. Once it was off the floor, I realized how much better the room looked without it. I told Yasmin to have it cleaned instead of throwing it away, figuring it might come in handy if whatever they were going to do ruined the floors. She directed

Nate to take it outside where she'd already scheduled a pickup service. Once dealing with the rug was finished, Yasmin checked the item off her to-do list with a flourish. She was good at this.

Under her direction, Adam and Tyler painted a large circle on the floor with the enthusiasm of kids armed with paint and a forbidden surface. Yasmin painted smaller symbols within the circle herself, using directions from her copy of the grimoire and handwritten notes from the one I'd burned.

I stood in the hallway and watched as my cousin destroyed the hardwood floor of my house. "What do I *do*?"

Miranda took me by the elbow and steered me to the wing-back chair in Annabelle's alcove. "Sit right there, love."

"But what can I do?"

"Do you know your part of the incantation?"

I nodded.

"Good." She looked at me with kindness and fond exasperation. "Then you can sit." She patted my knee and walked away.

All I could do was watch, feeling useless. It felt like waiting for Christmas as a kid, without the surety that at the end of the night, I would receive a gift.

"Are you all right, my dear?"

I jumped, startled at Annabelle's sudden appearance. She was standing at my elbow, halfway embedded in the floor so that her eyes were level with mine.

"Sorry, were you there for a while? I think I might have zoned out a bit," I said.

"I'm here," Annabelle said, not quite answering the question.

"What about you? Are you okay, Marley?"

"I must confess I'm a bit nervous," she said.

"Understandable." I rested my head on the back of the chair

and turned to look at Annabelle as she watched the preparations unfold. A lock of her hair escaped from behind her ear, and for the umpteenth time, I wished I could reach out and touch her, if only to tuck it back.

A lump formed in my throat as I settled back to watch Yasmin boss Nate, Miranda, and the kids around. Miranda playfully squeezed Nate's arm when he muscled an antique side table out of the way, causing him to blush all the way from the V-neck of his shirt to the tip of his hairline. The house, once so empty and silent, seemed full to the brim with life and laughter. The hole in my chest filled with feelings. These people were here for me and Annabelle, not because I had asked, but because they wanted to help.

A cold, ghostly hand gently stroked the back of my neck. Little tingles lit up my sensitive skin in the spots where Annabelle's fingers made contact. I remembered feeling this same sensation my first night in the house. Despite not knowing how I would react to the presence of a ghost, Annabelle had tried to comfort me the only way she could.

"Thanks, Marley," I whispered. "If this doesn't work—"

"It will," she said firmly. "And . . . I know."

~

Timing was crucial. Annabelle was to step into the magically drawn and charged circle exactly at sunset. The ritual would happen hours before the full extent of the eclipse. I assume there were magical reasons that had to do with the mystical properties of sunset versus midnight or whatever, but didn't ask. If it let Annabelle come back sooner, sunset was fine by me.

Yasmin had smeared a dark red liquid on her face and around the circle on the floor. I didn't want to know what it was or if it would stain but I had a feeling it would definitely stain.

Annabelle stood on the edge of the circle, fidgeting as the grandfather clock in the sitting room ticked down the seconds until she was to step forward. Yasmin had three different watches on her wrist and an alarm on her phone to get the timing right, but Annabelle kept her eyes on the old clock. All three of the magic books were infuriatingly vague about what would happen once she entered the circle at sunset on the night of the blood moon.

All Agatha's book said was: "She shall come to be as she no longer was, then shall come thrice more."

At 8:17 p.m., Yasmin clapped loudly. "It's time!"

Miranda, Yasmin, and I stood on the edges of the circle and held hands. We chanted a series of phrases. With her maroon dress and matching overcoat, Miranda looked exactly like a friendly witch you might find living in a cabin in the woods. Yasmin, however, was channeling a more modern version of witchcraft, wearing an off-the-shoulder patterned dress with long bell sleeves and knee-high boots.

Our intoned words bled into each other in my mind, adding an eerie soundscape to the darkness slowly falling on the house. Nate, Sage, Adam, and Tyler watched from the alcove. Tyler filmed the entire thing on his phone but had promised not to narrate.

Finally, it was time.

We stopped chanting and everyone seemed to take an anticipatory breath as we broke apart and allowed Annabelle to step forward into the circle. She looked around, bemused. She held her hands at her sides, twitching her fingers every now and then as if she wasn't quite sure what to do with her hands.

Yasmin grabbed my hand again and squeezed it. "Second

incantation."

"Right." I joined in with Miranda and Yasmin, my mouth slipping on the words I'd boasted about hastily memorizing while my head was still stuffy with painkillers. My ankle throbbed from bearing my weight for the minutes we'd been standing.

For a minute that seemed to hang suspended in time, nothing happened. Then all of a sudden, the energy in the room changed. Annabelle started glowing with a pulsing light. The radiance around her head reminded me of a halo, and I remembered the first time she appeared over my head. I had thought of her as an angel.

"Oh," Annabelle said, looking at her glowing hands.

Yasmin squeezed my hand again, and I realized I had forgotten to keep saying my assigned phrase. I squared my shoulders, ignored my aching body and resumed. Across from me, Miranda's face was a mask of calm.

There was a knocking at the door, but we all ignored it. Annabelle was still glowing, her body becoming brighter and brighter.

In addition to Annabelle's glowing radiance, the circle itself started pulsing with an ominous reddish light. I looked down at my feet. My toes were right on the outer line Yasmin had drawn on the hardwood.

The knocking got louder, turning into a pounding at the door.

"Don't break the circle," shouted Yasmin.

"What the hell is going on here?" Seymour Anderson burst in the door and stood in the entranceway holding a briefcase. He was wearing a Patagonia sweater, khakis, and a bewildered expression. "We had an appointment!"

Yasmin, Miranda, and I ignored him, focusing on the energy swirling through the room and surrounding Annabelle. I vaguely heard Sage shouting and a scuffle as Adam and Tyler tried to shoo Seymour out the door.

The circle was still humming with energy and emitting a bluish light. Yasmin tightened her grip on my hand, and I squeezed Miranda's with my other. Inside the circle, Annabelle looked calm, even as an unnatural wind whipped through the house, tousling her hair and rustling the wide legs of her trousers.

"I'm not sure if it's working, dears," she said. "I don't feel—"

Suddenly, Annabelle's head snapped up. She looked to the ceiling and seemed to see something no one else could. Her expression became puzzled. Like her train had arrived early and she wasn't ready to step onboard.

A bright light appeared over her head, shining down on her golden curls, making them glow fiercely in the dimly lit sitting room. Her face, always pale and shimmery, went translucent, then flickered, briefly into solidity. Her blue eyes opened wide in shock.

"Oh *fuck*," Annabelle said.

She took in a very deep breath, holding it, and flung her arms over her head.

Then she was gone.

# Chapter 25

The circle broke immediately, both literally and figuratively. It no longer seemed to hold any power once Annabelle disappeared. The three of us let go of each other's hands and stared at the center where she'd been, dumbfounded.

"What the hell just happened?" Seymour Anderson was still standing in the doorway, clutching his briefcase. No one answered him.

Yasmin fell to her knees, feeling the circle with her hands. "Where did she go? Did it fail? I can't believe we failed."

"But *something* happened," said Miranda. She looked around the sitting room as if Annabelle was simply hiding behind the television set.

"Will someone please tell me what the hell is going on here?" Seymour demanded from the hallway. Sage was watching the adults helplessly while Adam and Tyler conducted a search for the missing ghost. They ran from the alcove to the kitchen and back, shouting her name.

Nate stepped up, ushering Seymour out of the house with

a firm grip on his arm. I felt an intense rush of gratitude for the dorky electrician's apprentice and the kids, even though I somehow knew they wouldn't find Annabelle.

I stood in the center of the circle where Annabelle had disappeared, trying to sense her, but I couldn't. She was gone.

Yasmin stared at her hands, still smeared with blood. "I don't understand. Everything went to plan. She should be restored. Exactly how she would be if she hadn't—"

I didn't stay long enough to hear the rest of her sentence. I ran out of the house, rushing past Seymour and Nate.

"Gibson!" Sage followed, sprinting after me.

My ankle throbbed and my hip ached but I ran as fast as I could up the lane that led to the road that connected Abaddon with the rest of the island.

I knew exactly where Annabelle was.

~

Low voltage lights lined the pathway to the house. Red-tinged rays of sunset lingered, competing with deepening shadows. Sage caught up to me halfway down the lane to Mike's. "Gibson, where are you going?" they shouted.

I was breathing too hard to form words. All I could do was wheeze, "Annabelle."

In front of Mike's, two of the largest horses I had ever seen were hooked up to an old-fashioned open-air carriage. The whole thing was white, including the seats and even the spokes of the gigantic wheels. There was a Just Married sign with gold lettering attached to the back of the carriage.

Mike approached from the side of the house as Sage and I ran down the lane. He was wearing an old-fashioned top hat and a black suit, complete with a black bowtie.

"Please," I said, putting my hands on my knees and pulling air into my lungs. It felt like knives digging into my chest every time I took a breath, though I wasn't sure if it was from exertion or fear. "I have to get her."

"Whoa, slow down." Mike held out a hand to steady me as I straightened. To Sage, he said, "What's going on?"

Words haphazardly spilled out of Sage. "We did a ritual to try to bring Annabelle back, you know, the ghost from the other night, and I think maybe it worked, but maybe it didn't, and—"

"Annabelle came back and I know exactly where she is, but it'll take me too long to get across the island to her. Please, Mike." I pleaded, not caring if I sounded pathetic. All I knew was that I needed to get to Annabelle's cove and that in my current state, if I walked, it would be too late. "I need your help."

Mike shared a look with Sage, clearly trying to decide if I was nuts. While we talked, the motion sensor light on Mike's garage activating, adding a beam of white to the diffuse light of dusk.

"Please, Dad," they said. "I'll take Joan, and Gibson can ride with me. We need to go get her."

"Absolutely not."

"But—"

Mike held up a hand and looked at me. "You are not riding one of my horses again until you've done at least a week of riding classes."

I took a breath, ready to beg, but he gestured to the carriage. "I just finished a sunset wedding ride, and Britney and Eddie are still hooked up, so we might as well take them."

Sage jumped in the carriage gracefully and held out a hand to help me up. "Thanks, Dad!"

Unexpectedly, I flung my arms around his neck. "Thank

you, Mike."

He smiled, then shook his head. "Life sure has been exciting since you arrived." He took my arm and helped me into the carriage. "Let's go get your ghost."

~

The sun descended slowly while we rode across the island. I simultaneously wished we could hurry and was afraid of Mike losing control if we did. I knew that wouldn't happen with Mike in charge, but couldn't help remembering the sense of falling. Leaning out the side of the carriage and squinting, I told Mike to slow down as we approached.

I hopped out as soon as I could see the mile marker near Annabelle's cove. My ankle protested, but I limped as fast as I could toward the familiar bend in the path. Behind me, Mike was saying soothing words to guide the horses to a stop. Sage had followed behind us on their bike, and the bike's tires skidded on the dirt as they caught up.

Scrambling onto the rocks where I'd seen Annabelle disappear twice, I shouted, "Marley! Are you here?"

Sage followed me onto the rocks. "You think she's out there?"

I nodded, not tearing my eyes away from the choppy water. The wind was gusting, making white foam appear on the surface as waves formed. I had no idea that a lake could have such intense waves.

"She's out here," I said, scanning the water desperately. The horizon was marked by lines of purple and red above the dark blue of the water. "She has to be."

"Why here?" Sage stood next to me and put their hands to their eyes, searching like I was.

"She's connected to this place. I've seen her here before—as an actual ghost, like, a scary one." I swallowed, suddenly terrified that I was too late. Had Annabelle come back to life only to drown again? I tried to shove the possibility from my mind. "This is where she died."

Sage didn't say anything. Their presence next to me on the chilly beach was comforting, even as I started to panic.

After what seemed like ages, I spotted a pale hand sticking out from the dark water. "There!"

Her shoulders and hair were visible now, and it looked like she was conscious, struggling to stay afloat as the waves tossed her around.

"Marley!" I shouted and plunged into the water, not caring about the shock of the cold water seeping through my jeans and into my shoes. I rushed forward, shouting her name and waving.

I kept slipping on the rocks as I got deeper in the water, so as soon as I was in deep enough, I plunged in and did an awkward doggie paddle, keeping my head above the water so I could see Annabelle's waving arms. She did the same, reaching toward me and kicking.

When I finally reached her, she grabbed my hand. It was cold and slimy, but it was Annabelle's hand in mine. Pulling her close, I dragged us both toward the shore, kicking until I could reach the bottom and then awkwardly dragging Annabelle's dead, heavy weight. She was wearing a white gown that was much heavier than it looked and dragged behind her like a fishing net.

We stumbled on the slippery rocks on the little beach. Annabelle was a rag doll, barely able to move herself, and my own coordination was still hampered by my injuries. But I held onto her solid, shivering body, determined not to let her fall.

"It really is her," Sage said, their voice low with awe.

Mike took Annabelle's other arm, helping me keep her upright and holding her steady as she coughed. "We have to take her to the hospital."

"She died over two hundred years ago, Mike. She doesn't have a Social Security card or birth certificate. We can't take her to the hospital."

He frowned.

Annabelle's skin, hair, and gown were gray. She was solid, but looked washed-out, like she just walked out of a black-and-white movie. Her body shook, shivering so hard her teeth clattered. Her lips were as blue as her eyes. She wasn't wearing shoes.

"Marley, can you hear me?" I brushed her dirty, wet hair from her face. Mike, Sage, and I maneuvered her into the carriage. She let us move her, as limp as a rag doll. Once she was seated, I held her tightly, trying to will my body's heat into her. "We're going to take you home. How does that sound?"

Her eyes looked much darker in the light of the moon as it rose. The bloody red color hadn't appeared yet and the eerie light of the early night made her seem fragile. The skin around her eyes was shadowed with dark purple splotches instead of crinkling with smile lines. She looked more hollow than she ever had without a body.

At last, Annabelle spoke. Her voice was raspy and thin. It sounded like every word was dragged painfully out of her throat.

"I'd like some tea, please."

# Chapter 26

I talked to Annabelle nonstop on the ride back to Abaddon. She shivered constantly, shaking in my arms. I talked about the houses we passed and the weather, babbling. The words I said were completely irrelevant to our situation, but I felt like if I stopped talking, none of this would be real. Behind us, the Just Married sign flapped against the back of the carriage. Sage stood up on their bike pedals and pumped their feet furiously to keep up.

Mike expertly positioned the carriage next to Abaddon's front gate, talking softly to the horses from his position in the driver's seat.

"Here we are," he said.

Yasmin stood on the porch, peering out into the not-quite-darkness of the night. The eclipse hadn't started yet, the moon still rising. She ran to the carriage and started to scold me for leaving, with fire in her eyes and furious words halfway out of her mouth. But she stopped when she saw Annabelle in the backseat.

"Oh my god, Annabelle." The fear in her expression turned instantly to worry. Yasmin opened the gate and shouted back at the house, "They're here! Bring us as many towels as you can find."

Mike helped me lift Annabelle down to the ground, dripping wet and wearing a long nightgown that restricted her movement. Yasmin held her arm while I climbed out of the carriage as well, my jeans wet and sticking to my legs. My arms felt empty without her, and I finally felt the cold, my body convulsing in a sudden shiver. Sage arrived and slid off their bike, leaning it against the fence.

"Take her other side, please," Mike said to Sage. He glanced at the giant carriage horses, who were patiently waiting for instruction. "I need to—"

"I got it." Sage helped Yasmin walk Annabelle to the house, supporting her weight and guiding her down the path through the front yard.

"Mike . . ." I turned to him, still shaking, overcome with gratitude. His fancy suit jacket and shoes were wet, and we'd dripped lake water all over the back of his fanciest carriage. "I don't know how to—"

"I don't really get what's happening in this house. Like, at all." He looked at the path that led to Abaddon and shook his head. "But Sage adores you. Adam, too. Whatever this is, just don't let them get attached and then take it away from them." He nodded to the horses. "I need to take Britney Spurs and Eddie Van Horsen back to the stables. Good luck with your ghost. Or, whatever she is now."

I nodded, a lump forming in my throat.

~

When I stepped in the foyer, Annabelle had been covered in blankets from the house, some I'd never seen before. She was holding a steaming mug of tea. Everyone was talking at her while she stared blankly at the liquid as if she hadn't realized she could drink it now. Water dripped on the tile entryway as a puddle formed around her bare feet.

"Let's get you dried off, dear." Miranda gently used a towel to pat her hair, twisting water out of the damp strands. Annabelle started shaking hard enough to make the tea slosh out of the mug, joining the pool of lake water on the tile.

I followed as Miranda and Yasmin slowly led Annabelle up the stairs. Without asking, they took her up to the third floor. When I made it to the landing of the second floor, Sage put a hand on my elbow, holding me back. They pressed a clean towel into my hands and said, "Are you okay?"

"Yeah." I mustered a smile. "Thanks for all your help, Sage."

They nodded.

I continued up the stairs, not at all sure I was okay, but knowing I had to be, for Annabelle.

What if she regretted coming back? What did we do?

Once she made it up to the third floor and into the bath, Annabelle seemed to slowly come awake. She sat on the edge of the claw-foot tub while Miranda rubbed her feet with towels and Yasmin brushed her hair. They said reassuring things, fussing over Annabelle and acting like she was having a day at the spa instead of coming back from a near-drowning.

"There you go, dear," Miranda said, "we'll run you a nice bath, and Gibson will take care of you. Then we'll check on you in the morning." Her voice was calm and soft. I remembered thinking it was cloying when I first arrived, before I built a tolerance to the aggressive kindness of the people here.

"Okay," Annabelle said, staring at me as if she only now realized I was there. She looked a little like a wet cat. A sad ghost sitting on the edge of a claw-foot tub in the house she used to haunt.

Miranda started the bath and left, patting my back as she went.

"Will you two be okay?" Yasmin asked, wringing her hands. "I didn't—I'm sorry, I—"

"We'll be fine, cuz," I said. "Thanks."

"I'll be right downstairs." Yasmin left as well, leaving me and Annabelle alone.

I checked the running water and turned on the cold water tap to bring down the temperature.

"Don't want to warm you up too quickly," I said, finding the silence between us much too loud. "I remember that from . . . something or other."

"Yes, dear." A ghost of a smile played at her lips, which had finally returned to a normal human color.

"Let's, uh, get you out of these clothes." I didn't move to help her out of the nightgown, and she hadn't moved from her seat on the edge of the tub.

All of this was wrong. I'd imagined her without clothes many times. But in my mind, I undid the buttons on her shirt slowly while kissing her neck. Or I ripped the shirt open, laughing as she fussed over the damage.

"Marley? Clothes?"

She started, seeming to come out of a daze. Annabelle looked down at her body and frowned. "This won't do," she murmured, more to herself than me. It was a start.

I turned away while she undressed. When I heard her stand and step into the water, I gathered her soaked nightgown and put it in the sink to deal with later. Knowing Annabelle's love of warmth and comfort, I expected her to sigh as she sank into the warm embrace of the tub, but she didn't. She sat curled into herself, pulling her knees to her chest.

"I'll, um, leave you to it, then," I said, backing away. I didn't want to take my eyes off her, afraid she'd disappear again. "There's soap, and, uh, shampoo and everything if you . . ."

Annabelle held her knees and stared at the faucet. She nodded once.

"I'm not going to close the door." Sinking to the floor on the other side of the bathroom, I said, "I'm right here if you need me, Marley."

As I told her I was there for her, I wondered if she was really here or if this was an echo of her—a shell of the ghost I'd come to know and love.

I sucked in a few breaths and waited to feel a sense of relief. I had gotten what I wanted. Relief didn't come.

On the other side, Annabelle was quiet. Every once in a while, she stirred, the water in the tub sloshing around her. I couldn't stand the thought of her alone in the water—again—but I didn't want to crowd her.

I should've known this would go wrong.

But how could we have known? I trusted Yasmin to do the ritual according to the instructions written by Agatha and the other women in my family, trusting that Agatha wouldn't have set all this up only to harm Annabelle and her successors. But that didn't change the fact that I'd been so excited to have her return that I hadn't stopped to consider the consequences. I knew she had drowned, had seen her with my own eyes on the water, and yet I let Yasmin bring her back to life exactly as she had been when she died—in the depths of Lake Huron.

Closing my eyes, I rested my head against the wall.

Annabelle knew this would happen and she'd gone ahead with the ritual anyway. My chest felt too full, like there was a storm in my ribcage I couldn't calm.

Unable to bear the silence, I started singing the first song that popped into my head. After the second verse of "I'm a Believer," my voice stopped shaking. On the next chorus, I heard a splashing, then Annabelle joined in, her voice raspy and quiet. We finished the song together, and I wiped the tears from my eyes.

"Okay in there?" I asked.

"Yes, I'm . . ." She almost sounded like her usual self. Another splash. "I'm okay. It was very cold. In the lake. I didn't know if I could keep going."

I wished I could see her face. But if talking about it from the other side of a wall was easier for her, I would do that.

"The first time, I struggled, too, even though I was there because I . . . But I let go."

The breath I pulled in was sharp, the sadness I felt for her like a knife in my chest.

"This time I thought, 'Gibson is waiting. She'll find me. And she'll be worried. If I don't keep kicking, she might try to boil water for tea and burn down the house and what good will that do anyone?' It doesn't make sense, but that's what I thought."

"Marley—"

"I kicked and kicked and—I lost my shoes. Maybe I never had them? I don't remember."

Unable to stay on the other side of the wall, I scrambled to my feet and rushed to her. Annabelle wasn't crying, but I was. She turned her face to me, and I held it in my hands, feeling her soft skin and never, ever wanting to let her go.

"I'm here," I whispered. "I'm here."

She took a deep breath, her whole body expanding with it, then smiled a giant, brilliant smile. "I'm really back."

I returned her smile, then sat back on my heels. My drying jeans were chafing against my thighs. "You can use my toothbrush if you want," I said, not sure why that was what came out of my mouth.

She laughed. "I think I'll pass."

I handed her a towel and turned away again as she stepped out of the tub.

"I'll try the paste, though."

"You got it. I'll, uh, get us some clothes." I moved her soggy nightgown from the sink, tossing it on the floor, and left her standing, wearing only a towel.

While I struggled to peel off my own wet clothes and change into dry pajamas, she yelped in surprise. "Oh, it's mint!"

I smiled. "Mint, yeah. Did they have toothpaste in the 1800s?"

"It was powder. And it tasted terrible," came the reply. "Toothpaste is one of the many marvels of the modern world I've never had the occasion to try."

She spit into the sink, rinsed her finger, then ran the tap again. When she emerged from the bathroom, her hair was dark and dripping, but it looked more intentional than it had when she emerged from the lake. Her face was red from scrubbing instead of hypothermia. She looked fresh and a little wild, like a person who'd come in from a long journey away from civilization. In some ways, she had. Now that color had returned to her cheeks, I was again struck by how beautiful she was. Annabelle didn't glow the same way she had before, but her face was no less gorgeous. Her eyes were no less expressive without a ghostly gleam.

And she was only wearing a towel.

My cheeks heating up, I thrust a pair of boxers and a tank top at her and turned around while she changed.

"You can take the bed," I said. Standing side by side in the small room, I realized how Annabelle usually flowed into and around furniture, her ghostly form not taking up space the way a human would. Now that she was here, really here, the small bedroom felt crowded.

"Nonsense, Gibson. We can share." She sat down on the bed and looked up at me expectantly. When I didn't move, she added, "Can't we?"

"Of course." My heart sped up as I looked down at her face, so open and trusting and beautiful. The boxer shorts I'd loaned her were very short, riding up to show her pale, perfect thighs. I took a deep breath. "We can share. Of course we can share."

I mentally scolded myself. She literally just came back from the dead and I wanted to jump her? I took the far side of the bed, scooting all the way to the side so that Annabelle had as much room as possible.

She lay down next to me, her hands next to her sides. "Goodnight, dear."

"Goodnight, Marley." I said it like this was a normal night, as if we could somehow go back to whatever we'd been before. Seeing her hand waving from the water and knowing that she had been plunged into the depths of the lake alone made me ache. It made me angry, too. How was it fair that we found each other but couldn't be together like normal people?

I closed my eyes. The back of my hand was mere centimeters from Annabelle's. Instead of the tingling thrum of ghostly energy, I felt warmth. She was here with me. She was real.

Next to me, Annabelle breathed in and out evenly. She was so close I could feel the rise and fall of her chest and hear her breathing. Neither of us moved. A cool breeze drifted through the window, bringing with it the smell of the night air, and all the possibilities it held.

Slowly, carefully, I turned my hand over and reached for her, palm up.

Annabelle took a deep, halting breath, then I felt her skin, so soft against mine. Our fingers twined. I squeezed her hand tightly.

She held me back.

We both turned to face each other at the same time, and either I kissed her or she kissed me, I wasn't sure, but it didn't matter because finally—*finally*—we were kissing. I held her hand tightly, smashed between our bodies as we moved closer, removing every bit of space between us. Our mouths clashed at first, teeth clicking and lips sliding awkwardly. I didn't care one bit because I was finally kissing Annabelle, *really* kissing her.

We eventually found a rhythm. I tilted my head to one side, and she tilted to the other, and that was all it took for us to fit together perfectly. Annabelle moaned into my mouth and clutched tightly to my waist.

I pulled back and said, "I can stop, Marley—"

She grabbed me, sliding her hand on my waist lower and pulling me forward. "Don't you dare."

"We don't have to do anything," I said. "You're recovering from—and if you want to rest, I don't need to—"

Annabelle raised herself on her elbow, then pushed up to straddle me. She pulled back to look at me, her eyes darker than I remembered ever seeing them. "I do."

"Fuck, yes," I whispered, then any other words I might have had were drowned in a forceful kiss. She held me firmly and thrust her tongue into my mouth. I melted into it. She tasted like mint. Just ordinary toothpaste and spit and Annabelle.

Above me like this, she was in the same position she had been in before, hovering above me as a spirit. But now, her weight pressed me into the mattress, and I felt her soft curves against my body. Feeling her ghostly self above me had been sexy and strange—but this, this drove me wild.

I ran my hands up and down her sides, slipping my hands under her shirt to feel her skin. She made little happy sounds as we kissed, grinding against each other slowly at first, and then with more and more desperate thrusts.

When she pulled back, I nudged her to sit up again and slipped my hand under her shirt, watching her eyes flutter closed. She bit her lip and let out a little moan.

"Clothes off, now," she said.

"Yes, ma'am," I said, half joking, but her expression changed just enough to let me know that she enjoyed hearing it. She took off her shirt, exposing her glorious breasts, and tossed it aside.

She let me up so that I could take my own top and underwear off, then I helped her shimmy out of the boxers I had loaned her. Then she hesitated and looked away. "It's, um." She cleared her throat. "It's just that it's been about two hundred years since I . . ."

I pulled her back into an embrace and kissed her soundly. "I got you, Marley. I won't do anything you don't want."

She let me guide her back down against the pillows, then said, "But I want *everything*."

I grinned. "I'd better get started, then."

Kissing and licking my way down her body, I savored the

taste of her and relished every sigh, moan, and gasp I elicited. I took my time exploring her, doing my best to give her the pleasure she had been denied for so many years, both as a woman in an unhappy marriage and as a ghost, doomed to roam the island without a body.

She sucked in a breath, then cried out, "Oh god." I felt her muscles tense everywhere, then she fell limp, breathing hard. "Oh, wow . . . wow." She kept saying "wow" as I kissed my way back up her body.

"Okay?" I asked, pressing a kiss to her sternum.

She nodded. "Do you want me to, um . . ."

I shook my head, instead guiding her hand between our bodies and showing her where and how to touch me. She watched as I moved back and forth on her hand, finding a rhythm that worked. Keeping eye contact was too intense, so I kissed her and then screwed my eyes shut as I came.

Afterward, we rearranged ourselves, our limbs entwined.

"Will you still be here in the morning?" I whispered, keeping my voice low as if speaking at a normal volume might influence the answer.

"I don't know, darling," she replied as her eyes closed. "Yasmin thinks I can stay the night and on till morning, but Miranda isn't sure. The books weren't specific."

Instead of answering, I kissed her again, and she held me tightly as we both drifted to sleep.

# Chapter 27

As a person with a body, Annabelle snored. Loudly. She also hogged the bed, drooled, and twisted the sheets into a hopeless tangle around her legs. The room was still mostly dark when I woke, but my body's clock told me it was early morning. Despite the chaos of sharing a bed with a former ghost, I felt good. I wouldn't say refreshed, that would be taking things a bit far. But I felt—good. Whole.

My hand was numb from where it was wedged under Annabelle's body, but I left it where it was, resolving to live with pins and needles for as long as necessary to not disturb the beautiful slumbering woman beside me.

Annabelle woke with a start. She swiveled her head around, taking in the morning sun coming in from the bedroom window with wide eyes. Her hair was an unruly mess; it looked like a chaotic blonde cloud surrounding her head.

"Hi," I said. "We missed the eclipse."

"Oh! I was—" She wiped the drool drying on her chin. "I was sleeping."

"That you were." I reached out and tried to smooth the curls on her head, but only succeeded in making certain spots stick up even more. She stared at me, looking confused and beautiful. "How was it?"

"Perfect. I don't really sleep when I . . . normally, I just go away." Annabelle's face dissolved into a smile as she seemed to realize where she was and what had happened. "I dreamed I was a cow." Then she smothered me in kisses.

I ran my hands down her side, savoring the solid feel of her in my bed.

"Oh!" She pulled back, her mouth round with surprise. "Gibson, I . . ."

"Everything okay?"

She looked amazed and excited. "I . . . need to use the toilet! I haven't had to do that in so long."

"Perils of owning a body, Marley," I replied, chuckling. "Comes with pros and cons."

I stretched my arms and legs while Annabelle used the bathroom, shaking out morning stiffness and feeling all the aches I still had from my brush with equine disaster. Glancing down at my naked body, I grimaced at the bruises that had turned from bright purple to a sick green color. They painted my right side like a canvas splashed with the worst colors in a watercolor set. My ankle was back to its usual size but still bruised and stiff. I wasn't exactly at my sexiest, but thankfully Annabelle hadn't seemed to mind. I marveled at the fact that although she had seen the worst of me, she still came back to be with me.

In the bathroom, Annabelle spit into the sink, then ran the tap for a while longer. She hummed a little tune while she washed up, and though I couldn't see her, I could picture the way her hips would move along to the music in her head. I'd seen her do it several times, swaying in the kitchen while making me coffee, or as she sliced onions to add to a dish for dinner. I loved her nonsense songs and her terrible dancing. I—

Oh shit, I really did love her.

Annabelle peeked her head out the bathroom door but otherwise kept it shut. Her curly hair had been tamed with water and her face glistened, freshly washed.

"Gibson, I have a problem."

I did too, I thought. I was in love with a woman who might disappear any minute.

"Yeah? What's your problem?" I said out loud.

"I'm starving!" She pouted, sticking her lower lip out as far as it would go. "And I don't have any clothes!"

She crossed her arms over her chest to try to cover herself, but it just emphasized the shape of her breasts. She did a little awkward jog before jumping back in bed and covering herself with the sheets. Her chest and thighs jiggled a little as she hopped into bed, and it was the best thing I had seen in recent memory.

I couldn't help the grin that spread on my face. "I don't see a problem with that second thing."

And it was so easy, then, to kiss her. It felt entirely natural to take her in my arms, to lay her down and worship her. Between Annabelle's thighs, while she grabbed the sheets with one hand and my hair with the other, I was home.

~

We cobbled together an outfit for Annabelle since all she had was a nightgown from the 1800s. My shirts were too tight for her. I didn't mind this at all, but she didn't find them comfortable enough to wear, so she picked one of Yasmin's flowy white blouses. It was so similar to what she usually wore in her ghost state that I did a double take when she emerged from Yasmin's closet with it on. Nate's jeans were approximately the right size, and my shoes were a fit.

"Ta-da!" Annabelle did a little twirl when she'd assembled her outfit for the day.

I smiled but said, "I'll take you shopping if you want, Marley."

She clapped her hands together and said, "Yes, please." We both ignored the fact that she wouldn't need to keep them for long.

Annabelle insisted on making breakfast. She relished the turn of every knob on the stove and she couldn't resist sticking her fingers in the scrambled eggs just to feel the gooey mess on real fingers instead of ghost ones. At the table in our usual chairs, our legs pressed together, and she played footsy with me.

She looked so satisfied eating buttered toast that I flushed, recognizing the face she'd made last night. To distract myself from Annabelle's orgasmic breakfast bliss, I checked my notifications, then wished I hadn't. Seymour Anderson filled my email inbox and my texts with increasingly unhinged pleas for a response. That wasn't a surprise since I had ghosted him and then he walked in on an occult ritual in the house he was trying to buy. The text I didn't expect to see was from Babs.

"Saw the band last night. Not as good w/out u. New song sucks. Hope ur well, call me when ready for more work, there's a shit ton."

I started typing a long response about Brooke, the band, my new song and how I needed to take a break from the scene since I hadn't found a place in it, then erased it all. "All good here but wont be back for a little while, not sure when. Will call soon."

Brooke texted a few times, asking if I was okay and then giving me shit when I didn't reply. I stopped my thumb before I could swipe over to Instagram or YouTube to watch the band play without me. They weren't my band—they never had been. For years, I wanted to belong with them. But being on this stupid island put me together with a bunch of new weirdos who, like it or not, gave me a place to belong. And it made me write my own song. It wasn't finished yet, but it was mine.

"Oh good, you're here. I have an idea," Yasmin announced as she entered the kitchen. She looked refreshed and relaxed, with her ever-present notebook of ideas in her hand. "But you need to leave."

Annabelle looked affronted. "Excuse me? I just got here!"

"What I mean is, Gibson, you take Annabelle out for the day. Go see the world outside this house."

I put a hand on Annabelle's shoulder, and she laced her fingers through mine. "I did promise you a day out, you know. And I think you wanted to play games on my phone?"

She laughed. "That seems less important now."

"It's settled." Yasmin herded us toward the foyer. "You guys go have a day, and when you get back, we'll have a feast. I will cook for you to make up for all the meals you cooked for us."

I squinted at Yasmin as she shoved me out of my house. "Can you cook? Have you ever cooked for us? Is this your sneaky way of getting rid of me? Through poison?"

Annabelle swatted me. Both of us were surprised when she actually made contact—she hit harder than I expected her to, and I rubbed my arm.

"Ow," I said. "I'm just kidding. Dinner sounds nice."

Yasmin shut the door behind us, saying, "Do not come back to this house until six thirty!"

Annabelle and I looked at each other and shrugged. I took her hand as we walked down the front porch stairs and into the front yard.

"So, Marley, the island is your oyster. What do you want to do?"

~

The clothing stores on Mackinac Island did not live up to Annabelle's standards, but the fudge shops exceeded them. When we arrived at the third T-shirt shop, the former ghost actually stamped her foot in protest of the quality of the wares inside. The stores were full of mass-printed goods made overseas stamped with same-looking logos on brightly colored jumpers and shirts. I held up a bright orange vest with a stylized anchor to her chest to check the size, and the look she gave me made me think I was in danger of being slapped.

We found a store inside a resort that sold overpriced clothes to visiting golfers, and Annabelle sighed. "Finally, something that isn't horrid."

I walked around the shop with my hands shoved in my pockets, trying to look like I belonged there. I didn't.

After trying on half a dozen outfits, Annabelle found one that satisfied her. I enjoyed watching her try on clothes but didn't enjoy ponying up two hundred bucks for her final choices. She picked out a jumpsuit in a shade of cobalt blue that perfectly accented her eyes. And it was low-cut enough to perfectly accent her cleavage. I handed over my credit card and laughed as she tried on a series of increasingly ridiculous-looking pairs of sunglasses from the rack next to the counter. But the smile on her face as we left the store, her old clothes in the shopping bag on my arm, made the injury to my wallet hurt less.

With Annabelle properly outfitted, I followed her lead as we wandered the island, my hand never leaving hers.

She made friends at three fudge shops, talking with the owners and tourists alike. Annabelle smiled and laughed easily. Even while dead, she seemed to exude a natural charm that was heightened now that she was out in the world of the living. She touched everything she could, feeling the textures of knitted scarves for sale and poking her finger in her square of fudge. I touched her every chance I got, trying not to think about how short the time we'd have together in the real world would be.

"Bicycles," she said as we passed a rack stuffed with at least twenty of them in all different sizes. "So many bicycles."

"Do you want to ride one?" I asked. "I bet Sage would let you borrow theirs."

We were only a block away from the small office where customers went to book Mike's horseback rides and carriage tours.

"Oh, no." She held up her hands and physically backed away from the row of bikes like they were snakes ready to strike. "No thanks. I'd rather ride that lovely lady." She pointed to a woman riding a brown-and-white horse. It was bigger than Medium Sebastian but smaller than Sage's horse Joan. "But I don't want *you* anywhere near a horse."

I shrugged. "Suit yourself." I grabbed her hand, shifting her shopping bag to my other arm. "This is your day."

Her smile was as bright as the sun overhead.

We took a series of selfies at the beach, then I took a dozen photos of Annabelle posing by herself. She marveled at the giant bridge in the background while the wind whipped her hair and the sun kissed her cheeks. In the bright daylight, I noticed that she had a little cluster of pale freckles across her nose.

I offered to trudge up the hill to the fort, but she shook her head.

Shading her eyes, she scrunched her nose and regarded the imposing white building. "It looks basically the same as it did then. Let's get lunch."

While we walked up the hill to the Grand Hotel, Annabelle pointed out the flowers and native plants she saw. Her knowledge was a combination of experience with the island before it saw a burst of development during the Victorian era and many years afterward in which all she had for company was botany books. She was delighted by the Secret Garden and the view from the porch at the hotel. The stuffy formal atmosphere of the place made my skin crawl. But Annabelle, who was beautiful and looked gorgeous in her new clothes, fit right in, so I followed her as she admired the architecture and furnishings of the old-fashioned resort.

I nudged her in the direction of the lunch buffet, self-conscious of my casual attire. But I needn't have worried because ahead of us in line was a group of at least twenty tourists in cargo shorts and sweat-stained shirts. What I could see of the main dining room looked fancy as fuck, and I wanted to see Annabelle's reaction to it. She could finally sip tea in a setting that was worthy of her.

But after twenty minutes standing behind the tour group, my feet ached and my stomach growled.

Annabelle took my hand and led me back outside, past the line that had formed behind us.

"But, Marley, you wanted to have tea," I protested.

She shook her head. "I wanted to have tea, yes, but I'd be just as happy to have it with you in the kitchen, sitting on worn-out old chairs and drinking out of cheap mugs."

I smiled, wondering if she would ever believe me when I

said I didn't like tea.

~

We searched for it but couldn't find where Annabelle's father was buried in the Post Cemetery. Most of the graves from that era in the island's history weren't marked, and Annabelle couldn't remember the exact location. We didn't talk much as we wandered through the stone markers. Annabelle's face was serious but not pained. She walked through the cemetery, lightly touching the headstones, lost in thought. I let her be.

After half an hour of wandering through the plots, Annabelle nodded and said, "Thank you for taking me here. I'm ready to go."

I took her hand as we left through the iron cemetery gates. We passed the sign for Fort Holmes, but she didn't react one way or the other, so I let her lead me through the island's lush interior paths. We climbed up the steep steps to Point Lookout. Sweat stuck to my back and dripped from my elbows as we climbed. At the top of the small hill, we could see the weird rock formations that dotted the island, surrounded by dense green forest. Beyond, the water went from jewel green to stripes of brilliant blues that led up to the horizon, where the sky met it with its own shades of blue.

Annabelle breathed in deeply, turning her face to the sky. She reached for me, and I pulled her into a hug from behind, looping my arms around her neck.

"Are you ready to go home?" she asked.

"Yes." The question was as complicated as it ever had been. The answer was simple and clear.

# Chapter 28

Since Annabelle vetoed my bicycle suggestion and I didn't dare suggest a horseback ride, we walked back to Abaddon. We made it slightly ahead of Yasmin's six thirty deadline. I opened the gate and held it for Annabelle.

The smell of something delicious filled the house. We stepped up to the porch, but just as I opened the door and Annabelle started to walk through it, Yasmin appeared, wearing an apron that said "Witch, Please."

"You're early!" She pointed back out the way we came. "Out till six thirty!"

"But—" I poked my head in and sniffed, detecting the aroma of roasting vegetables.

Miranda appeared from inside the kitchen, also wearing an apron that looked like an immaculate addition to her elegant pantsuit. "We're eating outside. Why don't you two go around the house." She herded us back out the door but made it seem polite somehow.

I shrugged and guided Annabelle around the side yard. She

let me put my arm around her waist, and we walked side by side past the wood pile to the back garden, where a small crowd had formed.

Adam spotted us first. He raised his arms in the air and shouted, "There they are!"

Annabelle's mouth dropped open. "What's all this?"

In the backyard, Rebecca and Sara chatted with Pete, who looked as grumpy and strange as ever. Mike and Sage were on the lawn, setting up yard games, while Adam and Tyler watched. Nate emerged from the kitchen door with plates and utensils, which he set on the outdoor table. They had moved the kitchen table outside next to it and put every chair in the house around the two tables.

"Oh my gosh, you really are here!" Rebecca squealed. She bustled over to me and Annabelle, leaving Sara to finish her conversation with Old Pete.

I reintroduced Rebecca as the person who gave me an excellent haircut.

She was giddy at the prospect of meeting a ghost come to life. "I love ghosts. I watch those paranormal reality shows all the time. *Ghost Hunters*? Love it."

Annabelle's expression fell. "Hunters?"

"Oh my gosh, I'm so sorry. I didn't mean that as offensive to your kind."

"I don't think I have a kind. I'm just me."

As we talked, Sara extracted herself from Pete and joined us. I reintroduced her as the lead singer of the Thursday-night jam band at Helga's. Sara peered at Annabelle, squinting. She crossed her arms and said, "Hmm."

Rebecca stage-whispered, "She's having a hard time with the whole ghost thing."

"I'm not convinced this isn't a mass hallucination," Sara said. She got an elbow in the side from her wife and added, "But in any case, it's nice to meet you properly. We brought brownies." Sara pointed at a platter on the table.

Annabelle smiled. "Thank you for coming. I've never had a brownie." She peered at the brown mass but didn't seem eager to try it.

From the grass, Mike let out a shout as Sage completed a tricky frisbee catch.

"Is that—was he here? Last night?" Annabelle asked.

"Yes, that's Mike," I said. "He helped me get you home."

She nodded, her expression reserved. "I see." She approached Mike and Sage, clasping her hands behind her back nervously. They spent a few minutes talking, solemn looks on their faces, and then the mood shifted. Adam and Tyler showed Annabelle how to toss a beanbag into the hole of the cornhole board, and she joined their game, cheering everyone's tosses regardless of who was on which team.

I stood at the railing and watched. Pete thrust a low-quality beer in my hands, mumbled something, and then wandered off.

After a few rounds of increasingly competitive cornhole games, Yasmin emerged from the house. She clapped her hands and announced, "Dinner time! Everyone, come eat!"

We all found places around the tables. Everyone made sure I sat next to Annabelle, and that she had the best seat, next to the food.

Yasmin clinked her fork on her mug. "Before we eat, I'd like to say a few words." She launched into a witchy prayer that mentioned the earth and the moon so many times I lost count. When she got to the parts about healing energy, I zoned out. But Annabelle held my hand under the table, and my leg brushed against hers, so although my stomach growled, I was content. Finally, we ate.

The food was delicious. Yasmin and Miranda, with Nate's help, had made roasted chicken and vegetables, mashed potatoes, pasta salad, and asparagus. Mike supplied biscuits from a can and sodas for the kids. Miranda told us her lemon bar recipe was so famous it had won awards in the 1970s. Conversation flowed freely, with Annabelle fitting in among the strange ensemble perfectly. The kids had spent time before the ritual peppering Annabelle with questions, so now it was Mike and the Johnsons' turn. She told them stories about the island before the United States regained it, describing how people at the fort and in the small town survived the harsh winters and fondly recalling the gatherings of Anishinaabe fur traders that arrived with the seasons.

Eventually, scrutiny returned to me. Mike asked, "What about the house? I thought you got an offer on it."

Yasmin studied her nails.

I sighed. "Seymour Anderson gave me an offer, yes. But he also . . . walked in at an awkward moment while we were bringing Annabelle back. His offer went down by a million because he says the property is cursed, and I have a feeling that's an insult, given how much the Montclair property went for."

Mike frowned. "That's ridiculous. Shouldn't he be raising his offer to get you on board? You're the one with the house. Does he want it or not?"

"He doesn't want the house; he wants the land. Besides, it's a haunted dump," Pete said.

We all looked at Pete, aghast. "It is!" The strange old man cleared his throat. "Electrical aside. And that doesn't mean it has to stay that way."

Miranda clucked her tongue, and the rest of the group looked everywhere but me.

"Pete's right. To make Abaddon into a home, you'd have to do *so* many things." I shrugged. "I don't even know what all you'd need to do. Decorating? Drywall? Yeesh." I remembered my vision of the garden as a gathering place, full of people and life. The impromptu party Yasmin had thrown was close to being what I imagined, but not quite.

"Besides, no one wants to live in a haunted house," Annabelle said. "Witches aside, of course." She added a smile, but no one else did.

There was a moment of silence. It was broken by Adam, who spoke around a mouth full of mashed potatoes. "That's not true! People love haunted houses. Otherwise, why would they make a whole ride at Disneyland?"

We all laughed, but what he said stuck with me. The vision of the garden hadn't left my mind the whole night—it juxtaposed itself on top of reality in a way that was confusing but felt, strangely, comfortable.

Maybe I was just a witch late bloomer. The spells that Yasmin learned at four might come to me when I got to Miranda's age.

I turned to Nate and asked, "Could you put up string lights? Maybe out into the garden?"

He stroked his chin. "Of course. Might take me an hour or two, though." He craned his head back to see the electrical panel he'd worked on with Old Pete, then started mumbling to himself.

I laughed. "Not right now, man. But someday."

~

After dinner, Sage hooked up their Bluetooth speakers, and we cleared a space on the deck large enough for a makeshift dance floor. The kids did TikTok dances to songs that were popular when I was their age, and they dissolved in giggles when Miranda and Pete tried to imitate the moves.

Sage's playlist included a song that I instantly recognized as Call Me Kate Kane by Ivan's bassline and Brooke's scratchy vocals, but I didn't know it.

"What is this?" I asked. Sage showed me their phone—it was a new single, the one they released with Stephani on guitar instead of me. "Huh."

Sage took their phone back. "It's not terrible, but it's definitely not my fave."

I expected to feel angry or jealous. But I gazed at Annabelle and the people gathered on my porch and felt nothing but contentment. "Yeah, it's catchy. Pop. Not their usual style."

Sara and Rebecca Johnson swayed in an approximation of dancing for three songs, looking into each other's eyes and sighing. Then they left for the night, taking Tyler home. Soon after, Mike, Adam, and Sage departed, leaving me with Old Pete and the weird people I'd started to think of as family. Miranda, Yasmin, and Nate gathered around the table, nursing beverages. Annabelle and I joined them.

"What do you think is going to happen tomorrow? Will you go back to being a ghost?" Nate asked, his fingers intertwined with Yasmin's on top of the table.

She kicked him.

"Sorry."

Annabelle smiled, her usual mask back in place. "It's a good question, Nate. When Agatha and I discussed it, she wasn't sure if I would return to the world as I was or if I would . . . dissipate."

"Dissipate?" Pete echoed. "You were a ghost. Now you're not a ghost."

Annabelle nodded.

Nate picked up the thread from there. "But it's only for last night and today, then you'll dissipate? Why would a ghost dissipate after being real and getting a girlfriend?"

He looked at me and Yasmin for answers. She looked away, and my vision unfocused, my mind replaying the word "girlfriend" over and over.

"I think," Annabelle said, "that whatever happens tomorrow, I will be grateful for my time here. And grateful to all of you for summoning me." She looked around the tables, where we'd squeezed nine adults, three kids, and a giant spread of homemade food and dessert.

"If you're supposed to haunt this place, then wouldn't you keep haunting it?" Nate asked. He looked at the back of the house as if he expected to see a sign, something that made it obvious Abaddon Cottage was not a normal house. "I'm new to this ghost business, but . . . why would anything have to change if your spirit is still tied to the house?"

"It wasn't the house that brought me back to life, dears." Annabelle folded her hands on the table. She had tucked a napkin into her jumpsuit top to avoid getting crumbs all over it. She looked ridiculous with the napkin sticking out. I loved her so much I ached with it.

Annabelle continued. "At first, being a ghost was very confusing." She spoke as if she was telling someone else's story, not her own. "I wandered the fort for a long time, scaring the dickens out of people. I'm not proud to admit it, but at times, I enjoyed being spooky!"

She smiled and waved her hands in the air, making "boo"

sounds.

"But mostly I wandered the forest where I wouldn't scare anyone. I also didn't want to get attached. People used to die much earlier. This place, where this house was built, was a lovely meadow that made me happy. I felt it was where I was supposed to be, so I stayed. Eventually, a house was built here, and I found myself unable to leave it. I'm not sure why I came out of the lake when I should have moved on, but it must be part of a plan that I simply do not understand."

"A plan?" I scoffed, then remembered to be kind. "Sorry, Marley, but I just have a hard time with the idea that everything in life is preordained."

"What else am I to think, dear? That I'm a cosmic clerical error?"

I didn't have an answer to that. The adults around the table examined their drinks.

Yasmin wrung her hands. "I wish I could predict what would happen tomorrow. It seems like I should be able to, but . . . Maybe my mom could—"

Annabelle put her hand on Yasmin's shoulder. "You've done great, Yas."

"You can't know everything, dear," Miranda said. She looked directly at Pete and said, "Life is supposed to surprise you." To Annabelle, she said, "And death, I suppose."

I grabbed one of the terrible beers. "I'll drink to that."

We toasted, then Annabelle said, "I don't care." She stood and took the napkin out of her shirt collar, putting it down on the table with an air of finality. "I have an hour or so left before the moon returns to its place and whatever is slated to happen happens."

She gathered the empty plates and headed inside. I followed

her.

Annabelle washed the dishes. I stood next to her and started rinsing them, trying not to cry. In the bottom of the sink, the dishes shifted and I heard a delicate crack. I carefully pulled out the angel wings mug from the bottom of the pile. The point where the wings jutted out from the mug had broken, leaving one dainty wing hanging off.

"Well, that's a bit on the nose. I mean, honestly." A few tears escaped my eyes, and I wiped them, trying not to fall apart entirely. "If this is all the time we have . . ."

Annabelle wrapped her arms around me, soapy hands dripping on my shirt, and buried her face in my neck. "I don't think it is."

"But if it is—"

"No, darling, I don't think so. Though I wish I could've taken you up to Sunset Rock. The view is stunning." She hugged me even tighter.

"But what if it is? What if you cross to the other side, and it's all because I was selfish and—"

Annabelle loosened her hold on me so she could turn me around in her arms. "Gibson, listen to me. If this is all we had, then I'm grateful. I've had far more time to enjoy the beautiful things in the world than most. And even if all I had was this short time with you, then—"

I closed my eyes and held still while she raised up on her toes to kiss me, lightly, on the forehead.

"Then it was time well spent," she whispered. "I want you to live the rest of your life fiercely. Without regrets. Even if I can't be here with you, we'll have had these moments and, my darling, you won't ever be alone."

Fresh tears fell and she kissed them away.

I felt a desire, then, to protect this place and the people here who had helped me even when I didn't want to be helped. Annabelle kissed me again, more firmly this time.

"I'm still here," she said. "Let's make the most of the time we have."

I let her lead me upstairs. Annabelle closed the bedroom door behind us. She took off the jumpsuit I bought her and hung it up in the wardrobe carefully. Then she helped me pull off my clothes. We didn't speak. The moon rose over the bedroom at the top floor of Abaddon Cottage, and this time it cast a pale silver light instead of a burned red.

We went slow, touching and kissing tenderly until we couldn't take it anymore, and then we didn't go slow at all.

I let sleep take me, drifting away as Annabelle whispered nonsense in my ear and kissed the sweaty hairs on the back of my neck. The soft, human smell of her accompanied me into the darkness of dreams.

When I woke up in the small hours of the night, I was alone.

# Chapter 29

Nate spread too much jam on a piece of toast, and some of it plopped off the bread onto his plate. The kitchen smelled like coffee and warm bread. It seemed smaller than it had a week ago when I entered alone, grimacing at the dust and old appliances. Dust still crept into the crevices, and there were still a few unlabeled jars in the back of the cupboards. But the coffeemaker was burbling happily, and there were enough dishes in the sink to indicate an entire family lived in the house.

Surprisingly, I was calm when I entered the kitchen. I moved slowly, still sore and not sure how to feel about everything that had happened the previous day and night. I took a mug that said "Grab life by the beans" from the cupboard and poured myself a cup of coffee from the pot. Neither Nate nor Yasmin seemed to know what to say, so they didn't say anything at all. Nate got up and put a piece of bread in the toaster for me.

I sat down at my spot at the table. Annabelle wasn't there. I didn't know if she would come back or if she *could* come back.

"I'm not leaving." I pointed at Yasmin. "You're not either. I think I know how we can make this work."

Yasmin opened her mouth and then closed it, looking like a confused fish.

I shook my head. "Wait—I said that wrong. Do you want to leave Abaddon? Go back home to California?"

Nate busied himself at the toaster, making enough noise that we didn't forget he was there but not enough that it intruded into the conversation. Yasmin's gaze flicked to him before she answered, saying, "No. I don't want to leave."

I spied a smile playing at the corners of Nate's mouth as he buttered the toast that popped out of the toaster.

"Good. You're going to draft the business plan. I set up a meeting with Seymour Anderson to see if he'll fund us, but if he doesn't, I think my boss Babs might have some connections with a morally dubious venture capital firm."

"Wait, slow down. Funding for what?"

I grinned. "You know what they say, if you can't get along with your family, start a business with them."

"No one says that." Yasmin played with the lacy sleeve of her blouse, then undid the button at her wrist and stuck her finger through the buttonhole. "And I can't write a business plan no matter what the business is. I've never done anything like that."

Putting every ounce of sincerity I was capable of into my voice, I said, "Yas, out of the millions of people on planet Earth who might be able to write a business plan, I trust you to be the most capable and most annoying about doing so. Plus, Nate will help."

Nate set my toast down on the table, then stood behind Yasmin and put a supportive hand on her shoulder. "Heck, yeah, babe. Owning a small business is hot."

"You don't even know what Gibson is proposing." Her voice was withering, but fond.

Nate shrugged.

"Oh, good morning, folks. What's this about a business?"

Annabelle appeared in her spot at the table, mostly visible and fully dressed in her usual blouse and flowy trousers. She was wearing house slippers and a very bright smile on her not-quite-solid face.

I held out my hand, palm up, and she placed hers carefully on top of it. "Glad you made it back, Marley."

"Me too, Gibson, me too."

~

Seymour Anderson met me at an airy coffee shop on the bay that also doubled as an art studio. We sat in homey chairs and watched half-million-dollar boats go by.

I apologized for giving him the runaround and blowing off our deadline, explaining my fall from a horse and exaggerating my injuries to make it sound like that was the main reason for my delay. Then I took a deep breath and launched into my pitch. When I practiced with Annabelle, she listened with rapt attention, making encouraging noises and googly eyes at me. Which had been nice but didn't really prepare me for Seymour's furrowed brow and serious businessman face.

The pitch ended with, "I know it was rather strange for you to walk in on what looked like an occult ritual, and I apologize for the timing. But my spiritual advisor insisted that the lunar eclipse was the only time we could embrace the spirits in the house and turn the negative energy into a welcoming presence for guests."

He pursed his lips while I said this but didn't immediately

get up and leave, which was a good sign.

"It's not that *I* believe in this stuff, of course," I continued, with a gee-whiz shrug of my shoulders, "but after spending time in the house, I can see how *others* might. And I think we have a real opportunity to cater to a niche audience: bored rich people who want to believe in the supernatural. There are plenty of places on the island to get a standard Victorian revival bedroom or a soulless modern suite. But where else can you get a room with a ghost?"

He was extremely polite the entire time. But it was clear that all he was interested in was the land under my cottage's foundation and he thought I was insane. He implied that Miranda put me up to the whole thing, saying she had a corrupting influence on the year-rounders. I smiled and let him pay for the coffee.

His loss.

~

While walking back to the cottage, my phone rang.

Brooke's picture came up on the screen, and I almost pressed the red dismiss button to end the call. What did I have to say to her? "Thanks for not being my girlfriend and thanks for not letting me in the band we both considered family?" Nope.

But something made me take the call. Maybe the wind or the view of the Round Island Lighthouse or whatever.

I answered. "Hey, what's up?"

On the other end, I heard the sound of traffic and people shouting in New York at each other. A powerful wave of nostalgia hit me. To gird myself against it, I conjured a memory of the odor of Penn Station.

"Oh my god, hi." Brooke sounded breathless, like she was walking fast or had smoked too many pretentious cigarettes the night before. "I just . . . there's been a lot going on, and I hadn't heard from you since the show and . . ."

"Yeah." There was a lot in that "yeah," and we both knew it.

"I'm sorry," Brooke said. "I really am. You know that, right? Like, I think I depended on you more than I actually wanted to be around you? And that's not right. Right?"

I laughed. "No, it's not. And yes, I understand what you mean. I think I had an idea about what we could be . . . and that needed to change. It took me coming out here and you booting me from the periphery of the band for me to get that."

There was a loud honk and a profanity-laden screed from the other end. "Sorry about that, I'm going inside, hold on."

I heard the muffled sound of Brooke putting the phone against her shirt and then the chime of a bell ringing and the background hum of an espresso machine.

She picked up again, laughing. "See, the fact that you use the word 'periphery' when I'm just talking to you casually is, like, we are not the same."

I laughed with her, walking away from downtown past the row of picturesque bed-and-breakfasts. Bikes and horses joined me on the road, but I realized I was used to their presence now. Even the clop-clop of a giant draft horse coming up from behind didn't bother me. The spire of Ste. Anne's Church pierced the bright blue sky, and I headed toward it.

"How's Stephani?"

Brooke sighed. "She's good. Like, so good. And I think she gets the direction the company wants us to take."

"Company? Wait, did you get a deal?"

I could hear the grin on Brooke's face when she said, "Yeah, man! You really haven't been online, have you?"

"No, sorry. I've been . . . dealing with other stuff. Congrats." I looked up at the beautiful white building of the church, feeling genuinely happy for Brooke and the band I'd tried so hard to join. "That's really great."

"Thank you." Brooke sounded relieved. "It's a lot to deal with. I think Stephani will be a good collaborator. We're in the same microgeneration, you know? She understands where I'm coming from when I make references from 2009."

I rolled my eyes but chose kindness. "I get it."

The grin crept back in her voice as she said, "So, did you hook up with someone there? I hope you did."

"I mean . . ." I was grinning, too.

"You totally did, you slut!"

I laughed. "She's . . . quite a bit older." I paused, then added, "Than me."

"Fuck yeah! Get it, Gibson." After a moment of pleasant silence, the ambient sounds of a city coffee shop from her end and the wind whistling through trees on mine, she said, "Are we okay?"

I thought about my answer, then said, "I was pissed at you. But yeah, I think this will work out."

"I'm so glad. I was dreading this conversation, if I'm honest."

Before a week ago I would have too. But so much had happened that the anxiety and desire and jealousy I felt whenever I thought about Brooke had dissipated like morning fog.

"We're okay," I repeated. "I'm happy for you and the rest of the band."

I walked around the grounds of the old church, wondering if Annabelle had seen a similar view of the building when she was alive. While I wandered, Brooke chattered about the record deal that the band was deliberating over.

"Have I told you that they want six new songs? Which is, like, doable, but we can't decide on a place to go write because Ivan is being a little bitch and Stephani is super insecure as the newest member, so she's zero help. I'm like, guys, can we just go to New Jersey or something?"

"How much did you say they're giving you to write and record?"

She named a ridiculous sum of money.

A new grin spread across my face as inspiration struck. "Does everyone in the band have a winter coat?"

"Uh, yeah, I think so."

I paced, already making plans in my head. "And is anyone allergic to horses?"

"Not that I know of. Gibson, what are you talking about?"

I left the churchyard, stopping to allow a horse-drawn carriage to pass by before turning my feet toward home. To get there, I would pass through residential neighborhoods, swanky old-fashioned resorts, and wild forest. Next to my house was Mike's property, which would be empty of horses during the winter when the herd went to Pickford to fatten up and prepare for next year's tourist season. I pictured his garage, where he kept thousands of dollars' worth of dormant music equipment.

"Hear me out, Brooke, I have an idea. Could you get the company to pay for a flight to Michigan? And is anyone in the band deathly afraid of ghosts?"

# Chapter 30

*Seven months later*

Helena Cartwright arrived in early spring, about a month before the wedding, when most businesses on Mackinac weren't yet open for the season. Yasmin was simultaneously a complete wreck and totally in her element. I stayed out of the wedding plans, letting her, Annabelle, and Miranda handle things like dresses, tuxes, a gender-neutral option for me and Sage, flowers, speeches, and the guest list. I would never tell her, but one of the happiest moments in my life was when she asked me to be in charge of the music.

Nate and I escorted Yasmin's mother to Abaddon from the airport, where she'd arrived on a private flight instead of waiting for the thaw that would allow the ferry to start for the season. After looking Nate up and down, she greeted him warmly.

To me, she said, "Darling, you look just like your mother, and I'm going to pretend that I'm okay with that until we can talk."

I nodded, and we resumed our walk back to the cottage.

Once there, she immediately told Yasmin everything she thought was wrong about our soft launch plan, the website, the curtains, my hair, Yasmin's hair, our logo, and the house in general. My hair was in an awkward almost-to-the-chin stage while I decided whether to grow it into a mohawk, so she was correct about one thing.

After touring the house and garden, inspecting the guest rooms carefully, and surveying the back deck where the reception would be held, Yasmin showed her mother to her room. I couldn't hear their conversation, but when Yasmin returned downstairs, her eyes were red and puffy.

"Okay?"

She nodded. "Hard but necessary conversation." She sighed and wiped her eyes, then said, "Why is growing up so hard?"

"I wouldn't know since I've never done it."

She laughed. The next few days with Helena in the house were easier but not easy. She clashed with Yasmin over small details and had an infuriating habit of siding with anyone's opinion except her daughter's. The only thing that made the situation tolerable was the fact that she also adored Nate. I resolved to throw her out of my house if she didn't approve of the good-natured electrician.

Helena's relationship with Annabelle was equally fraught. Somehow, my aunt had a sixth sense about her, making it impossible for the ghost to sneak around her or appear without warning. She followed Annabelle from room to room, asking her metaphysical questions and seeming to know she was there even when she was invisible.

"It's impossible, Gibson," Annabelle whispered to me a day before the ceremony, while she and Yasmin were having a mother-daughter spa day. "She won't let me—"

"Sneak up on people?"

Annabelle huffed, then proving my point, disappeared.

~

Yasmin Cartwright and Nate Phillips were married in a beautiful ceremony at Mackinac's famous gazebo. Yasmin was gorgeous in her flowy black dress; Nate cried the entire time. Yasmin's brothers, standing in a stoic line behind Nate, kept their composure long enough to see their sister down the aisle, but started sniffling when the vows began. Nate's mother and sister never once stopped smiling, overcome with joy even when there were no cameras in sight to capture their happy faces.

Throughout the ceremony, I longed to hold Annabelle's hand. She still couldn't leave the house without fading, but Adam volunteered to be the wedding filmographer. He pointed his phone screen at the happy couple and live-streamed the event for Annabelle, who dressed up and watched from the tablet I set up in the living room at home. My desperation for her ebbed like a tide. I let gentle waves of feeling tickle my feet, but the need didn't pull me under. Not anymore.

The reception was held in the garden at Abaddon, which had been outfitted with strings of fairy lights that connected to the house and extended out into the garden. They filled the backyard with a magical yellow light that snuck into the garden's dark crevices and made my chest feel funny when I stood back to take in the tableau.

Before I left to put tin cans on the back of a carriage with Yasmin's brothers, Helena pulled me aside. We sat in the empty front room of the house while the party continued out back. She handed me a package wrapped in simple black paper.

"This is a gift for you. And your ghost," she said.

I accepted the gift warily. "What is it? You didn't need to . . ."

She waved my hesitation aside. "Just open it."

Inside was a clothbound book. The cover had a graphic illustration of the moon phases on it. I flipped to the back, which had the text that we'd chanted to bring Annabelle back printed in gold leaf. "It's beautiful. But why . . ."

"Oh, for Pete's sake, Gibson," she said, "open the book."

I put on a wry smile. "Given my history of family members and old books, I think you'll forgive me for being cautious."

Nonetheless, I opened the book to reveal a calendar of sorts, with a detailed listing of months, phases of the moon, and more celestial details for a span of the next twenty-five years. The dates of upcoming lunar eclipses were marked and circled with a shiny gold ink. I felt like my ribcage needed to expand several sizes to accommodate the rush of emotions swirling around inside.

"Are you saying—"

"That she can come back again? Of course. Wasn't that obvious?"

"No! No, it wasn't."

Helena smiled at me and patted my knee. I wasn't sure where Annabelle was, but I couldn't wait to show her this. She would love the ornate lettering and the intricate binding.

My heart pounded, overwhelmed by the possibility that Annabelle could come back again on the next eclipse. And all the eclipses after that. "I don't know how to thank you."

"You don't need to. You know, before I sent Yasmin here, I consulted tea leaves. The imagery I saw was quite strong."

"She, um, didn't mention it." Even if she had, I probably,

no, *definitely*, wouldn't have been receptive to hearing about it at the time. "She was focused on the book."

Helena nodded. "She has always been a very serious child. Very focused."

"Can't imagine why," I muttered.

"The leaves left behind a pattern that suggested to me great love and intense loss. I saw an angel with wings of moss from which new life was allowed to grow and flourish. And I saw a bridge that connected life and death."

I leaned back against my seat as if pressed down into it. I couldn't have responded to that if I tried.

Helena continued, "This house, Abaddon Cottage, it's—"

She looked around at the sitting room. We kept some of the original furniture but cleaned and refinished it. Yasmin, Annabelle, and I had argued bitterly over the wallpaper, entering a standoff that resulted in a tense three-day stretch in which Annabelle refused to cook for anyone and started throwing things while invisible just to scare us into finding a resolution. Nate was the one who solved it. We removed the old, peeling, yellowing paper. The process was disgusting and sticky, and the substances I found under the paper I wished I could wipe from my memory. But the new pattern we found online, an updated version of the old one, worked perfectly as a trim around a new coat of warm yellow paint. The look was classic and homey, but updated and clean.

"You've made this house into something no one could have predicted," Helena said. "I'm sure Agatha never intended for strangers to pay to stay here. But it has charm. And it has you in it, too."

I nodded. Somehow, I knew that if I deflected the compliment, she would call me on it.

"I've never doubted my daughter, though I'm sure she says otherwise. Now that I'm here, and I've seen this thing you're doing together, I don't doubt you, either." My aunt folded her hands in her lap and looked down at them. "You didn't have a mother to believe in you as a young adult, and I'm sorry for that. I should've tried to be there for you after she…"

"I understand," I said. And I actually did. "I'm not sure I would've wanted anything to do with you at the time."

The grandfather clock we hadn't discarded chimed, intruding to remind me to keep breathing.

Helena slapped her thighs and stood. "Well, I've welcomed several interesting people into my family today. Old Pete has the most confusing aura of any man I've ever met. Anyway, I wish you all the success in this bed-and-breakfast venture. You have not grown up to be the person anyone expected Veronica Cartwright to grow into, Gibson."

I waited for my hands to stop shaking before I joined the tin-can brigade.

~

*Two years later*

The owners of Helga's, neither of whom were named Helga, let us reserve a seat in the bar located directly in front of the band. Rebecca brought a little stand and put my phone on it. She propped it up carefully, moving it around to make sure Annabelle could see me through the video feed. Every week while the bar was open, I set up the tablet in the living room so Annabelle could watch us play from home.

We went through several drummers when Sage left for college. The new guy, Kevin, was also a dentist that set up shop on the island part time. He was no Sage, but he was good enough and he showed up to jam every week. Mike and I rotated bass and guitar based on vibes and mood, pushing each other to become better at both.

My song, as arranged by me and the members of Call Me Kate, was released on the album they wrote during a frigid winter on Mackinac. It wasn't usually a hit with the patrons of Helga's, but it was the band's third-best performing single. The band toured but never made it back to Mackinac before taking a hiatus so that Brooke could launch a solo career.

Sara brushed her hair out of her eyes and announced, "This next song is a special for our guitar player and her sweetheart."

There was a chorus of *aww* from the crowd, and I held my hand to my heart to show them I appreciated it. Kevin counted us down with his sticks, and I joined Sara at the mic. We poured our hearts into "I'm a Believer," knowing the crowd that had come in for the July yacht race and stayed to have a few drinks would join in and sing along.

From the stage, I couldn't really see Rebecca holding my phone. And Annabelle still didn't show up in photos or videos, so I couldn't see her dancing, but I knew she was there. Every week, she watched us from the living room at Abaddon, dancing wildly and singing along at the top of her lungs.

~

*Three years later*

Annabelle sat on the bed while I stood at the wardrobe and contemplated throwing all of my clothes in the fire pit and starting over. Abaddon's current guests were making the most of the summer, burning s'mores and telling scary stories in the backyard at the moment, though, so I gave up the idea.

"You're going to have to learn the difference between Camembert and Pont l'Évêque." Annabelle kicked her slipper-clad feet as she babbled about cheese. "And in my experience, the streets are more pungent there, but that's to be expected for people who have such a vibrant food culture."

"Marley, I love you, but your experience with France is a little dated."

She clicked her tongue.

"Are you going to help me pick out clothes or are you going to pout?"

"I'm not pouting," she said, pouting. She floated over to the wardrobe to pout there. "Their tea selection might not be what you're used to."

"That's true. I'm accustomed to the finest curation of teas this side of the Atlantic and this side of the twentieth century." My internet search history included so many inquiries about bringing back tea from overseas that tea ads followed me around on my devices.

"Don't make fun of me, Gibson." Impossibly, she pouted even harder. "I just want to be sure you'll be okay while I'm gone!"

"I'm the one who's going to France, and I'll be fine. You wanted me to go see the world."

"I do! And I have my list of things to bring back."

"I'll get you everything on your list and then some. Rebecca has the iPad now, so you can watch the band while I'm gone. And I'll video call you from the Eiffel Tower."

She sighed. "I will watch the band, but it won't be the same without you. You simply must see the view from the Sacré-Cœur, dear, I watched a video program about it. But you mustn't bring a lock, or buy one, even if you're tempted to. They're weighing down the bridge, you see, and . . ."

She chatted at me while I filled my suitcase with a half dozen black shirts and durable underwear. I bought an extra suitcase halfway through my trip and filled it with things that reminded me of her, along with gifts for Yasmin and Nate, the Johnsons, and Big Mike and the kids.

When I returned, the porter who helped me bring my luggage from the ferry to the house was a college kid making a buck on Mackinac for the summer. He had enormous arms and laughed when I told him I owned the famous Mackinac haunted house.

When I opened the door to Abaddon, the guests were out for the evening and Annabelle had forgotten to turn on the lights. She was sitting in her alcove alone, an unmoving, half-visible facsimile of a person with eyes that stared out of her face like cold, dead glass.

The look was gone as soon as I turned on the lights, replaced by her usual cheer.

~

*Five years later*

"Will I be a ghost when I grow up?" Lily shoved a piece of watermelon in her mouth, then spit out the black seeds. She took one of them and put it gently in her brother's hair. He smiled and drooled, trusting her completely.

The adults looked at each other around the picnic table.

"No, dear," Annabelle said gently. "You'll be a very lovely, vivacious, strong young lady and you'll do great things."

"But I want to be a ghost like you!"

"Lil, remember how we talked about Auntie Annabelle?" Yasmin said, removing the seeds from her son's hair. I held my palm out and she deposited them in my hand, holding it briefly before letting go. "Auntie Annabelle is a special auntie, remember?"

"I 'member."

"And remember how she came to visit last year? We went out to the beach and found her."

Yasmin, Annabelle, and I studied the little girl's face, waiting for her answer.

"Yep. I saw her kissing Auntie Gibson behind the shed," she said, matter-of-fact.

I cleared my throat, but Yasmin didn't miss a beat.

"That's because Auntie Gibson loves Auntie Annabelle very much," she said. She'd taken to motherhood, and everything else she'd decided to do, like a duck to water.

I met Annabelle's eyes and felt a flush rising to my cheeks. Last year, we held a grand party at the house to celebrate Annabelle's return. I'd taken her hand and led her behind the shed, grinning and shoving her against the wall and kissing her—and kissing her and kissing her—until a gang of small children mounted a search party determined to find their wayward ghost friend.

"You wouldn't like being a ghost, dear one," Annabelle said, turning to Lily. "Walking through furniture isn't all it's made out to be. You wouldn't be able to hug your brother Jack."

Lily made a face at the toddler seated next to her, clearly uninterested in any hugging that might occur between her and her sibling.

"And just think of all the delicious food you'd miss out on!"

Lily frowned, clearly not liking that answer, either. She took a giant bite of watermelon, and the juice dripped down her chin to her chest, staining her shirt.

I said, "I think I'll be a ghost. I've decided."

Lily's face lit up like a little sun while Annabelle's clouded.

"I'll come back and haunt you, little monster," I said, putting down my own slice of fruit, then slowly approaching Lily with my hands poised to tickle her. "I'll find you when you're sleeping and I'll put spiders in your nose!"

I pretended that I was going to grab her but gave her plenty of opportunity to escape. I chased my goddaughter, screaming with laughter, across the lawn until we both collapsed in a heap. When I looked back at the group at the picnic table, Annabelle wasn't there.

~

*Eleven years later*

This far into autumn, Sunset Rock was mostly empty. The bruised sky faded from a deep amber wash into shades of purple as it met the still line of the lake at the horizon.

A few blinking buoys winked at us from afar. Gulls swooped overhead, searching for scraps. A flying V of geese zoomed by them, reaching to catch up with their already migrated counterparts. I held tightly to Annabelle's hand, solid and warm in mine. We were both sweating a little, and I savored the slide of Annabelle's palm against my palm. I ran my thumb over her knuckles, feeling the little bumps and trying to memorize them.

"Will you be okay?" I asked.

We hadn't spoken much since climbing up here. I carried the picnic basket on the hike up to the high spot, while she carefully held the wine.

Annabelle gave me a surprised look and squeezed my hand. "What do you mean?"

"When I'm gone." I brought our clasped hands to my lips and kissed her fingers softly. I pressed a kiss to each one, taking my time. When I finished kissing her hand, I met her gaze. The sadness in that familiar depth of blue filled me with a familiar ache. "Will you be okay?"

"Oh, darling." She pulled me forward and kissed me as lightly as I'd kissed each finger of her hand. We held each other gently as the sun set on our only day together for the next three years. Wet tears streamed down her cheeks, and I kissed them away.

"My darling," Annabelle said again, not answering the question. She kissed me until her body faded in my arms and the sky was lit only by stars and the pale light of the moon.

~

*Many years later*

"Next year, have Jack do the pruning and clean up the garden, dearest," Annabelle said, rocking back and forth gently in her chair. The first snow was falling on Mackinac, bringing with it the peaceful silence of winter. I brought a blanket and two steaming mugs out to the back deck. I handed Annabelle her tea and arranged myself in the chair, groaning as I lowered down.

She said, "See? I can tell it's bothering your back. You don't need to do it yourself. The grandkids like to gather the leaves and jump on them, so let Jack do it while they're here."

"Okay, okay." I put my hands around my cocoa mug, feeling its warmth.

I watched the moon. It was a sliver of steel barely visible in a cloudy, dark blue sky. The cold wind coming off the lake ruffled my hair. I'd grown it out, gathering it in a ponytail and letting it fall down my back like a silver rope. "We'll make a day of it next year. Have the kids over and tell them garden cleanup day is a national holiday."

"Gibson," Annabelle said, and there was something catching at the edges of her voice. There was an echo to the way she said my name, some shadow I couldn't see. "Darling, I—"

I turned to her.

Annabelle looked the same as she always had. She glowed faintly from within, with that ethereal light I had found beautiful from the moment I saw it. Her fluffy white-blonde hair had never changed, nor had all the ways her face expressed what she was feeling. The other half of my song sat with me, smiling sadly and looking at the moon.

"I need you to know that I will always—it will always have been worthwhile, loving you. My afterlife, for whatever purpose I was allowed to remain, has been the greatest gift I could possibly hope to receive."

"Marley—"

"I just need you to know." Annabelle reached out a hand, palm up. She held it between us, hovering in the air between our chairs. Together, we rocked back and forth, watching the gradual wilting of our garden as autumn faded into winter.

I reached for her.

"I'm still here, Marley," I said, smiling. "But when my time is up, wherever you are, I'll find you on the other side."

# About

Cat Washington is the pen name of an author who loves to write stories where the fantastical brushes up against the mundane world. Follow Cat on Instagram @catwashington_author and on Bluesky @catwashington.bsky.social. Find more social media profiles and links at: catwashingtonbooks.com and https://linktr.ee/catwashington.

# Soundtrack

Music is integral to *The Ghost of You Lingers*. Gibson falls for Annabelle while playing guitar for her, despite their very different musical tastes.

Follow their journey with playlists found at: catwashingtonbooks.com/pages/soundtrack

# Acknowledgments

Writing isn't a solo sport, though it often feels that way.

This story wouldn't exist at all without racket, the best ghost I know, and the people they scooped and put in a lovely little internet hole. We've swapped stories and art; debated topics both important and mundane; supported each other through life and world events; shitposted and shared memes; and most importantly, made each other laugh. You know who you are. Thank you for being wonderful and weird. Please never stop.

Thank you to Sarah, my first draft beta reader and cheerleader, who helped shape the story and provided encouragement for me to finish it.

Many thanks to my Rocky Mountain Fiction Writers critique group, the Tattered Cover (formerly Panera) gang: Rick, Sue, Tom, Bill, Cathy, Susan, Dallas, and others. I've learned so much from working with you all. Thank you to beta readers Urvashi Pahwa and R. Wade Hodges, as well as Nancy Houser-Bluhm for your moral support and encouragement.

Lauren and Shari, thank you for being my friends.

Carolina VonKampen provided the final polish and vital editing to this manuscript, but I touched it last, so any mistakes are on me.

Thank you.